## *Pra*

## LOST AN

"If I get one wish this year, let that be reading *Lost and Lassoed* for the first time again—OR moving to Rebel Blue Ranch and never looking back. Sage crafts and delivers yet another deliciously addictive romance. The banter is explosive, the chemistry is electric, and the journey is as sizzling as it is emotional and vulnerable. Simply perfection. I'm down bad for the Rebel Blue Ranch series and anything Lyla Sage will give us."

—Elena Armas, *New York Times* bestselling author of *The Spanish Love Deception*

"Teddy and Gus are spicy, sizzling, enemies-to-lovers perfection! I loved every moment of their feisty banter, their steamy sexual tension, and their touching emotional journey as they found home in each other's hearts."

—Chloe Liese, *USA Today* bestselling author of the Bergman Brothers series

"Lyla Sage delivers another scalding hot romance; this one is also a tender rumination on fathers and daughters, and the love that makes a family. *Lost and Lassoed* burrowed deep into my heart, and I know it's going to stay there for a good long time."

—Kate Stayman-London, bestselling author of *One to Watch*

"*Lost and Lassoed* has everything I've come to expect from a Lyla Sage novel; delicious tension, heartwarming vulnerability, characters you can't help but root for, and more simmering heat than a Rebel Blue summer sun. Readers will be alternately clutching their pearls and their tissues. Lyla once again pours her heart lovingly into each page on another delightful trip to Rebel Blue."

—B.K. Borison, author of *Lovelight Farms*

By Lyla Sage

*Done and Dusted*

*Swift and Saddled*

*Lost and Lassoed*

# LOST AND LASSOED

# LOST AND LASSOED

*A Rebel Blue Ranch Novel*

LYLA SAGE

The Dial Press
New York

A Dial Press Trade Paperback Original



Published in the United States by The Dial Press, an imprint of Random House, a division of Penguin Random House LLC, New York.

The Dial Press is a registered trademark and the colophon is a trademark of Penguin Random House LLC.

Dial Delights and colophon are trademarks of Penguin Random House LLC.

This book contains an excerpt from the forthcoming book *Wild and Wrangled* by Lyla Sage. This excerpt has been set for this edition only and may not reflect the final content of the forthcoming edition.

LIBRARY OF CONGRESS CATALOGING-IN-PUBLICATION DATA

Names: Sage, Lyla, author.
Title: Lost and lassoed / Lyla Sage.
Description: New York: The Dial Press, 2024. | Series: Rebel Blue Ranch;
3 Identifiers: LCCN 2024005975 (print) | LCCN 2024005976 (ebook) |
ISBN 9780593732458 (trade paperback; acid-free paper) |
ISBN 9780593732465 (ebook)
Subjects: LCGFT: Western fiction. | Romance fiction. | Novels.
Classification: LCC PS3619.A384 L67 2024 (print) | LCC PS3619.A384 (ebook) |
DDC 813/.6—dc23/eng/20240216
LC record available at https://lccn.loc.gov/2024005975
LC ebook record available at https://lccn.loc.gov/2024005976

Printed in the United States of America on acid-free paper

randomhousebooks.com

1 3 5 7 9 8 6 4 2

*Book design by Virginia Norey*
*Wildflowers : Olena Panasovska/stock.adobe.com,*
*horseshoe: RealVector/stock.adobe.com, cowboy boot: Ann/stock.adobe.com*

For everyone who got to chapter three of *Done and Dusted* and immediately wanted Gus and Teddy. I'm so happy to finally share their story with you. Thank you for waiting.

And for my dad, the proudest man alive.

# LOST AND LASSOED

# Chapter 1

## Teddy

Nothing said "Good morning" like the smell of stale cigarettes and spilled beer. Walking into the Devil's Boot at night was one thing; honestly, it was one of my favorite things. But during the day, it was an assault on the senses. I could almost feel the ghosts of bad decisions clinging to my suede jacket (cream-colored, vintage, covered in fringe, totally adorable yet badass).

So why was I walking into Wyoming's dingiest dive bar at seven o'clock on a Sunday morning? Because my best friend had asked me to, and there wasn't anything I wouldn't do for her.

Emmy Ryder and I had been friends since birth—almost literally. My dad started working on her family's ranch when I was only a few months old and Emmy was only a couple of months older than me. My first memory is of the two of us jumping over one of the narrower parts of the stream that cuts through Rebel Blue Ranch. We went back and forth over and over again until Emmy slipped and fell into the water. I can still hear the splash and the clattering of river rocks that accompanied it. Her ankle swelled up like a balloon almost immediately—even at five or six, I knew that that was not what an ankle should look like. I helped her out of the stream, and she leaned on me the whole way home.

We've been leaning on each other ever since.

Her fiancé, Luke Brooks, was the owner of the Devil's Boot. He'd inherited it from his dad a few years ago, and he was actually kicking ass as its proprietor. Brooks had a lot of dreams for the bar. His biggest one was installing a mechanical bull—no, I'm not kidding—which is why I was about to spend my Sunday sifting through boxes and sweeping up layers of thirty-year-old dust and grime and god knows what else to clear the way for it.

I didn't mind, though. Plus, I kind of owed him, considering I'd kicked him out of his and Emmy's bed last night so she and I could have a sleepover.

Emmy and Brooks were standing at the bar talking with their heads close together. I'd left their house earlier to grab us some coffees and give them some alone time, which they'd probably used to have sex in the shower—horny little shits.

Sometimes I wanted to get a spray bottle so I could squirt them—you know, the way you do with a cat or a dog when it's misbehaving—when their public displays of affection got a little too intense.

But Emmy and Brooks were made for each other, and I loved them both. A lot. I loved Emmy more, obviously, but Luke Brooks had grown on me over the past couple of years. It was a beautiful thing to watch your best friend be loved in the way you know she deserves.

"Coffee's here," I said, announcing my presence.

Emmy turned to me. "Oh, thank god, you're a hero." She

was wearing the tank top I got her for her birthday—it said LUKE PILLOWS right across her boobs—and a pair of black leggings.

It occurred to me that I was overdressed for a day of cleaning out the Devil's Boot's second floor—Wranglers, black tank top, and the jacket, obviously. But I liked clothes, the way I felt when I put together an outfit I liked, and I really liked this one. Clothes were like armor, and armor would be needed if a certain older brother of Emmy's was going to show up today.

Not Wes. I loved Wes.

I handed over her cup, which she took gratefully. She curled her fingers around it and took a sip. The diamond-studded gold band that now adorned her left ring finger glinted in the light. She looked at the cardboard drink holder I was carrying. It had two more cups in it—an iced brown sugar latte for me and a black coffee for Brooks.

Emmy arched a brow at me. "Funny," she said, "I remember asking you to grab a cup for Gus, too."

"Huh," I said with a shrug. "Must've forgot." Gus was Emmy's oldest brother, Brooks's best friend, and, most important, my archnemesis.

Small towns wove complicated webs.

It wasn't that I hated Gus . . . well . . . actually, scratch that. I did kind of hate him. I don't remember how it started (that's a lie, but it's not important). Mostly, I just always felt like he didn't like me, so I didn't like him, and then it spiraled into our being delightfully mean to each other all the time.

He was just so . . . grumpy. Men who are that good-looking should not be allowed to be such assholes. It was false advertising.

And he was getting worse with age.

Emmy sighed. "How do we feel about trying to be nice today?" she asked.

"Not great," I said. Brooks laughed from his spot at the bar. I walked over to him and handed him his cup. He lifted it in a "Cheers" motion.

"Thanks, Ted," he said. "Gus won't be here for a little bit, so you've got time to prep your verbal arsenal."

"See?" I said, looking at Emmy. "He gets it."

Emmy shot Brooks a pointed look, but he just winked at her. I watched her soften a little. "I just thought it would be nice if our best man and maid of honor didn't hate each other," she said. The words "maid of honor" sent a little pang through my sternum.

Of course, I was thrilled to be Emmy's maid of honor. I was excited about her wedding, her life, everything. But sometimes, when the topic of the wedding came up, I got sad. Not inconsolable or anything, but it felt like my happiness for my best friend and my sadness for myself were both staking claim in my chest, punching each other as hard as they could to see who would get knocked out first.

It was a reminder that we were in different phases of our lives, and it scared me. Emmy had always needed me. We were each other's number one. Now she had Brooks, and I was terrified that she wouldn't need me the way she used to—that she wouldn't need me the way I needed her anymore.

"Then maybe Brooks should pick a best man that isn't so hateable." I shrugged and looked over at him. "She's got two brothers, you know."

All he did was smile and say "Noted."

Emmy sighed and moved on. She tried to get Gus and me to get along a couple of times a month. It never worked, but I admired her persistence. My best friend never gave up. She directed my attention to a piece of paper on the bar where she and Brooks had laid out a checklist for the day. The goal was simple: Get all the trash out of the second floor and move anything that was to be saved to the basement.

Brooks and Gus would take the basement, which was okay with me because that place was straight out of a horror movie, and I wasn't really in the mood to get possessed by a demon today. Unless it was a hot demon—then I could be persuaded. Emmy and I would take the second floor. Brooks's eventual plan was to put a smaller bar and new seating up there and remove some of the seating on the first floor to make room for the mechanical bull.

Once we were armed with garbage bags, gloves, and cleaning supplies, Emmy and I started toward the rickety stairs that led to the second floor of the Devil's Boot. At that moment, the back door to the bar opened and Gus Ryder sauntered in. I could feel my blood pressure rising.

He was wearing a tight faded blue T-shirt, gray joggers, and a Carhartt baseball cap. His dark brown hair was longer than I'd seen it in quite a while. Last year, he had started sporting a mustache instead of the short, neatly trimmed beard he'd adopted in his twenties. The mustache was still going strong, and even though I thought it looked good on him, the first thing out of my mouth was "Hey, pornstache. Nice of you to join us."

"Fuck off, Theodora," he said without even glancing my way. His voice was bored. The way he said my full name made me grind my teeth.

"Did you steal that shirt out of Riley's closet?" I asked, gesturing to his tight blue shirt. Riley was Gus's six-year-old daughter, and the way his shirt was hugging his chest and biceps, it looked small enough to be hers.

"You know," he said, finally throwing his emerald eyes toward me, "the way you're ogling me is making me uncomfortable."

"Well, the way I can see your nipples through your shirt is making *me* uncomfortable," I countered. "Brooks," I said, glancing over at him, "I can't work in these conditions."

Brooks shrugged and said, "Take it up with the boss," nodding toward Emmy, who was looking at Gus and me. She was unamused.

All she said was "Gus, you and your nipples are in the basement. Ted, let's go." I followed her up the stairs but turned back toward Gus to give him a wave.

He flipped me off.

I hoped he'd get eaten by a demon.

A few hours later, Emmy and I were in the double digits on full garbage bags, and the grime of the Devil's Boot had formed a film on my skin. I had severely underestimated the muckiness of the bar's second floor. I'd had to drape my suede jacket over a chair and cover it with a plastic bag in hopes of keeping it clean. On the bright side, I'd found a few old vinyl records that Emmy said I could take home. I texted my dad and told him we were going to have a Tanya Tucker and Willie Nelson listening party tonight.

Sorting through some boxes in the corner, I found a bunch of old newspapers. I pulled out a *Meadowlark Examiner* from 1965 and saw a story featuring the Devil's Boot as one of Wyoming's best bars.

"Emmy," I called. She looked up from where she'd pulled a

wet, dirty piece of fabric from the other corner of the room. "Have you seen these?"

"More newspapers?"

"Yeah," I responded. "Are there more than this?"

Emmy nodded. "We found a few boxes in the basement. Luke wants to keep them. I think he wants to frame a couple of them. You and Ada could probably come up with something cool to do with them, too." Ada was Wes's girlfriend. She was an interior designer and impressively creative. I liked to paint and do things with my hands, so she and I got along.

"They're really rad," I said, thumbing through more of the papers. There were stories about the Devil's Boot and pictures of it throughout its history. A copy of the *Jackson Hole News* named it the most unique bar in Wyoming.

"Will you take that box to the basement? There's a small closet at the end of the hall where we put all of the others."

"You know how I feel about the basement," I whined.

Emmy laughed and said, "I guess this is your chance to live out that demon romance you told me about last night." I let out a huff. I couldn't believe she was using my book recommendations against me.

"Fine," I muttered. "But if I get murdered down there, or taken to some evil dimension, you're going to feel really bad for making me do this." I slid on my jacket; I didn't want to let it out of my sight. Plus, I had to look cute in case the hot demon showed up.

Emmy put a hand over her heart. "I promise to throw you the best funeral that Meadowlark, Wyoming, has ever seen," she said.

"Don't forget, I want to be cremated and shot off in fireworks," I responded.

"While Kiss performs 'I Was Made for Loving You,'" she said with a wave of her hand. "I know, I know." I decided on that when Emmy and I were in sixth grade. Talk about going out with a bang, am I right?

I picked up the box and started down the two flights of stairs. The basement was dark. This was the first time I'd made it all the way down here, and it was seriously creepy. Where were Brooks and Gus?

The smell of cigarettes and stale beer wasn't as strong in the basement. It mostly just smelled old. It was also a lot cooler—probably because of all the paranormal activity lurking in the nooks and crannies. The floorboards creaked under my feet. Just when I started to relax a bit, a loud bang startled me, and I hurried toward the closet at the end of the hall.

I needed to get out of this creepy basement immediately—hot demons be damned. When I got to the closet, my jacket snagged on the doorknob, slamming the door shut behind me and leaving me in total darkness. I dropped the box of newspapers and heard a frustrated grunt.

There was someone else in the closet.

I turned back to the door, trying to unsnag my jacket and get the door open. I succeeded at untangling my jacket, but I could feel a tear where it got caught in the door. The door, on the other hand, wouldn't budge.

"What the fuck, Theodora?" came a deep and angry voice from right behind me.

And that's how I locked myself in a closet with Gus Ryder.

Well, shit.

# Chapter 2

# Gus

I had heard her fucking boots coming down the stairs. I shook my head, annoyed that I could tell it was her. No one else stomped around like they owned the place—not even Brooks, and he did own the place.

I slipped into the closet to avoid her. So imagine my surprise when she barreled into that same closet with all the grace of a goddamn tornado, dropped a heavy-ass box on my foot, and proceeded to slam the door shut behind her—leaving us in total darkness.

Peachy. Absolutely fucking peachy.

She was too close to me—way too close. Much to my annoyance, Teddy is always around—always has been, probably always will be. "Open the door, Teddy."

I heard her jiggle the doorknob and throw her body against the door. "I'm trying," she said. "It won't budge."

*Christ.* I didn't have time for this. "Move," I said as I tried to shoulder Teddy out of the way. As soon as my body touched hers, I got a jolt like I'd touched an electric fence—not a pleasant feeling, in case you were wondering.

One of the most annoying things about Teddy? She was familiar, even though I didn't want her to be.

*Don't think about it.*

But here I was seven years later still thinking about it. Here was the fucking kicker: I didn't even like Teddy. At all.

Teddy Andersen was trouble. And loud.

"If it's not budging for me, it's not going to budge for you," Teddy snapped, then muttered, "unless it's got a thing for assholes." I heard that.

She moved out of my way and I felt for the door, then down to the doorknob. I tried to turn it, but it was jammed.

Fuck.

"I told you." Teddy's voice wasn't quite behind me but also not quite next to me—wherever she was, she was still too fucking close.

"What did you do to it?" I demanded.

I could almost hear her eyes roll. "You're kidding me, right? This door is older than you," she said. "So, basically, ancient"—yup, caught that dig—"and you're blaming me?"

"You're the one that shut it," I said, my temper already flaring. My fuse always seemed to be a hell of a lot shorter around Teddy.

"Not on purpose. It got caught on my jacket, which now has a hole the size of your ego in it." God, she was annoying. "This is vintage suede," she complained.

"We're indefinitely locked in a closet in the basement of a bar, and you're worried about your stupid jacket?"

"It's not a stupid jacket," she said. "And we're not locked in here indefinitely. Just call Emmy or Brooks."

That was a good idea, but I wasn't about to tell her that. I reached into my pocket, but when I didn't feel my phone there, I cursed under my breath. I'd left it on the front seat of my truck.

"You don't have your phone, do you?" Even though I couldn't see her, I knew she'd probably crossed her arms across her chest, narrowed her eyes, and tilted her head, which meant her stupid bouncy ponytail would move with her.

Even in the dark, I had to fight the urge to find that copper-colored ponytail and yank it.

"No," I snapped, "I don't have my phone. You call them."

"Well, Gussy," she said—I prickled at the nickname, and at her tone of sickly-sweet annoyance—"I don't have my phone either. It's upstairs."

Goddammit.

I ran a hand down my face and let out an annoyed grunt. Of all the places I wanted to be, locked in a closet with Teddy wasn't anywhere on the list. But I knew there were a lot of people who'd like to trade places with me.

Even though I was loath to admit it, Teddy was a knockout. I'd never noticed when we were growing up. Teddy was eight years younger than me, and I wasn't a fucking creep. But then, when Emmy and Teddy graduated from college, Teddy wore this dark green dress that just . . . Never mind. The point is that I know Teddy is pretty. Beautiful, even. But beautiful like a lion or an elk or any other large and dangerous animal. Beautiful to look at, but you didn't want to get too close because it'd rip your throat out or trample you or spear you to death with its giant horns.

So yeah. Teddy was beautiful or whatever.

But I wasn't looking to get eaten alive.

I started banging on the door and hollering for Emmy and Brooks.

Teddy let out a sigh. "Emmy will come looking for me as soon as she realizes I've been gone for more than a few minutes. Chill out."

"How do you know that?" I demanded.

"Because I know Emmy. She's not going to leave me in this horror movie basement." She was probably right, but I didn't care. I ignored her and kept banging on the door. "For god's sake, August, take a breath."

"Don't tell me what to do," I spat. This woman's mere existence got under my skin like nothing else. Why couldn't Emmy have a friend that wasn't irritation incarnate? A nice, normal friend that didn't make me want to bash my head against the wall?

Or a friend that wasn't always at the scene of the crime when Emmy did something she shouldn't have.

"Don't tell me what to do," Teddy mimicked me, and I let out a growl. "Are you afraid of the dark, Gussy?"

"No, but if I remember correctly, you are," I shot back. I'd known Teddy her whole life—literally—her dad had started working for mine when she was barely three months old. I remember the day Hank Andersen rolled up to Rebel Blue Ranch in his gold El Camino with Teddy in tow. I was seven or eight then, and Teddy was a hell of a lot less infuriating—probably because she couldn't talk yet.

Teddy smacked my arm. "I am not!" Why couldn't this woman keep her hands to herself?

"Then why were you running through the basement like a spooked horse?"

"Because I was avoiding you, obviously."

"That worked out really well, didn't it?" I asked. She was so close to me. When she talked, I could feel her breath. It reminded me of how it felt against my neck. *Fuck. Get it together, Ryder.*

"Well, it would've, if you weren't the type of creep that hides in closets. What were you even doing in here?" I couldn't tell her that I was hiding from her. That would give her too much satisfaction.

"Can you stop talking?" I said. "You're giving me a headache." I did have a headache, but for once, it wasn't because of Teddy. I hadn't been getting a lot of sleep this week, and it was catching up with me.

I could tell Teddy was about to volley something back at me, but just then there was a loud creaking somewhere else in the basement. Teddy gasped. Her hand found mine as she jumped closer to me. "What was that?"

Again with the touching. *Christ.*

"Now who needs to chill out?" I asked, and yanked my hand away from hers. I didn't like the way holding it made me feel. "It's an old building. There are noises everywhere." Teddy stayed quiet—not convinced. "Anyway, I thought you weren't afraid of the dark."

"I'm not," she said. She must've straightened up, because I felt her chest brush against mine. *Fuck.* "I'm afraid of what's lurking in the dark. There's a difference."

"What do you think is 'lurking' "—I used air quotes even though she couldn't see me—"in the basement of the Devil's Boot?"

"Demons," Teddy said. "And I don't think it's the hot ones." What the hell was this woman on about?

"You're insane," I said. I moved to run a hand through my hair, but it brushed against Teddy's waist instead. I felt her go still, and I snatched my hand away immediately.

"And you're an asshole," she said, but not with her normal authority. Her voice sounded . . . breathy, almost?

We needed to get the fuck out of here. I started banging on the door again. This time Teddy joined me. I guess she was thinking the same thing.

After a minute or so, I heard Brooks's voice—thank fucking Christ—just outside the door. "Gus? Why are you in the closet?"

I sighed. "Because Theodora wreaks havoc wherever she goes." Teddy smacked my arm. One more touch from her and I was going to tie her hands behind her back.

No, wait, not like that. Goddammit.

"Teddy is in there with you?" Brooks asked.

"Yes," Teddy shouted. "And she would desperately like not to be." Brooks stayed silent.

"Let us out, man," I said. "The stupid door is jammed."

"I don't know if that's a good idea," Brooks said. I could hear the smile in his voice. *Bastard.* "Might win some points with Emmy if I leave you guys in there to work out your issues."

"Don't. You. Dare." Teddy's voice was venomous.

"It won't win you any points with Emmy if we kill each other," I said. "And I swear to god, Brooks, I will haunt the shit out of you."

"Same," Teddy chimed in.

"Is this the first time you guys have ever agreed on something?" Brooks asked. His tone was even more amused now. It wasn't, though. There was one other time Teddy and I had agreed on something, but that agreement meant keeping our fucking mouths shut. "Seems like the closet is doing its job." The doorknob jiggled, and within a second, the door was open and light flooded into the small space. "Better quit while we're ahead."

Teddy and I stumbled out of the closet. It was dark enough in there that the dim light of the basement made me squint.

As my eyes adjusted, I heard Teddy say "Thank god." I looked over at her. Her chest was heaving slightly and her skin was flushed.

The way she looked made it seem like we'd been doing a lot more than arguing while we were locked in the closet.

I gritted my teeth.

"How did that happen?" Brooks asked, gesturing toward the closet.

"Hurricane Theodora," I remarked with an eye roll. "How else?" Teddy flipped her russet ponytail over her shoulder and smirked like I'd just given her a compliment. "You know, being compared to a hurricane isn't a good thing," I said to her.

"Really?" she asked sarcastically. "I don't know. Powerful, relentless, fierce . . ." she counted off the adjectives on her fingers.

"Destructive, devastating—" I countered.

"—ly beautiful?" Teddy said before I could finish. I rolled my eyes so far back in my head that I thought they'd never come back around.

I opened my mouth but then closed it. I couldn't think of anything to say back, which was the worst thing that could happen in a sparring match with Teddy.

"It's okay, Gussy," she whispered, "I won't tell anyone you

think I'm beautiful. It's this gossip you have to worry about." She nodded toward Brooks, who looked as if he was about to deny it, but then Emmy's voice came from the staircase.

"Ted?" Emmy called. "You okay?"

"Yeah!" Teddy yelled back. She turned to me again. I thought she was going to deliver a closing blow, but instead she walked past me. As she did, she pointed a finger at my chest and said, "What's that?"

I looked down, and she moved her finger up to flick me in the nose.

*Damn it.* I fell for that every fucking time.

Her annoying laugh echoed through the basement as she made her way back up the stairs.

# Chapter 3

## Teddy

"Stupid fucking piece of shit!" I shouted at my sewing machine—a vintage Brother Coronado that—until this moment—was my pride and joy. I was trying to fix the giant (three-inch) tear that the Devil's Boot closet doorknob had ripped in my favorite jacket, but the mint-green sewing machine had other plans.

"I thought you were supposed to be running *from* the demons," Emmy had said with a laugh when I told her what happened in the basement. "Not straight into their arms."

"Okay, first of all," I said, "I wasn't in *anyone's* arms"—even if they were annoyingly nice arms—"and I feel the need to make that *very* clear, considering you're engaged to Meadowlark's biggest gossip. And second of all, are you finally admitting that your brother Gus was sent from hell?"

"Hell in general? No," she responded with a small smile. "But your own personal hell? Maybe."

I couldn't decide which was worse: the fact that I'd gotten stuck in a closet with Gus or the fact that my sewing machine was screwed up. Every time I stepped on the pedal, thread was piling up, getting tangled, and creating something akin to a bird's nest on the underside of the fabric. I'd done everything—rethreaded the machine, tried different thread, checked that the bobbin was seated correctly, reset the tension settings—but no dice.

I dropped my head onto my sewing table. It met the wood with a resounding thud. I could try to sew the tear by hand, but the vintage suede was too thick for me to get the neat, unobtrusive stitches that I could with the machine.

The thought of not being able to repair my jacket brought tears to my eyes. *It's just a jacket, Teddy.*

But it wasn't.

It was my jacket. I'd had it since I was sixteen. I had dragged Emmy out of bed before sunrise—she was not a morning person—and we'd driven to Cody, a big city compared to Meadowlark. It was the end of the summer, so all of the seasonal workers had dropped their stuff at the thrift stores, and they left a lot of good stuff behind. We dug through bin after bin. I encountered a lot of questionable stains, and Emmy nearly came to blows with an old woman over a Wrangler vest with the Marlboro Man stitched into it.

But then I found this jacket. I cleaned it. I cared for it. I made sure it didn't smell weird and vintagey.

I gave it a new life.

I loved this jacket. It was timeless, unique, and . . . Teddy. And now I didn't know whether I could wear it again without causing more damage.

I wished I could blame Gus for this, but I was the one who'd been running from demons in the basement.

Tears poked at the back of my eyes. I know it sounds ridiculously dramatic that I was crying over a jacket, but I wasn't just crying over the jacket. I was crying over what it meant to me, and the memory attached to it, one of the many moments when Emmy and I had been completely in sync. Partners in crime. And, truthfully, it hadn't felt like that in a while.

I had been so excited when Emmy moved back home, but I didn't get to spend a lot of time basking in that feeling because she and Brooks got together almost immediately.

Emmy's my best friend, so I was thrilled for her, but it's been weird to watch the way our friendship has changed—for me, not for her, I don't think—in the two years since she came back from Denver. I'm still reckoning with that—a life where it's not just her and me against the world.

Emmy didn't really come to me anymore—I went to her. A lot of the time we spent together now was at her house—sometimes it was just us, sometimes Brooks was there, which I generally didn't mind. But we didn't do things together the way we used to. I did things on my own, and when I wanted to spend time with Emmy, I prioritized where she was at instead of where I wanted to be—like at a thrift store in Cody.

Coming to terms with that has been more difficult than I thought it would be. I was happy for her but sad for me.

It's just weird to be happy for her and sad for me at the same time.

I contain multitudes and all that shit, I guess.

But now it felt like this jacket was just another piece of my life that was going to get left behind, another part of *me* that was going to get left behind.

The other day, one of the girls I work with at the boutique announced that she was pregnant, and my first thought was that we weren't old enough to get pregnant—especially on purpose.

My second thought was to ask her if she knew who the father was.

And then I remembered that we're in our late twenties, and she's been married for nearly five years.

It just feels like everyone is moving on . . . without me. Even Luke Brooks—former manwhore extraordinaire—is settling down, for Christ's sake. And here I am, twenty-eight, working at the same boutique I've been working in since I was twenty-two, in the same small town I grew up in, with no change in sight.

Growing up, I was always ahead of everyone else. I made my own path, and I forged ahead fearlessly. I was the leader in my life.

In fourth grade, I thought it was bullshit that we only got pizza every other Friday in the cafeteria, so I organized a recess protest—nearly the entire first-grade class, except Kenny Wyatt, the fucking coward, stayed outside when the bell rang until the principal agreed to hear my complaint. It took a petition that I stored in the back of my math binder and a lunchroom cleanup assignment, but the next year, we had pizza *every* Friday.

When I decided I liked clothes in junior high, I went all in. I taught myself to sew. I saved money for supplies by walking people's dogs or babysitting. I wanted to learn a craft, and I got good at it.

I was the girl who all the other girls came to for advice—what to wear (everyone loved my style), whether they should break up with their boyfriend (almost always yes), how to talk the sheriff out of calling your parents if you got caught at a party (cry—cry a lot). It was my way of taking care of the people around me and taking the lead.

Growing up, it was always Emmy's goal to leave Meadowlark. She felt stifled here—like our small town was sitting on her lungs. Me? It felt like the only place I could take big, true breaths. I left for college, fucked around Europe on my own for a little bit right after, but I always had every intention of coming back home. I just . . . I loved it here. It was the place my dad chose for us, and that meant something to me.

And in Meadowlark, I shone. People loved me, and I loved to be loved. There was only one Teddy Andersen. Here, I was ahead of the game.

So how did I get so behind?

I'd always been happy in Meadowlark, but over the past few months, I had begun to wonder if I had started to resent it at the same time. It felt as if Meadowlark was taking care of everyone but me. Everyone I loved in Meadowlark seemed to be doing big things—getting married, renovating houses, having babies, falling in love. It was a silly thing to feel—like the place I lived didn't care about me, even though I loved it so deeply—but I felt it anyway.

And then there were the smaller parts of these big feelings that I'd started to notice in real life. The other day, at Emmy's house, I'd noticed she'd put a bunch of pictures in frames—nearly all of them of her and Brooks—hiking, on vacation, at Rebel Blue. I realized that the pictures I had framed in my room were of Emmy and me.

And that made me sad.

Life had begun to feel bittersweet, and I was getting all of the bitter and everyone else was getting the sweet.

I told myself not to cry. I didn't like crying. I didn't like seeing my world through watery and swollen eyes.

There's nothing wrong with crying—I've spent a lot of time

comforting others, telling them it's okay to cry—but for some reason I've never been able to allow myself that same courtesy.

Except for certain occasions, like right now.

No one else here. It was just me, my jacket, and a Bob Seger record. And so I let myself cry, head down on my sewing table, clutching the fringe of my suede jacket. I don't know how long I stayed that way, but it wasn't until I heard my dad making his way down the hall that I quickly lifted my head, took a deep breath, and hoped the small smile I was attempting didn't look like a grimace.

He was using his cane today. That meant he felt good enough to be up and about, which lightened my heart a little. Both of his hands were gripping the top curve of his cane, which meant his knuckle tattoos were on display. On one hand, four fingers read THEO, and on the other, DORA.

I loved all my dad's tattoos, but those were my favorites.

Hank Andersen was a badass in every sense of the word. His long hair, which used to be jet black but now was more salt-and-pepper than anything else, was pulled back into a ponytail. Today he was wearing a Thin Lizzy T-shirt, faded blue jeans, and light blue socks with wiener dogs on them.

"You okay, Teddy Bear?" he asked as he leaned against my doorframe. It took some weight off his right leg, which was the one that gave him the most trouble—probably from spending too much time behind a drum set. "Bob Seger stopped playing ten minutes ago." He nodded toward my record player, where the *Night Moves* album was still turning and a crackling noise was coming from the speakers.

I hadn't even noticed the record had finished, which was saying something because that album ends with "Mary Lou"—one of my favorite songs of all time.

"Yeah," I said. I quickly got up and went to my record player, lifted the tone arm, and switched off the turntable. "Just a rough day."

"Seems like you've had a few of those lately," my dad responded. I just shrugged. "Scale of one to ten?" That's how we talked about bad days, pain, sickness, and all the things in between.

I thought about it for a second. "It was a six." My dad's icy blue eyes flashed with concern. "But I think we're closer to a five now that I've seen your socks."

He looked down at his wiener dog socks and grinned. "And what if I told you VH1 is airing its Hundred Greatest Songs of the Eighties tonight?"

I sniffled a little but smiled back at him. "Down to a four."

"Do you want to call Emmy? Is she around? We can order dinner." I nodded. My dad made his way a little farther into my room until he was only a step and a half from me. He brought one of his old, weathered hands up to my face and used his thumb to wipe away one of the tears that was sitting at the corner of my eye. "I'm sorry you had a bad day."

I shook my head. "Not for much longer," I said. Hank smiled at that. "I can handle dinner, though."

My dad shook his head. "It's okay. Aggie's coming over. That's a lot of people to cook for." Aggie was my friend Dusty's mom and a very talented carpenter. She and Hank had become quite fond of each other over the past few years, and now Aggie was sharing the load of taking care of my dad without even trying—coming over on Friday nights or bringing him food while I was at work.

I loved Aggie; she was badass and funny and kind. But it also twisted the knife just a little bit more that even my dad—my sixtysomething dad—had a romantic prospect, something new in his life, something that was pushing him forward. I was grateful, of course, but I couldn't help but sometimes feel a . . . twinge. My dad didn't seem like he needed me as much anymore either.

And I thrived on being needed.

"Okay," I said. "Sounds good."

"I'll order the food." He turned and went back down the hallway toward the kitchen.

Once he was gone, I called Emmy. She picked up on the first ring.

"My sewing machine is broken and I can't fix the rip in my fringe jacket," I said as soon as she picked up. She might not need me the same way anymore, but I still needed her. "And the Hundred Greatest Songs of the Eighties is on VH1 tonight. Come over?"

"I wish I could," she said, and I felt my entire body deflate. "Luke's mom is coming to dinner tonight."

I opened my mouth to respond, tell her it was okay, that I hoped her dinner went well, that I loved being my dad and Aggie's third wheel, but nothing came out.

"I'll call you later, though?" Emmy said after a few beats of silence.

"For sure," I choked out. "Love you."

"Love you," Emmy said, and hung up.

*Don't cry, Teddy. It's going to be okay.*

# Chapter 4

# Gus

"Everything's fine, Cam," I said with as much enthusiasm as I could muster. "Seriously. There's nothing to worry about."

"Are you sure?" she said on the other end of the phone. I know the mother of my child well, and her tone was laced with concern.

"Totally," I said. Everything was completely fine. I didn't accidentally shrink all of my and Riley's clothes by washing them on hot, serve cereal for dinner three nights in a row, or get a brush stuck in Riley's curly hair.

None of that happened.

"You sound"—Cam paused for a second—"stressed." That was an understatement if I'd ever heard one.

Cam was in Jackson Hole for the summer, shadowing at a law firm there and doing an immersive bar prep course. I was happy for her. She'd had a difficult time last year after she failed the bar exam the first time. She hadn't told me or anyone else in our family, and she'd put a lot of distance between us all in those few months. She wouldn't respond to my texts or calls unless they had to do with Riley, which would've been fine, but our co-parenting relationship was built on a pretty solid friendship foundation, so it worried me.

My brother's girlfriend, Ada, was able to get it out of her a few months after it happened. She said she felt like a failure, even though she was the furthest thing from it. Ever since I'd known her, Cam had wanted to be a lawyer, and I was glad she decided to take the bar again. Her fiancé, Greg, is some big deal investment banker, so he jumped at the chance to go to Jackson to be closer to a lot of his Richie Rich clients for a few months.

From what I know, he's not the biggest fan of Meadowlark.

So I encouraged Cam to take the opportunity in Jackson, which meant I had our six-year-old daughter all to myself. Over the past six years, Cam and I had perfected our custody arrangement, and I was able to structure all my responsibilities at Rebel Blue around it. Plus, we had my family to help out, and Cam and I could always lean in when the other needed it.

I was a single dad, but I'd never had to be a single parent.

Until now.

It had been a week and a half since Cam left—she left two Wednesdays ago. It was Friday now, and she was right. I was stressed.

Summers at Rebel Blue were always a busy time of year, but this year was also the first time we had a fully operational guest ranch added to the mix. So not only did I have nearly fifty ranch employees to keep track of, but in a couple of weeks, I would also have city folks running around my ranch.

And city folks were fucking idiots.

"Gus?" Cam's voice came through the phone again, pulling me out of my thoughts. "You there?"

"Yeah, sorry. I'm good. We're all good." I fucking loved my kid. I just had to get used to our new routine.

"Are you sure?" Cam asked.

"Yes, and Riley's great. She's doing riding lessons with Emmy right now." My little sister was my daughter's favorite person. She was mine too.

"Don't forget she has soccer this afternoon."

"I know," I said. "She and Emmy hang out after lessons, so Emmy will get her ready and take her to soccer, and I'll pick her up after I finish up for the day."

"Okay . . . you'll let me know if you need me?"

"Yes." *No.*

"Okay. I'll let you know if I can call for bedtime." I hoped she could. Riley was starting to miss her mom.

"Sounds good. Talk to you later."

A few hours later, I was deep into the hills of Rebel Blue, checking on the tanks that we used to gather rainwater. Once the tanks were full, we would drag them to a pasture for the cattle. I hadn't planned on going this far out today, but after I checked the first few tanks, I was running good on time, so I kept going.

Less work for me tomorrow.

The one thing you need to know about ranchers? We're fucking obsessed with water—especially in the summer. The West is dry, and even though a lot of Rebel Blue is irrigated, we still rely on rainwater for our cattle. It replenishes the grasses they eat and the streams and ponds where they drink. We're always looking for ways to use our resources more efficiently and sustainably. It's important to us.

Wes and I normally checked these together, but we hadn't had time this week, so he and I had to split up. Dusty—who was somewhere between a ranch hand and a second-in-command—was taking some too. I was actually happy to be on my own today. It was nice. Quiet.

None of the tanks on my docket were full yet. It wasn't a surprise—there hadn't been a lot of rain lately—but it still worried the hell out of me to see each one nearly half empty.

I walked back to my horse, Scout, who was waiting a few feet from the tank, and mounted. Scout was jet black on his front half, but his back half was splotched with white paint. He was one of my dad's rescues. I'd been riding him for about five years—he was probably in his late teens. He was a damn good horse. I took one of my deerskin gloves off and gave his neck a few rubs.

When I glanced at the sky, the sun was farther down than I was expecting it to be. Had this taken me longer than usual? My phone vibrated in the pocket of my vest. I didn't recognize the number that flashed on the screen, but it was a Wyoming area code, so I answered.

"Hello?"

"Hi, is this Gus Ryder?" a woman's voice asked on the other end.

"Yes ma'am."

"Hi, Mr. Ryder. It's Nicole, Riley's soccer coach."

Fuck. *Fuck.* Riley.

"We finished up here a little bit ago and just wanted to

know if you were close by?" My throat went dry, and my heart fell to my stomach.

I forgot to pick up my kid from soccer practice.

"Shit," I breathed. "I'm so sorry. I lost track of time. Someone will be right there to grab her." It wouldn't be me. I was at least forty minutes from the stables, and that's if Scout and I pushed it all the way back. I had to call Emmy or Brooks or my dad.

"No worries," Nicole said. Her voice felt a little too warm for telling a dad he'd forgotten his kid. I tried to picture Nicole's face, but I couldn't. I knew she had red hair—dyed red hair. Not copper like Teddy's. Wait, why was I thinking about Teddy right now? "It happens. I know Camille is out of town for the summer." Cam normally coached Riley's soccer team. "A change in routine can be hard."

A change in routine didn't mean I could forget my kid at soccer practice. Fuck. "I'm really sorry."

"All good. I'll hang out with her until you can get here."

"Thank you," I said. When I hung up, I immediately dialed Emmy. She lived closest to town. It took twenty minutes to get there from Rebel Blue—fifteen from Emmy and Luke's. She picked up after a few rings.

"What's up?" my sister asked in greeting.

"Can you pick up Riley at soccer?" The question was rushed, my voice distraught. Emmy didn't respond right away.

"Gus," she said worriedly, "soccer was over a half hour ago."

"I know, I know," I said. "I was checking the rain tanks, and I lost track of time. Scout and I are all the way up on the east side of the ranch. There's no way I can get to town in less than an hour."

"Luke and I went for a drive. We're like thirty minutes outside of town . . ." Her voice trailed off.

"Please, Emmy," I said. If she couldn't get there, I would need her to help me find someone who could.

"Okay," she said. "I'll take care of it."

"Thank you," I said, relieved.

"Ride safe, okay?"

"Yeah," I said, and hung up the phone. I slid my phone back into my vest, grabbed Scout's reins, and kicked at his middle. "Let's go, boy. I gotta get home to my baby girl."

## Chapter 5

# Teddy

"Hey, Cloma," I said with a smile. "What brings you in so late?" I was working on inventory—making sure all the sales from this week were updated and that what was in the store matched what we had in our records.

I'd been working at Cloma's boutique on Main Street since I came back to Meadowlark after college. It was technically called Lace and Lavender, but I couldn't get behind that, so I just called it the boutique. Plus, it was the only one in Meadowlark, so it couldn't be confused with anything else.

I started out as a regular sales associate, but pretty soon Cloma recognized that my fashion merchandising degree could be of use to her. Now I was the buyer for the boutique, and I had also built out our website and e-commerce presence from the ground up.

E-commerce made up over sixty percent of our revenue. We sold unique, high-quality Western wear, and we shipped it all over the world. I spent about half of my working hours at the boutique and the other half at home, which was nice; I liked to keep an eye on my dad.

Plus, Cloma let me produce my own designs and sell them locally. There were two racks of Teddy Andersen originals at the front of the store, and they sold well—the best sellers in the boutique this week, according to the inventory I'd just checked. I was proud of the work I did here.

And Cloma was great. She was in her midfifties. She wasn't from Meadowlark, but she'd been here for over ten years. Her long hair was dyed a deep purple. Her eyeliner was always smudged perfectly, and she was always wearing a Stevie Nicksesque shawl.

She rarely came by so late in the day, but I was happy to see her, and I greeted her with a hug.

She hugged me back.

"I'm glad I caught you," she said as she pulled back from the hug. She gave me a smile that didn't quite reach her eyes. "Do you have a second to chat before you go?"

"Sure," I said, feeling uneasy. Something about Cloma felt . . . off. She walked toward the counter, and I followed. I noticed that she was carrying a good-sized brown paper bag. She sat on one of the tall stools behind the counter, and I took the other one. "Is everything okay?" I asked.

"Everything is great," she said, but her tone wasn't convincing. "I have something exciting to tell you." For some reason, I doubted that. This conversation was weird. I'd never had a weird conversation with Cloma.

"Okay . . ."

"I've sold Lace and Lavender. I signed the contract yesterday."

I was . . . confused. She'd sold the boutique? "Like, the building?" I asked dumbly.

The smile Cloma gave me was knowing. "No, honey. I sold

the boutique. The name." I blinked a couple of times—at a loss for words (rare, I know). "A brand bought it—the rights to the name," she said. "I trademarked the name Lavender and Lace a long time ago—which turned out to be a damn good decision. A few years ago, a brand reached out and was interested in buying me out of the name. I said no. This time when they called, I said yes. I could either rebrand or let this place go."

"Why?" I asked.

"Why did they buy it?" I mean, sure, but that's not what I was asking.

"No, why did you say yes this time?" My voice was softer than I wanted it to be. I didn't know how to process what was happening.

Something flashed across Cloma's face. Sadness, maybe? "I've been selling clothes my whole life," she said. "That's all I've ever done—all I've ever wanted to do—but you know as well as I do that it's not always lucrative." That was true. The profit margin on clothing was . . . not great. "But I'm getting older, and it's time for me to move on. This sale gives me a chance to do that and to be comfortable while doing so."

"What does this mean?" *For me* is the part of the sentence I don't say.

Cloma sighed. "It means that the boutique is closing." Fuck. I stopped looking at her. I looked at the wall behind her instead. The silver of a belt buckle caught my eye. I focused there.

*Don't cry, Teddy.*

"Why can't we just rebrand?" I asked. My voice was unrecognizable, even to me. "I could do it," I said. "I could do the whole thing. I know I could." But Cloma shook her head.

"It's not worth the cost, Teddy," she said. "Not just in money, but in time and energy. Sometimes things just run their course, and you have to let them go. That doesn't mean that it wasn't worthwhile and wonderful, it just means that maybe we should try something new." Cloma sighed. "It's time for a change. For both of us."

"But I'll be out of a job." My voice broke on the last word, and I hated the way it sounded. My emotions were all over the place lately, and my hold on them was getting less and less stable.

"I'm so sorry, Teddy," Cloma said. It sounded like she meant it, but that didn't make me feel better.

"When?" I asked.

"I'm closing the store next week." *Fuck.* Next week?

"I want to thank you, Teddy. I am so impressed by you," Cloma said quickly. "You are whip-smart. You're observant and creative and tenacious and all sorts of wonderful things that are going to take you so far. I could never thank you enough for everything you've done for me and this store, but I have something to try." She handed me the paper bag she was carrying.

One thing about me? I love presents. I love them in every form—giving them, receiving them, thinking about them—and Cloma knew that. She'd given me a lot of great ones over the years—a vintage Dior bracelet, a pair of handcrafted silver cowboy boots, and my own Stevie Nicks shawl—but I didn't know if I wanted this one. I'd rather have my job.

But I took the paper bag from her anyway. I opened it and saw black leather, and the smell of leather conditioner hit my nose as I reached in to grab what was inside. When I pulled it out, my jaw dropped.

Goddammit, this woman was good. She knew how hard it would be for me to stay mad at her when I was holding this beauty in my hands.

I'd been coveting a 1996 Coach City Bag for as long as I could remember, and now I held one in my hands. It had the perfect silhouette and understated hardware. It was items like this that made me cling to the hope that I could bring my possessions with me to the afterlife.

"It's beautiful," I said, wondering when the lump in my throat had started to form. I didn't know whether it was from the gift or the fact that the gift felt like a goodbye to something I didn't feel ready to say goodbye to.

"I've been saving this for you for a few years. Picked it up at a consignment store in Portland a few years back," Cloma said.

"I can't believe you've been holding out on me," I responded, with as much of a smile as I could muster.

"I have this for you, too." Cloma reached into her back pocket and pulled out a small piece of paper. A check. "It's six months' pay." I shook my head, but Cloma went on talking before I could voice my protest. "Take it, Teddy. It's the least I can do. This place is just as much yours as it is mine."

I felt like this place *was* mine. Maybe that's why this hurt so much.

Or maybe it was because it felt like everything was changing at once?

"Thank you" was all I said. It would be nice to have some cushion. My dad had racked up a fair amount of medical bills last year, and the at-home caregiver who came a few times a week wasn't cheap. Amos, Emmy's dad, helped us where he could—my dad had worked as his number two at Rebel Blue for twenty years—but I tried to do everything I could on my own.

"What will you do next?" I asked, genuinely curious about what could possibly make this woman leave something that she loved so much.

Cloma smiled. "I've got a grandbaby in California that I don't see nearly enough. I'm going to start with going out there for a few weeks, and then I'll figure the rest out. You and Emmy are more than welcome to raid the racks and shelves this weekend. You can have anything you want." That made my smile a little more genuine, but it didn't meet my eyes. I definitely couldn't say no to that. "I'm sorry I didn't give you more notice. I didn't know what my decision would be until I made it."

"It's okay," I said. "I understand." (I didn't.) "I'm going to miss you," I said honestly. Cloma leaned over and hugged me tight.

"I'm going to miss you too, Teddy girl. It's been an honor working with a lion like you."

*Don't cry, Teddy.*

When I walked out the back door of the boutique, the sun was setting. It felt like a metaphor for my life.

Well, fuck that.

I looked up at the sky, took a deep breath, let out a good solid "God fucking dammit," and stamped my feet a few times.

Something rustled in the dumpster just behind my Ford Ranger, and after a few seconds, Wayne's head popped up. Wayne was the Meadowlark raccoon guy. His house was in a holler outside town, and I swear, it had more junk in the front yard than the Meadowlark dump. He was a tinkerer and could often be found in dumpsters looking for metal and wood and other materials.

Wayne removed the old ski goggles he was wearing and looked at me. "You okay, Miss Teddy?" he asked in his backwoods drawl.

I sighed and waved him off. "Yeah, Wayne, I'm fine. Just one of those days."

Wayne tilted his head. "You sure?"

"Yeah, I'm sure," I said. I motioned to the dumpster. "Find anything good today?" Before Wayne could answer, my phone buzzed in my back pocket. "One sec." I pulled it out. "It's Emmy." Wayne nodded.

"Hey, babe," I said when I answered the phone.

"Hey, Miss Emmy!" Wayne called.

"Hi. And hi, Wayne," my best friend said. I could hear the smile in her voice.

"She says hi," I said to Wayne as I opened my truck's passenger door.

"Are you busy right now?" Emmy asked.

"Just leaving work, why?" I wasn't ready to tell her it was the last time I'd be leaving work—at least at the boutique.

"I need a favor, and you're going to want to say no, so I'm reminding you how much you love me before I ask—you love me a lot, right?"

"Some might say too much," I responded.

"Can you pick up Riley from soccer practice?" Emmy said quickly. "Gus got caught up on the ranch, and Luke and I are pretty far out of town right now." Well, that wasn't what I was expecting.

"You know he's not going to want me to pick her up. I think

he'd rather have Riley get a ride home with a motorcycle gang than with me," I said.

"Well, he put me in charge of finding someone to get her home, and I don't know any motorcycle gangs," Emmy said. "So you're it."

I didn't mind picking Riley up. I loved that kid. Yeah, she was the spawn of Gus, but she was also half Cam, which meant she was at least half cool. "Fine," I said. "Where is she?"

"The field behind the elementary school."

"On it," I said.

"You're a hero. I'll call you later. Everything okay? You sound a little . . . down." I wasn't expecting that, but I guess I should've. I hadn't really talked to her in the past couple of days—a few texts that I answered, a few calls that I didn't.

"Long day," I said as an explanation.

"I'm sorry for making it longer," she said, and she meant it.

"It's okay. We can blame Gus."

Emmy laughed at that. "Text me when you have Riley, okay? I love you."

"Love you back."

# Chapter 6

## Teddy

When I pulled in to the Meadowlark Elementary School parking lot, I could see Riley sitting on the bleachers in her pink soccer uniform. A woman with dark red hair and another girl in a matching uniform were with her. It looked like they'd been there awhile.

I got out of my truck, and when the door slammed, all three heads turned toward me. I waved, and Riley got up to run to me, but the red-haired woman, who I recognized as Nicole James from school days, blocked her with her arm.

"Hey," I called out. "I'm here to grab Riley."

"Hi, Teddy!" Riley called and waved.

"Hey, kid." I smiled. Riley was the perfect mix of her mom and dad. She had Cam's dark, curly hair and thick eyebrows and Gus's dark green eyes. She also had a set of dimples that matched her dad's, but Gus didn't smile a lot, so I wasn't convinced they were still there.

"Teddy Andersen, is that you?" Nicole asked. She was older than Emmy and me—maybe Wes or Brooks's age—I couldn't remember for sure. She was younger than Gus, though, and he was ancient at thirty-six or fifty—however old he was.

"Yes ma'am," I said. "Hi, Nicole."

"You're here to pick up Riley?" she asked. She was still blocking Riley with her arm for some reason.

"Yep," I said. I popped the *p* for emphasis, considering I'd already said that.

"I called her father, and he didn't mention that you were coming. He said he'd be coming to pick her up." Did I detect a hint of disappointment in her voice? Oh god, did this woman have a crush on *Gus*?

Yuck.

"He got caught up, but I promise I'll get her home safely." I gave Riley a "C'mon" nod, which she understood. She ducked Nicole's arm and ran over to me.

Nicole folded her arms. "I didn't know you and Gus were close." Her tone was prodding.

Yeah, Nicole was *definitely* hoping for a little Gus Ryder action. I had to stifle a gag. "We're not," I said as I draped my arm over Riley's shoulders, "but Riles and I are tight. Isn't that right, Sunshine?" I used the nickname we'd all been calling Riley since she was born.

Riley nodded. "Teddy and I are like this." She held up a hand with crossed middle and pointer fingers.

"I'd feel more comfortable if I double-checked with your dad, Riley." Nicole pulled her phone out, dialed, and then put it on speaker. I rolled my eyes, and Nicole definitely saw.

The phone rang and rang before it went to Gus's voicemail. "He's probably still riding back from wherever he was on the ranch—kind of hard to hear your phone when you're on the back of a loping horse, you know?" I said.

Nicole let out a *hmph.* "Do you want to try Cam?" I asked. "Or were you calling Gus for something else?" I said it in my most pleasant tone and watched her eyes narrow.

Nicole tapped her phone screen a few times. Cam picked up after a few rings. "Hey, Nicole—is everything okay?"

"I'm afraid not," Nicole said. *Really?* "I've got Teddy Andersen here to pick up Riley, and I wanted to make sure that was okay with you before I sent her home."

Cam was silent for a second before she said, "I'm sorry—is that all?"

"Yes," Nicole said. The confidence with which she delivered her opening line faded a little.

"Teddy is on Riley's approved list of pickups." At that, I shot Nicole a saccharine smile. "And she has been since Riley started playing. I appreciate you checking with me, but it is absolutely fine to send her home with Teddy."

"Thanks, Cam!" I called, and Riley followed it up with a "Hi, Mama!"

"Love you both," Cam said. "I've gotta get back to work. Anything else, Nicole?"

"No," Nicole said, and hung up before Cam could say more. She was really rubbing me the wrong way—difficult to do unless you were Gus Ryder. Maybe these two were meant to be. "Okay, you're good to take her." Nicole waved me off.

"Thanks, Nikki," I said sweetly. I didn't know if she used that nickname, but I didn't care. "I hope you have a really lovely Friday night." I steered Riley back toward my truck.

Riley waved back at her teammate. "'Bye, Sara!"

I opened the passenger door for Riley—it was tricky—and made sure she got in and fastened her seatbelt before I shut it. I rounded the truck and got in on the driver's side.

"How was your day, kid?" I said as we pulled away.

Riley sighed—it was quite the sigh for a six-year-old. "Long," she said. *Tell me about it, sister.*

"Anything new and noteworthy?" I asked, prodding a little bit more.

She shrugged. "Not really. I had riding lessons and soccer today."

"A packed schedule," I said. Riley was a talkative kid, but she was quieter than usual. "Tell me one good thing that happened at both."

"Um . . ." She thought for a second. "I got to feed Sweetwater today." Sweetwater was Riley's horse. Amos had rescued her last year. She wasn't ready to ride, but Riley was helping Emmy and Amos take care of her—earning her keep.

"That's really cool," I said. "And what about soccer?"

"I scored two goals," Riley said with a shrug.

"Way to bury the lede, kid! You were holding out on me. We'll call your mom back later and tell her! She's going to be so proud of you."

Out of the corner of my eye, I saw Riley's shoulders sag. Ah, there it was—the reason she was so quiet. When we were stopped at Meadowlark's single traffic light, I reached my hand across the bench seat and grabbed Riley's small one. "You miss her, huh?"

Riley didn't answer. She just nodded. I gave her hand a squeeze.

"Is my daddy going to be home?" she asked quietly.

"Maybe not right when we get there, but really soon after," I said. "Are you hungry?" Riley nodded. "I'll make us some dinner while we wait, okay?"

✪

About thirty minutes later, Riley had finished her bowl of instant mac 'n' cheese—Gus was severely lacking on the groceries—and I turned on the TV to a show I knew she liked. I saw a call come in from Cam a few minutes later.

"Hey," she said. "Thanks for picking Riley up. Sorry about Nicole."

"Any time," I said. "Between you and me, I think Nicole's got a little crush on your baby daddy."

Cam laughed. "I got that vibe when she started pelting me with questions about him a few months ago. Then, at the game right before I left, she hit him with a very strategic hair flip and arm touch."

"She seems kind of . . . not great," I said. "They might make a good match."

An amused snort came from the other end of the phone. "I don't even know what his type would be at this point, it's been so long since I've seen him with *anyone.*" I tried to think back to the last time I'd seen Gus with a girl, and nothing came up.

*Huh.* Interesting.

"Anyway," I said, switching subjects as I walked to the living room, where Riley was watching TV, "I'm still with Riley, waiting for Gus to get home, if you want to talk to her. I think she's missing you something fierce."

"Me too," Cam sighed. "Hand me to my baby."

"Kid," I said, "it's your mom." Riley's face lit up. She hopped off the couch and grabbed the phone from me. Once she had the phone in her little hand, I left the living room to give them some privacy.

I walked out onto the front porch and sat in one of the Adirondack chairs Gus had placed there.

God, he had a good setup. He was on the west side of Rebel Blue—far enough from anything else that it felt like this place was all his. He had panoramic views of the mountains, and one of the streams that cut through Rebel Blue went right past the front of his white two-story house.

I closed my eyes and listened to the water flow, letting the sound wash away all the weight of my day.

It was just starting to work when I heard a truck rumbling down the dirt road. I opened my eyes just as Gus's Chevy pickup came to a screeching halt in front of his house. He cut the engine and was out of the cab before I could blink.

Gus stalked toward the house, his gloves and chaps still on, along with the dark brown cowboy hat that he typically wore. Gus always looked like he literally had a stick up his ass, but I'd never seen him the way he looked now—stressed, tired, disheveled.

As soon as he saw me, he stopped.

"What the hell are you doing here?" he asked—spat, rather.

"I think you mean 'Thank you, Teddy, for picking up my kid from soccer practice, getting her home safely, and making her dinner,'" I shot back.

I saw Gus's jaw clench. "Where is she?"

"She's inside talking to Cam," I said, coming to my feet. "Let them talk for a while. Riley misses her." I didn't mean for it to sound harsh, but it did.

"You think I don't know that?" Gus snapped.

I shook my head. "That's not what I meant," I said. Gus pulled off his gloves and rolled his eyes.

"Whatever, Teddy. I don't need you to tell me what my kid needs."

The annoyance that usually accompanied Gus Ryder started to bubble up under my skin. "But you do need me to pick her up, apparently."

"I asked Emmy to do it," Gus said as he came up the front porch steps.

"No, she told you she couldn't, and you wouldn't budge, so she said she'd take care of it, and here I am," I said. "If you didn't want it to be me, you should've been more specific."

"She should know I would never want it to be you," he grumbled.

That was it. I'd had a bad fucking day, and I didn't need Gus's shit on top of it. I mean, he couldn't even thank me. "Well, at least I didn't forget about her."

I watched Gus's face fall and immediately regretted my words.

It was a low blow—even for me.

"I didn't mean that," I said quickly, but the damage was done. Gus looked like I'd just kicked him in the balls and then in the stomach for good measure.

He sank onto the porch steps and ran a hand over his face. He didn't say anything, and it made me nervous.

"Gus," I said. "I'm serious. I didn't mean that. I'm—" Fuck, was I really about to apologize to my archnemesis? "I'm sorry."

Gus let out a sound that might've been an attempt at a laugh, but I couldn't tell. "How'd that taste coming out of your mouth?" he asked.

"Not great, honestly," I said with a sigh.

"You're right, though," he whispered. Never in my life had I heard August Ryder sound so . . . dejected. I didn't like the way it gnawed at my heart. "I did forget."

His voice cracked.

"You have a lot going on," I said quietly. Gus and Cam were a seamless co-parent team. I'd bet it was a tough adjustment to do it alone. Gus's shoulders sagged, and I didn't know what to do. I didn't even know Gus could *feel* things this way. I didn't know how to react. I'd always been good at caring and comforting, been the person people could depend on and talk to if they needed it, but I didn't know how to be that for Gus.

He hated me. And I wasn't his biggest fan either.

"I forgot to pick up my child, Teddy." God, he was so defeated. "What kind of father does that make me?"

I couldn't just stand here, so I did what I would do with anyone else: I sat down next to him on the porch steps. He tensed when he felt me near, but I stayed there anyway.

"At least you didn't accidentally leave her at home while you went to Paris for the holidays," I said. "By all standards, the Meadowlark Elementary soccer field is pretty tame." I hoped the *Home Alone* reference would lighten the mood a little. Growing up, it was Gus's perennial request for the yearly Ryder holiday movie marathon.

He didn't say anything. He took off his hat and put his head in his hands. "Am I a bad father, Teddy?"

Even though I was right next to him, I could hardly hear what he said. His voice was so low, so broken.

Before I could think about it, I put my hand on his back and rubbed it up and down a few times. "You are many things, August Ryder, and some of those things aren't great, I'll be honest," I said. "But a bad father isn't one of them."

# Chapter 7

# Gus

Riley and I rolled through the door of the Big House at half past eight, which meant we were thirty minutes late. Both Riley and I must've been tired because we slept in longer than usual, and then she got into my bed with one of her picture books and wanted to read to me for a while.

I didn't know how long she'd want to spend her mornings with me, so I certainly wasn't going to say no, but I did feel bad for being late to Sunday breakfast.

I hung my hat on one of the hooks by the door and walked toward the kitchen—Riley bounding ahead of me—where I could hear the voices of my family.

My dad built the Big House before I was born, and it was where we all grew up. It sat about a mile from the entrance to Rebel Blue, and it was set on a small hill—slightly elevated above everything else. The Big House was one of my favorite places on earth. It was a big log-cabin-style home that always smelled like leather conditioner and pie crust. There was always hot coffee in the pot, food in the pantry, and a place to hang your hat.

Now my dad was the only one who lived here. I moved out to my own house on the ranch before Riley was born; Emmy hadn't lived here since before she left for college and now she and Brooks lived together. My brother Wes was the last one here, but he moved to another house on the property last year. He and his girlfriend, Ada, were renovating it.

Honestly, I worried about my dad being here alone—Amos Ryder wasn't as young as he used to be—but all of us were close by. I didn't think he was lonely, it was just a big house—literally—for one guy.

When I walked into the kitchen, I saw my dad stationed in front of the stove with a kitchen rag draped over his shoulder—still cooking. Wes and Ada were looking at something on her iPad. Well, Ada was looking at something on her iPad—Wes was looking at her like a lovesick idiot. Wes's dog, Waylon, was sitting at their feet.

Riley had found her way onto Emmy's lap and was deep in conversation with her and Brooks. I watched Brooks tuck a piece of my sister's hair behind her ear.

It has taken me awhile to get used to Brooks and Emmy as a couple. Luke Brooks had been my best friend since elementary school. I'd found some kids picking on him—he was a lot lankier then, hadn't quite grown into his height or his ears—and stepped in. I gave him half my lunch and brought him home after school.

He's been around ever since.

Emmy and he started seeing each other in secret after she moved home and retired from barrel racing a couple of years ago. I found out when I saw them sticking their tongues down each other's throat after Emmy's last race. Let's just say I didn't handle it well. I punched him in the face. I still remember what it felt like when my knuckles connected with his cheekbone. And for the first time since I'd known him, Luke Brooks didn't hit back.

That's when I knew I'd fucked up.

Yet every time I think about that day, I feel like I'm the one getting the wind knocked out of me. Not because I didn't want them to be together, but because I hated that neither of them had felt they could tell me. I prided myself on taking care of my people, and it felt like the two people I loved most in the world didn't trust me to show up for them.

Brooks and I forgave each other pretty quickly—I was man enough to admit that I couldn't live without the bastard. But it still took me awhile to accept the fact that my best friend and my little sister were hat over boots for each other. After a couple of months, I finally stopped flinching every time he touched her—which was a lot, by the way. Who knew he was such a touchy-feely motherfucker?

Still, when I looked at them, I felt a gut punch. Not hurt anymore, but something different. The sense that when I looked at them, I saw the type of life I'd really like to have.

Emmy looked up at me when she heard me enter the kitchen. My daughter was playing with my mom's engagement ring, which now sat on Emmy's left hand. "Are you running on Brooks Standard Time now?" she asked with a smile. Brooks was perpetually late.

"Sorry," I murmured. "You guys could've started without us."

"Wouldn't dream of it," my dad called from his spot at the stove. "I think we're ready here. Everyone come grab a dish."

Each of us filed into a line to grab the serving platters heaped with breakfast food—eggs, bacon, sausage, French toast—pancakes for Emmy because she didn't like the texture of French toast—and fruit.

My dad never went less than all out with family meals. I got my love of cooking from him, but you wouldn't know how much I loved to cook by looking at my cupboards right now. I really needed to hit the grocery store.

We sat down at the big oak table that hadn't moved since before I was born. Dusty's mom, Aggie, had made it for my parents as a wedding present. There was an inscription on the underside of it—FOR AMOS AND STELLA, A LOVE STORY FOR THE AGES. JUNE 6, 1986. I had memorized it.

I'd spent a lot of time under this table staring at those words after my mom passed away. I had been diagnosed as dyslexic at the age of six, so it took me a bit to unscramble the letters, but once I did, I held the words close to me. And when I got older and started to think about the kind of life I wanted for myself, I thought of that inscription.

We all sat down at the table and started passing dishes around. I piled my plate high and made sure Riley had enough food and a good amount of fruit on hers.

Brooks talked about how everything was going at the bar—the second level was mostly cleaned out and ready for Ada. She, and Teddy apparently, were going to do some sort of cool wall art thing with some of the old Wyoming newspapers. Ada was an interior designer. She and Wes met when she came to Rebel Blue to renovate our guest ranch—Baby Blue.

"I'm so excited," Ada said when the project was brought up. "I've always wanted to modpodge an entire wall. Teddy sent me some pictures of the newspapers. It's cool that the Devil's Boot has so much history."

"Those newspapers caused her a lot of grief!" Brooks laughed, and I shot him a warning look. "When she went to put them downstairs, she ended up locked in a closet with Gus."

*Bastard,* I thought. Everyone else laughed too. I rolled my eyes.

"Wait," Wes said. "You and Teddy were in a small, dark, confined space with each other and both of you lived to tell the tale?"

"Barely," I grunted.

"God, I would've loved to be a fly on that wall," Wes mused. "What did you guys do in there?"

I didn't respond. If there was one thing I didn't want to talk about, it was being stuck with Teddy fucking Andersen in that stupid closet.

"So," Emmy said, changing the subject, "how's Cam? Is everything going okay in Jackson?" Her question was directed at me.

"Yeah," I said, honestly. "She likes the law firm she's shadowing at." Cam was doing great. I was the one that was struggling with her being gone. *I'd forgotten to pick up my kid, for Christ's sake.*

My mind flashed to Teddy—how she'd tried to rub the tension out of my back, how she'd told me I wasn't a bad father, and I'd believed her.

I'd never seen Teddy like that before—soft, I guess. But why the hell was I still thinking about it?

"But she misses me," Riley piped up.

Emmy smiled at her niece. "Of course she does, Sunshine. Who wouldn't?" There were a million reasons I was happy about my little sister moving home, but one of the big ones was that she could spend time with Riley—she worshipped Emmy, wanted to be a barrel racer just like her. "And you," Emmy said, looking at me, "how are you doing?"

I rolled my eyes and grunted.

"Riley," Ada said out of the blue, "I haven't seen Sweetwater in a while. Do you want to walk down to the stables with me?" My daughter lit up and nodded excitedly.

"Can I, Dad?"

"Yeah, Sunshine. No treats, though, okay?" I said. Riley nodded and pushed back from the table. She grabbed Ada by the hand and dragged her toward the back door.

Wes stayed seated, which I thought was weird. He normally followed Ada around like a lost puppy.

After the slider door shut, Emmy nudged again. "Gus, are you okay?" She was looking at me with worry.

"Yes, Emmy," I said, annoyed that she'd asked me again.

"Son," my dad began, "I know things have been a little tricky since Cam left, and I think it might be a good idea to look into getting some help."

*What the fuck?* "Cam's been gone for two weeks, Dad," I said, annoyance clear in my tone. "Riley and I are just getting used to our new routine."

"I know," he said. "But I'm worried you're stretching yourself too thin, August. You can't be everything for everyone—father, son, rancher, brother—all at once."

I gritted my teeth. Was my dad calling me a failure?

"You and Cam had such a good system," Emmy jumped in. "And we think getting some help on the days that Riley would normally be with Cam might help you a bit."

*We?* Had my family been talking about me behind my fucking back?

"I'm fine," I said again, trying to keep my temper under control. Normally, it only flared this quickly around Teddy.

"You're wearing two different boots, and your shirt is on inside out, man." That was Brooks. I looked down. *Shit*—he was right. I hadn't noticed.

"And Teddy said you don't even have any food in the house." Fucking Teddy. "And that it's not as . . . clean as usual."

"I don't see how that's any of Teddy's fucking business," I snapped. "I didn't know she was an expert at owning a home or having a kid. Oh wait, she's not."

"August." My dad's voice held a warning. I ignored it.

"Dude," Wes said. Great, all of them were piling on now. "What's the harm in getting a little help? I'm sure Cam would be thrilled to hear that you weren't having to do everything alone."

"I'm not bringing a stranger into my home because my family thinks I can't take care of my kid," I said.

"No one said that you can't take care of your kid," Emmy replied gently. "We're worried that you don't have time to take care of *you*."

"You're one to talk, Clementine," I said. "Remember when you had that riding accident that could've *killed* you? And instead of telling us and letting us help you, you came home and shut us all out? And started sneaking around with my best friend at the same time?"

Emmy shrank back a little, and Brooks shifted protectively. *Too far, Gus. Too fucking far.* "Talk to her like that again, I dare you," Brooks said. He hadn't hit me back a few years ago, but that didn't mean he wouldn't throw the first punch if he thought I was being shitty to Emmy—which I was. My family had hit a nerve. "She's worried about you, asshole."

"I. Am. Fine," I growled.

"And no one said anything about a stranger." Emmy spoke up again as Brooks's hand was rubbing her shoulder. "I was thinking Teddy could help you out."

I was stunned silent for a minute. Was she insane? "You've got to be fucking kidding me, right?"

"Riley loves her, and she's the closest thing to one of us watching her. She's been around since Riley was born," Emmy said, "and she needs a job, Gus."

"Last time I checked, Teddy had a job," I said.

"The boutique is closing. And I think she'd be really good at it." That almost made me laugh.

"Fuck no. She is careless and loud and . . ." I grunted in frustration. "I don't want my kid around her." I had my reasons for not liking Teddy, and most of them had to do with the fact that every time Emmy had gotten herself into a bad situation, Teddy had been nearby—drinking, smoking, sneaking out—basically everything you didn't want your little sister doing, Emmy did. With Teddy. I didn't need that happening to my kid too.

My dad's fist hit the table, scaring the shit out of all four of us. "That is *enough,* August." I couldn't remember the last time he'd raised his voice like this with me. It was cold and hard and communicated that Amos Ryder meant business. "You won't talk like that at my table. I won't allow it, August."

I leaned back in my chair, embarrassed that I'd just been yelled at by my father like I was a teenager and not a thirty-six-year-old man. Emmy, Wes, Brooks, and I were all quiet.

"Now," my dad said after some uncomfortable beats of silence, "I think Teddy helping out is a great idea. It sounds like it would benefit both of you."

"You don't get to make that decision, Dad," I said quietly. He was right to call me on my temper, but Riley was my kid, and I got to decide who was good enough to be in her life.

Not him. Not Emmy. Not anyone else but Cam.

"No, I don't, but August"—he sighed—"if you don't get some help, then I'm going to have to rethink your responsibilities at Rebel Blue until Cam comes home. You can't do it all, and I'm not going to make you try."

My mouth dropped open. No, he couldn't do that. I mean, I guess he technically could. He was in charge here, but I was too, in my own way. I looked around the table. My brother, sister, and best friend all looked as shocked as I did. They didn't know this part was coming.

"Dad . . ." I said, trying to find some words.

My dad held his hand up and asked, "Did you approve payroll on Friday?" Which stopped me dead in my tracks. Of course I had.

Right?

"I"—I stumbled, embarrassed that my siblings were here for this—"I don't know."

My dad let out a sigh. "We have nearly fifty employees on this ranch, August. That's fifty people and their families who depend on us to provide them with a living in exchange for their hard work." He didn't have to say the part about the people who depended on that including my brother, my sister, my best friend, and my daughter. "And all of those people are going to get paid a day late next week." I swallowed hard, properly chastised. He didn't need to mention that I'd been late most days since Cam left, or that our maintenance schedule had been thrown off because I had trouble keeping track of the days and sent the cowpokes off in the wrong direction.

"I'm not trying to berate you, August, but I know what it's like to be a single dad trying to do it all." Amos's voice was soft and gravelly again—the one we were all used to. The one that put us at ease and comforted us. "It takes a village, son."

I looked down at my hands. He was right. I thought about the early days after my mom passed away. My dad had tried so hard to hide the fact that he was broken, but he'd depended on Hank and Aggie to help. My situation could hardly be more different, but his point still stood: He hadn't been able to do it alone.

I took a deep breath. "Okay," I said stubbornly. "I'll talk to Cam, and if she's okay with it, I'll get some help."

"I'll talk to Teddy," Emmy said.

"I didn't say Teddy," I shot back quickly.

"She could literally start tomorrow, Gus. You said you didn't want a stranger. You might not like her, but at least she's the devil you know. And she loves Riley."

"She's got a point, Gus," Wes chimed in, and I shot him a dirty look.

I sighed, unable to believe what I was about to say. I was a stubborn ass, but I was also a logical person.

"Fine. Talk to her."

# Chapter 8

## Teddy

"How much money do you think it took to get Cloma not just to sell the name of the boutique, but to close it altogether?" Emmy asked. It was Sunday night, and I'd taken Cloma up on her "You and Emmy can have anything you want" offer. We'd been going through every rack and trying on clothes for the past hour.

"A lot," I said. "She gave me six months' pay, and I don't think she would've done that unless it was a drop in the bucket."

"That's insane," Emmy said. She had just come out of the dressing room. She was wearing a pair of black jeans, a white tank top, and a handmade leather vest. She did a little spin. "The vest has to be one of yours, right?"

I smiled. "Yeah." I'd made five of them last month—well, six, if you count the one I made for myself. Three pieces of leather panels, cut to perfection and stitched together using a thin leather cord. The result was slightly edgy and delightfully Western.

"It's incredible. You're so talented, Ted." I'd made and repaired a lot of clothes for Emmy over the years, and no matter what, she always made me, and my clothes, feel special.

"Too bad my sewing machine shit the bed last week, huh?" I said dryly.

Emmy looked at me like I'd just told her I was going to die tomorrow. "Still no fix?" I had never gone this long without a sewing machine. I nodded. "Shit, Ted. Is it broken for good?"

"I don't know, but the closest certified repairman for the vintage model is in Jackson, and I feel like I should know for sure if it can be fixed before I haul it all the way down there. And if I can't get it fixed, I'll need to replace it."

"So your jacket . . . ?" she asked.

"Is still hanging in my closet all sad and mopey."

"A casualty of the great Teddy and Gus lock-in." I rolled my eyes at that. Why couldn't he have sustained the casualty?

"Your brother is the worst," I said.

Something flashed from Emmy's eyes. "Speaking of Gus . . ." She wanted to say something but was hesitating.

"Spit it out, Clementine," I said, motioning for her to keep going.

"Well," she started, "you know Cam is in Jackson, so Gus has Riley full time." I nodded. "He wants to get some help—someone who can be with Riley at the house on the days she would normally be with Cam."

"That sounds like a good idea," I said, and it did. Considering the breakdown I'd witnessed on his porch, it was obvious that he needed help.

I didn't know why Emmy was telling me about it, though.

Emmy was quiet, so I looked up from sorting through a bunch of skirts trying to find the one (short, leather, crimson) that I'd had my eye on for a while. My best friend was looking at me the way she looked at me when she wanted something.

Then my brain clicked.

"No," I said immediately. "Absolutely not."

"Ted—"

"No," I said again. "No. No. No. No." Gus might need help, but I was not the woman for the job. Not unless Emmy wanted a double homicide on her hands. "No," I said, hoping this one held some sort of finality.

"Teddy. He needs help, you need a job." Emmy's eyes were so soft. "It's not permanent. It's just until Cam gets home, so you can take the summer to figure out your next move."

"No," I said again. Emmy sat down on the small love seat outside the dressing room and patted the space next to her. I groaned but went and sat beside her.

"I'm worried about you, Teddy," she said. There it was.

"I'm fine," I said with as much enthusiasm as I could muster.

"Really? Because yesterday I sent you a picture of a carrot that looked even more phallic than usual, and you didn't say a thing."

"You're worried about me because I didn't have anything to say about the penis carrot?" I mean, she was right, normally I would've been all over that girthy carrot, but it felt like she was reading too much into it. Plus, it was the first time she had texted me first in a while, so it didn't really seem fair to judge how I responded.

"No, I'm worried because of what your not saying anything about the penis carrot represents."

"Enlighten me," I said.

"Usually, when you're sad or upset or anything, I hear

about it. You say you're over it, but then we harp on it a little longer. If it's really bad, we go buy cheap plates at the thrift store and break them. We paint your garage. We *do* something about it.

"But not this time," Emmy continued. "This time, you're acting like . . . well . . . you're acting like me, and I don't like it."

In the past, I've willingly leaned on Emmy, but I just didn't know how to right now. I felt like my emotions were too jumbled to even begin to talk them through. And if I was being honest with myself, I didn't want to hurt Emmy's feelings. I didn't want to have to tell her that part of the reason I was sad was because of her. I just wanted to deal with this on my own and get over it.

Wow, I did sound like her. Emmy was a bottler—she would hold everything close to her chest and try to work through it without inconveniencing anyone. I knew when something was wrong, but I knew when to push and when to let her be inside her own head.

I guess this was Emmy trying to push. I let out a sigh. "I get what you're saying, Em, I really do," I said. "And yeah, I haven't been feeling awesome lately, but I don't see how watching Gus's kid a few days a week is supposed to help with that."

"Do you trust me?" Emmy asked.

"Duh," I said with an eye roll.

"Then trust me on this: I think this is a good thing. You don't have to worry about looking for a job right away, you can save a good chunk of that check Cloma gave you, and you get to spend the summer running around with Riley at Rebel Blue."

All of that sounded great, until I remembered who Riley's dad was.

I did not want to spend my summer with August Ryder.

"It's low-risk, high-reward," Emmy said, and looked expectantly at me. That was the exact line I fed to her when she was freaking out about having feelings for Brooks, and the look she was giving me told me she knew that.

"That was a different situation, Emmy," I said, reading her thoughts just as I'd been doing since we were babies.

"Yeah, but it still applies," she said. "Where would I be if I hadn't listened to you?" Honestly, probably engaged to Luke Brooks anyway. They still would've found each other.

I bit the inside of my lip and thought about what Emmy had said.

"Teddy," Emmy said again, more seriously this time. "Gus is struggling. He's always loved Rebel Blue so deeply, and he's always been the most devoted father I've ever seen, besides our own, and now both of those things are pushing and pulling at each other, and I can't watch him get torn up by them. He feels like he's failing. He feels guilty about it. Cam feels guilty for leaving. She called my dad after the soccer situation. She's worried that she put too much pressure on Gus and she's asking if she needs to come home." I knew what was coming next. "And he'll never forgive himself if she does."

And I'll never forgive myself if she came home and I could've helped.

"Don't say it," I said, holding up my hand. "You don't need to finish your guilt trip, I know where you're going with this."

Emmy scooted closer to me and laid her head on my shoulder. "So, what do you say, Teddy Andersen? Fancy a summer job?"

# Chapter 9

# Gus

Theodora Andersen was sitting across from me at my kitchen table. Her hair was pulled up in that stupid fucking ponytail, and the cold stare she was giving me made me wonder if her eyes had always been that icy. Or that blue.

It was early—six-thirty. Riley was still asleep. Which was good. A lot of things could go wrong while Teddy and I figured out the logistics of this new arrangement.

"Cam usually had Riley on Monday and Tuesday, and we'd switch at some point on Wednesday, depending on when I was done with everything for the day," I said.

"And that's the schedule you want to keep?" Teddy asked.

"Yes," I said. "In the summer, Riley hangs out with me on the ranch on Thursdays, and Emmy and Brooks on Friday afternoons after riding lessons. One of them takes her to soccer"—I swallowed, thinking about the event that had caused this whole thing—"and I'll pick her up there."

Teddy arched a brow at that, and I let out a growl, daring her to challenge me on it.

"No weekends?" she asked, undeterred by my demeanor.

"No weekends," I said, which was the plan. I wanted that time alone with my daughter. "So you can continue to terrorize the town. Or whatever it is that you do on the weekends."

Teddy rolled her eyes. The morning sun was streaming through my thin curtains and lighting Teddy's face. Her eyes had been blue a few seconds ago, but now they were silver.

She didn't dignify my jab with a response, which annoyed me. Teddy was normally all flames and chaos. Right now, she was cool and stoic.

For some reason, I didn't think I liked it, which was a weird feeling for a man who spent half of our interactions begging her to shut the fuck up. Still, I moved on.

"I normally leave the house around five-thirty"—I gritted my teeth at having to say this next part—"so Emmy suggested it might be easier for you to stay in the guest room Sunday through Wednesday so you don't have to commute." Teddy and Hank lived on the other side of town—it would probably take her half an hour to navigate the mountain roads up to Rebel Blue from her house.

"You want me stay in your house?" Teddy sounded amused.

"No," I shot back, "I really don't." The smile that grew on Teddy's face was infuriating. She was staying in my house, with my kid, I was going to pay her non-Monopoly money, and she still somehow found a way to get the upper hand.

Fuck.

Teddy flipped her ponytail, and I got a prime view of her stupid neck. "I'll see if the accommodations you're offering are up to my standards," she said in a languid tone.

I clenched my fists on the table, which she must've seen, because her smile grew again. I was trying to keep my cool. I didn't need to wake up my kid because Theodora Andersen decided to bring her boxing gloves out so early in the morning.

She started digging through her purse for something, I couldn't tell what. She pulled out pepper spray, a pocketknife, a lighter, a small sewing kit, a half-empty plastic water bottle, a protein bar, a bunch of gum wrappers, and Jesus Christ, it didn't look like the inventory was going to end any time soon.

"Do you live in there or something?" I asked. Why did she have so much stuff? And why was she throwing it all over my clean kitchen table? "What the fuck are you looking for?" I asked.

"A pen and some paper," she responded. She kept digging—now elbow-deep in her purse. She pulled out a small pink rectangle that looked like—

"Are you carrying a taser?" I asked. Teddy gave me a terrifying smile and pushed a button on the side of the hot pink rectangle, and two electric currents zapped between the metal points on the end. I wiped my hand over my face.

*This* is the woman I was trusting with my child?

She pulled out a pen with a chewed-on cap and a napkin from the coffee shop on Main Street.

"So, Gussy. Let's talk compensation, shall we?" Teddy bit the cap off her pen and wrote something down on the napkin before flipping it over and sliding it across the table to me.

"Are you serious?" I said with a sigh. She just smiled at me with the pen cap still between her teeth. "You're ridiculous." I flipped the napkin over and saw the number she'd written down, which was not the number I'd told Emmy—it was at least double.

I looked up at Teddy, but before I could speak, she slid the pen over to me and said, "Write down your counteroffer."

"Theodo—" I started to protest, but she cut me off.

"Write down your counteroffer or I walk, August." God, her fucking cocky smile was driving me insane.

I grudgingly grabbed the pen and wrote the number—$500 a week—that Emmy and I had already discussed and slid the napkin back over to Teddy, who looked at it and said, "Is this your final offer?"

"You know that's my final offer, Theodora."

"That's what you think I'm worth?" she asked.

"I don't think you want to know my answer to that." I sat back and folded my arms. I felt my jaw ticking.

"Asshole," she breathed.

I pointed my finger at Teddy. "Watch your mouth around my kid."

"You called Brooks—and I quote—'the biggest fucking dumbass on the whole fucking planet' in front of her like a week ago," she said.

"I don't see your point."

"Has anyone ever told you that you don't have great people skills?"

"Has anyone ever told you to shut up?"

"You, usually," she said with an eye roll.

"Shut up."

"See?" Teddy grinned, and it didn't seem malicious—more like amused. I didn't like the way it made me feel, so I moved on.

"Five hundred a week, Monday through Wednesday, and no calling me an asshole around my kid. Do we have a deal?"

"Can I call you an asshole around you?" Teddy asked.

"As long as Riley's not around, fine."

Teddy reached her hand out. "Deal," she said. I reached across the table and shook her hand. It was soft.

It was then that I heard a little voice coming from the hallway. "Dad?" Riley said, her voice still sleepy. She was wearing light blue pajamas with horses on them—a gift from Emmy—and holding a stuffed horse—also a gift from Emmy. Her curly hair was a disaster.

Cutest fucking kid on the planet.

"Hey, Sunshine, good morning." Riley padded over to me, and I pulled her onto my lap. When she saw Teddy, she smiled and gave her a little wave.

Teddy winked at her, and Riley giggled. As much as I hated to admit it, Riley really liked Teddy—thought she was funny and all that shit.

"Sleep okay?" Teddy asked. Riley nodded. She was quiet in the mornings, but after ten, all bets were off.

"Teddy is going to stay with you today, Sunshine." We'd talked about it yesterday—that Teddy would be here a couple of days a week and hang out with her while I was at work.

Much to my dismay, Riley was thrilled.

I looked at the clock on the wall. It was a little past seven. "I've gotta get going." I kissed Riley's head, and she nuzzled into my chest for a minute—still sleepy. I looked at Teddy. "There's breakfast for you guys in the oven, coffee in the pot, and"—I motioned to the notebook on the table—"I wrote down Riley's schedule and all that good stuff in there. I usually get back around six." I stood up, still holding Riley, which got me another giggle.

I gave her a squeeze and a kiss on the cheek before walking

around the table and depositing her into Teddy's lap and open arms. Something about Teddy taking her from me felt so . . . natural, it made my chest feel weird.

I walked away from them but risked a glance back. Riley had her head on Teddy's shoulder, and Teddy was gently rocking her on the kitchen chair. Seeing them like that—already so comfortable—almost convinced me that this was a good idea.

But as I was walking out, I heard Teddy say, "So when's the last time you were arrested?"

"Never?" Riley said.

"Well, tomorrow you're going to say yesterday," Teddy said. "Lucky you're mom's a lawyer."

Jesus Christ, what had I done?

## Chapter 10

# Teddy

"How's it going?" Emmy asked on the phone as I did the dishes. After a leisurely morning on the couch with Riley, I'd grabbed the breakfast Gus had left in the oven—pancakes and bacon—and we ate together. I didn't know if breakfast was a thing that Gus made every day before he left, but if it was, I could absolutely get used to it. Apparently he'd inherited Amos's cooking skills, and I loved Amos's cooking.

"I mean, considering I've only been here for two hours, it's great," I said.

"How does the house look?" Emmy asked. The last time I'd been here, after picking Riley up from soccer practice, Gus's house looked like a disaster area. It was so out of character that I actually felt *bad* for him. He thrives on regimen and routine, and his house normally reflects that. Every time I'd been here, aside from Riley's toys, the place had been immaculate. The blankets were usually folded with such precision they could probably have been classified as weapons.

The interior of the house itself is simple and homey,

so Gus's clean-freak tendencies don't make the place feel cold or impersonal—kind of hard to be impersonal when Riley's drawings are taped up all over the walls in the kitchen, anyway—it just feels like Gus.

"The house looks better. I think *you* telling him it was a mess probably got to him," I said with a laugh. I wasn't a clean freak by any means, but Emmy was on another level. She had a thing for piles. I have no idea how she found anything, but she always seemed to know exactly where something was—even if it was behind her nightstand under a sock.

The opposite of Gus.

I'd already snooped in his pantry and fridge, and I wondered what would happen if I broke his label maker. It might kill him. I stored the possibility of Gus's death by missing label maker away for later—just in case I needed it.

"Does he have food?" she asked.

"Yes," I said, "he has food. Have you thought about getting a job as an interrogator?"

"Shut up, you know I'm worried about him."

"He's going to be fine, Em. He seemed totally put together this morning—he was wearing a clean shirt and everything, and he was able to refrain from reacting to most of my digs."

Emmy sighed. "You two should cut each other some slack. Don't you get tired of the constant sniping?"

"Nope," I said. Then Riley walked into the kitchen again. She'd gotten herself dressed and was absolutely rocking a princess dress and a pair of cowboy boots. I took the phone from my ear and put it on speaker. "Emmy, say hi to Riley."

"Hi, Sunshine!" Emmy said, her tone very different from the one she was about to use to lecture me about being nice to Gus.

"Hi, Auntie," Riley shouted, and waved, even though Emmy couldn't see her.

"Have you shown Teddy her room yet?" Emmy asked. Right: I was going to stay here. I kept forgetting that, even though Emmy and I had discussed this at length. She was right—it would definitely be easier and more convenient—but I still worried about my dad.

Normally, if I was going to be gone for more than a few hours, I had a plan in place. I wasn't a planner in general, I preferred to go with the flow, but not when it came to taking care of my father. I coordinated with his nurses, asked Amos if he could stop by—that sort of thing.

When Emmy sprang this arrangement on me yesterday, and I—for some crazy reason—decided to agree, I hadn't done any of that, but when I talked to my dad about it, he didn't seem fazed at all. He just said, "Sounds like a hell of a summer" and went back to his crossword puzzle.

I hated leaving him. I was always worried that something was going to happen when I wasn't there. I pushed that fear down and focused on my best friend on the phone.

"Not yet," Riley said to Emmy.

"I think you should," Emmy affirmed. "You know, Teddy is my best friend, so I need you to take care of her, okay?"

"I will," Riley said. "I promise."

"Good. I gotta go, Sunshine, I can see your dad and Scout coming. I love you!" Riley and I both gave Emmy a "Love you too" and hung up.

I grabbed Riley's hand and had her do a little twirl.

"Incredible outfit choice," I said. "What do you want to do today, Your Majesty?" Riley grinned.

"I'll show you your room." Riley still had hold of my hand and started dragging me toward the hallway. "My room and Daddy's gym are upstairs"—she pointed at the stairs at the mouth of the hallway. I knew that, and I also knew her room had a kid-sized daybed and more stuffed animals than a carnival, but I wasn't about to steal the queen's thunder, you know?

"I'm not allowed to go in the gym because one time I dropped a weight on my foot, and it really hurt," Riley said, talking away.

We walked past the staircase. Riley skipped the first door on the right, but I knew that that was a bathroom, and then we came to a door on the left. My room. I looked at the last door on the right—Gus's room.

A little too close for comfort, but whatever.

The door to my room was open, and Riley pulled me inside. Like the rest of the house, the room had hardwood floors, but this one was mostly covered by a plush rug. The walls were cream-colored, and the large window faced the mountains.

The bed was a sofa bed that had been pulled out and made up. The sheets and comforter were mismatched shades of green, but I liked it. And you bet your ass the corners of the bedding were tucked and crisp. The thought of Gus having to make this bed for me and not being constitutionally capable of half-assing it made me smile.

He had brought in an end table to function as a nightstand. There was a mason jar on it with water and wildflowers. That was . . . nice.

"This used to be my room, but I got big," Riley said.

"I remember," I responded. If memory served, the room that Riley was in upstairs was much more spacious, but this one was still nice. And I could get used to this view. There was no such thing as a bad view in Meadowlark, but Rebel Blue definitely had the best ones.

Riley and I went out to my truck and got the backpack and duffel bag I'd brought—clothes, toiletries, a few paperbacks—the essentials. She helped me unpack, and she was chatty today. She told me that her dad had spent all day yesterday cleaning—which Riley hated—and that they'd then gone to the grocery store past her bedtime—which she loved. I also learned that the princess dress wasn't her first outfit choice but that she didn't know where all of her clothes were.

After I made us some sandwiches for lunch, I went into the laundry room behind the kitchen and solved that mystery real quick.

Gus's laundry piles were bigger than Emmy's, but substantially more organized. Riley's clothes were in pink baskets and his were in white baskets. I quickly threw one of the pink baskets in on Quick Wash and set a timer on my phone to make sure I put them in the dryer.

The rest of the day was nice—easier than expected. We walked down one of the trails near the house—I wanted to scope out some picnic spots—and we saw a couple of sheep; Riley took a nap, we folded her laundry, and we were sitting on the back porch playing Guess Who when Gus came home.

Listen, I was no fan of Gus Ryder, but watching Riley light up and take off like a shot to greet him when she heard the front door open was one of the top five cutest things I'd ever seen—right after the way she'd nuzzled into his chest this morning. I practically heard my ovaries go *ka-boom,* and I didn't even like him. Imagine if Gus was nice and all of this was happening—I'd never recover.

I wasn't sure what to do—greet him or stay where I was—so I stayed where I was. I leaned back in my chair and closed my eyes, basking in the glow of the evening sun. He was home later than he said he'd be. It was past six.

One thing about cowboys? After they've been working all day, you can hear them coming, so I knew when Gus was starting to make his way toward me. Leather chaps, and all the buckles they require, are not quiet.

"Hey," he said when he came out the back door.

I didn't turn to look at him. "Hey," I said. A shadow blocked the sun, and I opened my eyes.

It would never not be the most annoying thing in the world that he was so fucking handsome.

"How'd it go today?" he asked as he untucked and unbuttoned the Western pearl-snap shirt he was wearing—not that I noticed.

"Good," I said. "Your kid is much more pleasant than you." He shrugged like he already knew that. He had unbuttoned his shirt all the way, and the tight white T-shirt underneath was clinging to him. "Thanks for setting up the room," I said as a way to distract me from the fact that he was now removing his chaps.

He arched a thick, dark brow at me. "I don't think I've ever heard you say thank you," he said.

"I say thank you—I have manners, you know—just not to you," I said.

"Fair." He laid his chaps down on the chair next to me. "I'm going to shower and then make dinner. You okay with grilled chicken?"

"I can go get dinner," I said. "You don't have to make anything for me."

Gus rolled his eyes. "Never once have I seen you turn down a free meal," he said. "You entered every eating contest at the county fair a few years ago just so you wouldn't have to pay for any food all day." Huh. I didn't know he knew that.

But he had a point.

"Fine," I said. "Don't poison me, though."

"No promises."

## Chapter 11

# Teddy

Dinner was . . . surprisingly pleasant. Riley told Gus about our day in excruciating detail. He seemed okay with everything, until she told him about the laundry. His eyes flashed with annoyance.

After dinner, Gus and Riley fell into a routine. He rinsed the dishes, and she put them into the dishwasher. I tried to be helpful by clearing the table and putting leftovers in the fridge, but Gus shook his head. "I've got it. You're off for the day."

Something between us felt stilted right now—like we didn't quite know how to communicate without arguing and shooting insults at each other, so instead of responding, I just gave him a nod and wandered off to my room.

My phone buzzed with a text from my dad.

Hank (Not Williams): How was your first day?

Me: Good. Easy.

Me: Is Catherine there with you?

Catherine was one of my dad's home nurses. He had two—her and Joy. They came a couple of times a week while I was working.

HANK (NOT WILLIAMS): No, Aggie is here, so she sent her home. She's taking good care of me.

I didn't know how I felt about that. Usually, stuff like that was my decision. Maybe it was because I didn't remember the last time I'd spent a Monday night away from my dad, but apparently he was just fine without me.

ME: You scoundrel.
HANK (NOT WILLIAMS): You can take the man out of the rock band, but you can't take the rock band out of the man.
ME: Word.
ME: I miss you.
ME: Have a good night.
HANK (NOT WILLIAMS): Miss you. Tell Gus and Riley hello from me.
ME: I'll tell Riley for sure.
HANK (NOT WILLIAMS): Be nice, Teddy.
ME: GOODNIGHT LOVE YOU

I threw my phone on the bed and looked around my new room. My eyes caught on the wildflowers again, and I tried to picture Gus picking them and putting them in here. It seemed so out of character for him.

I'd had a good day with Riley. I felt at peace in this room. In this house. I felt tired, but relaxed, in a way I hadn't felt in some time. I wouldn't tell Gus, but I was grateful for this.

I guessed now was as good a time as any to take a shower—it had been awhile since I washed my hair, and although I felt weird about taking a shower in Gus's house, I figured I should just bite the bullet and get it over with.

When I walked out of my room—toiletry bag in tow—the house was quiet, which meant Gus was still with Riley. I didn't really know how this part of our arrangement would work—just the two of us in the house while Riley was asleep. Would I just sit alone in my room with a book so I didn't have to deal with him? Would he ignore me if we were in a common space like the kitchen or living room together? Or would we have to talk?

The guest bathroom was just like the rest of the rooms in Gus's home—simple and neat. There was one sink, a bath/shower combination with a dark green shower curtain and matching bath mat. Green was a recurring color in Gus's home décor. It suited him.

So far, being behind enemy lines wasn't as bad as I thought it would be.

## Chapter 12

# Gus

Riley went down for bed with less fight than usual. She'd probably worn herself out from talking my ear off all through dinner and bath time.

Teddy this, Teddy that. Teddy and me saw a sheep poop on another sheep's head today. Teddy liked my princess dress. Teddy made me a sandwich for lunch today. Teddy called me Your Majesty all day, Teddy, Teddy, Teddy.

Too much fucking Teddy, if you ask me.

But I was happy she'd had a good day. I was happy she'd talked my ear off—Riley had been far too quiet for my taste the last couple of days.

Still, it was too much Teddy.

That thought was only affirmed by the fact that when I went downstairs to the living room with a stack of picture books from Riley's room, Teddy was sitting on my couch. This was worse than being locked in a closet with her, because I had no escape even in my own house.

She must've taken a shower, because her copper hair was damp and hung loose around her face. She was wearing a giant T-shirt that had a wolf howling at the moon on it and held a paperback book in her hands. And—fuck. Was she not wearing any pants? I looked at her long legs. Her toenails were painted red.

She looked up at me and shifted a little. My eyes moved to her thighs and I saw the hem of some black shorts peeking out. *Thank fuck.*

"She go to bed okay?" Teddy asked.

"Yeah," I said. "Rare for her. She's a night owl."

"Like Cam." Teddy smiled, not the menacing smile she usually gave me, but a nice, warm one. "But unlike either of you, she talks a lot."

"Tell me about it," I said. Riley always had something to say, and I hoped she never stopped using her voice.

"Did you—" I started, and then trailed off. I swallowed—"have a good day?"

Teddy laughed a little. "Do we really hate each other so much that you can't even ask me how my day was without struggling?"

"Apparently," I mumbled.

She shook her head. "I had a nice day. I like being here." Something in me felt . . . kind of satisfied that she had a good day at Rebel Blue—at my home. "What about you?" she asked.

"It was fine," I said. I looked at Teddy, who was looking at me like she was waiting for me to say more. "There's a lot going on." I shrugged.

"Like what?" She seemed genuinely interested.

"Growing pains," I said.

"You're not giving me a lot to go on here, August," she responded, and she was right, I wasn't. I just didn't know how to talk about all of this with her.

"We're getting bigger every year—more cattle, more horses, more sheep, more hands and cowpokes, and now we've got wranglers for Baby Blue in the mix," I said. "And it's just a lot to manage."

"I thought Wes was in charge at Baby Blue," Teddy said.

"He is," I conceded. "But I need to be involved."

"Do you?" Teddy raised an eyebrow at me. "I mean, obviously you're involved because it has to do with the ranch, but do you have to know the inner workings of everything going on down there and be involved in every decision?"

I shook my head. She wasn't getting it. "I need to be there for him. I need to support him, and I need to be able to take over if something goes wrong."

"Has he asked you to do that? To be all up in his business just in case he fails?"

"I'm not 'all up in his business,'" I said. My temper was starting to flare. I was just looking out for my brother.

"It kind of sounds like you are." Teddy shrugged. "Wes is a very capable guy, and he's also substantially less stubborn than you or Emmy. If he needed help, I think he would ask you."

"He shouldn't have to ask me," I shot back. "I should just be there."

"You don't have to be everywhere all at once to be a good rancher," Teddy said. "It seems like you're just carrying weight you don't have to."

"You don't get it," I said.

"I think I do, actually," Teddy remarked. "You think that it's okay for people to depend on you, but you don't want anyone else to have the pressure of you depending on them." I didn't like the way she said it—like me looking out for the people I cared about was a bad thing—and I didn't want to get into this with her.

I sat on the other end of the couch with a stack of children's books—new ones that Riley and I hadn't read yet. I cracked one open and saw Teddy glance over with an eyebrow raised. She went back to reading her paperback—which I could now see had a shirtless man in a kilt on the cover.

*Christ.*

It was quiet for a few minutes, and I focused on the book in front of me. One of my favorite things that my dad did when I was a kid was read aloud to me, and I wanted to do that for Riley.

But because I was dyslexic, I had a hard time reading new material out loud without stumbling, and it made me feel like a fucking idiot, so when we bought new books, I read them to myself a few times before I read them out loud to her. It helped.

"Is that your preferred reading material?" Teddy asked from the other side of the couch.

"Yep," I said, not wanting to explain any further about why I was reading about a piglet making friends with a bunny.

"Interesting choice," Teddy said.

"Says the woman who's reading porn on my couch right now," I quipped. I knew a bodice ripper when I saw one.

"This is way better than porn," Teddy said, holding up her book. "Plus, I haven't gotten to the sex yet. The hero and heroine are too busy fumbling around each other to realize that the reason it feels like all the oxygen has been sucked out of the room every time they touch is because they're in love." She sighed.

"Nothing says love like suffocation," I grumbled.

I could practically hear Teddy roll her eyes at me. "You know," I said without looking over at her or her legs, "if you keep rolling your eyes like that, they're going to get stuck."

She let out a little puff of air that could've been a laugh, but I didn't really know what Teddy's laugh sounded like—at least her real one. I knew the maniacal villain one that she often used with me—like nails on a chalkboard.

"Yes, Daddy," she said sarcastically, and I straightened my spine, trying to stop the blood from rushing downward. What the fuck was wrong with me?

"Don't call me that," I snapped.

Teddy laughed—the maniacal villain laugh—and said "Why? Does it get you all hot and bothered?" I gritted my teeth and didn't answer, which was a mistake because Teddy laughed harder and said, "It does, doesn't it? Is that what you're looking for, Gussy? A nice girl to call you Daddy?"

"Fuck off, Teddy."

"I knew you had a kinky side," she said, still chuckling.

I slammed Riley's book shut and stood up, hoping that my briefs and sweatpants were doing enough to cover what was happening to me below the waist—as if she couldn't get any more infuriating. "Good night, Teddy," I gritted out, and stomped toward my bedroom.

"Good night, Daddy!" she called after me.

## Chapter 13

# Teddy

I'd always been an early riser, and even if I wasn't, I wouldn't have had a choice but to be one. My dad used to bring me to Rebel Blue every day before I was old enough to start school. Emmy and I would spend the day barefoot in the grass or running along the trails that ran through the ranch. It was still one of my favorite things—feeling the earth beneath my bare feet and looking up at the big blue sky. Rebel Blue was the only place where I felt like I could be grounded and steady while also having my head in the clouds.

Oh, to be so free again.

So I wake up early. I always have. That didn't change when I stayed at Gus's—even though my sofa bed was surprisingly comfortable—everything about Gus's house was comfortable.

Except Gus, obviously.

When I woke up on Wednesday morning and looked at my phone, it was almost five. I usually ran on Wednesday mornings, and running through Rebel Blue Ranch—with shoes these days—sounded like a good way to start my day.

So I rolled out of bed, threw on a pair of leggings, a sports bra, and a sweatshirt, grabbed my sneakers, and quietly slipped out Gus's back door.

At the edge of his backyard, a little trail led to one of the larger trail systems at Rebel Blue. I didn't know the trails as well as Emmy—not even close—but I could find my way around just fine.

When I ran on the road, I always had my headphones and a playlist that made me feel like I could run through a wall—in a good way.

But I didn't like to listen to music when I was hiking or trail running—obviously because of safety, but also because nothing beat the way the sounds of the mountains cleared and calmed my head.

I ran along the trail, watching the sun come up, breathing in the cool morning air, and listening to the breeze rustle the trees, until my phone said I'd hit two and a half miles and it was nearing five-thirty. Gus would be leaving soon, so I turned around and headed back the way I came.

It took me about twenty-five minutes to get back to Gus's. I walked up to the back door and stripped off my sweatshirt before I walked in. I dropped it on the back porch—I had worn it through my whole run, so I was disgustingly sweaty. And smelly. I'd let it air out before bringing it inside.

I opened the door as quietly as I could and I tried to do the same when I closed it behind me. I used the back of my hand to wipe some of the sweat off my face before turning toward the kitchen and coming face-to-face with Gus.

He had a forkful of eggs halfway to his mouth, which was open, and he was frozen as he stared at me. His eyes tracked up and down my form.

The intensity with which he was looking at me made me want to run and hide.

But I didn't run and hide from anything.

Or anyone.

Instead, I walked over to the coffee pot, which was full to the brim, and grabbed a coffee cup out of the cabinet right above it. I'd become partial to a mug from a place called Moon Lake. It was a deep forest green and had a chip in the handle. I'd been drinking out of it every morning I'd been here.

"Coffee?" I asked Gus without turning around.

"What are you wearing?" Gus grumbled.

"Running clothes," I said in a tone that I hoped communicated that I thought that was the stupidest question in the history of the world. What the hell did it look like I was wearing?

"You ran through the ranch like that?"

"Yes," I said, not bothering to tell him about the sweatshirt. It didn't matter—what I was or wasn't wearing was none of his business. I knew which Gus was coming out to play right now. It was the same one who'd punched Brooks in the face when he saw him kissing Emmy. Of all the Guses, this one was my least favorite. All of them were pretty bad, but that one lit a fire under me that I was desperate to burn him with.

"You're practically naked," he said angrily.

"God forbid someone see my stomach." I rolled my eyes. "I am nowhere near naked, and guess what, Gussy? If I wanted to run through the ranch in my birthday suit, that would be my prerogative—not yours."

"This is my ranch, Theodora."

"No, this is your dad's ranch, August." His jaw ticked. I thought back to the conversation he and I had had a few nights ago. It was obvious to me that the man needed to learn to delegate. "And if you keep running it the way you do now, you're going to be burned-out by the time you're forty, and then it's never going to be yours anyway because your dad isn't going to leave his life's work to someone who can't take care of it."

"You don't know what the hell you're talking about," he spat.

"At least I know how to ask for help," I said, even though I didn't, but he didn't need to know that this was the pot calling the kettle black.

"I. Don't. Need. Help," he said, punctuating every word.

"Then why am I here?" I asked, fighting the urge to step closer to him.

"Because apparently I was a murderer or someone who kicked puppies in a past life, and the universe was interested in dishing out some karma."

I leaned against the counter, took a sip of my coffee, and watched his eyes survey me again. Even though he was angry, his perusal was not.

It was . . . heated. Intentional. Appreciative.

He set his fork down and walked over to me until we were almost touching. My breathing hitched, and I saw his nostrils flare.

It reminded me of something I tried to forget—something Gus had obviously forgotten. I wished I could forget it, too—since it obviously hadn't meant anything.

I didn't back down, though. I held his gaze, daring him to try me. He reached out, and it felt like someone had kicked me in the back of the knees.

I thought he was going to touch my face, or tug on my ponytail. Instead, he reached into the cabinet behind me and grabbed a mug.

Then he put one of his big hands on my waist and pushed me aside so he could fill his cup.

# Chapter 14

# Teddy

I made it through my first week as Riley's part-time babysitter mostly unscathed, except for that weird shit in the kitchen last week. The way Gus's eyes had tracked up and down my body kept pushing its way to the front of my mind no matter how hard I tried to push it back. I had to shake my head to loosen all of the dirty thoughts that came with the memory.

You would think that after I'd slipped my vibrator (yeah, I brought my vibrator to work—leave me alone) between my thighs last night to the thought of someone I don't even like, this would be out of my system. He wasn't. Every time my thoughts drifted, I thought about the way his nostrils had flared and the way he'd looked at me and the way his hand had felt on my waist.

Dirty thoughts about Gus Ryder? Gross. Maybe I needed to start sleeping with the vet again. The vet had a name—Jake—but it was so much more fun to refer to him as just "the vet."

I spent Thursday and Friday at my house, catching up on laundry as much as I could, hanging out with my dad, making sure he was set with meals while I was gone, mowing the lawn.

It was a little past six on Friday when I got a text from Dusty.

Dusty Fucker: Dinner?

Dusty was a few years older than me—Wes and Cam's age—and had always been a good friend. His last name was Tucker, but he'd been in my phone as Dusty Fucker since I got a phone in seventh grade.

After high school, he'd disappeared. Left Meadowlark and spent over a decade cowboying around the world. He started in Montana, went to Utah and then Canada. A few years later, he was in Argentina and then Australia—always riding horses, always doing seasonal jobs, never staying in one place for too long.

Until last year.

He'd come back home to work for Gus at Rebel Blue and hadn't shown any signs of leaving yet. But I had a feeling he would later this fall, after Cam's wedding, when the girl he'd been in love with since he was sixteen was officially married to another man.

I texted him back.

Me: Diner in twenty?

Dusty Fucker: Need a ride?

Me: Happy to hear chivalry isn't dead, but no.

Dusty Fucker: See you there.

I did a quick change into a pair of jeans and a black tank top with thicker straps, then slid on my silver cowboy boots for that little extra something. I left my hair down, since I'd put some effort into washing and styling it this morning.

I looked at myself in the mirror, double-checking that the outfit I put together in my head looked as good in real life as it did up there.

When I went out to the living room, my dad was sitting in his chair playing his guitar. It sounded like Clapton.

"I'm going to dinner with Dusty," I said. "You going to be okay?"

My dad smiled. "Teddy. You've made me enough meals for the next three weeks. I'm fine. I'm the parent here, you know."

"And a damn good one," I said with a kiss on his head. "I'll be back soon. Or do you want me to stay out so you and Aggie can have an illicit rendezvous?"

Hank let out a hearty chuckle that told me I might be right. "Get out of here, Teddy." I blew him a kiss and headed out the door.

The bummer about going to the Meadowlark Diner was that it was right across the street from what used to be the boutique. The red FOR RENT sign on the front door felt like a kick in the shin.

When I'd started getting serious about the boutique—started trying to make it something bigger than a small-town clothing store—I had this dream that someday when Cloma was ready to retire, she'd leave it to me.

And now I was faced with the ghost of my dream every time I drove down Main Street.

I turned down the alley right before the diner. There was parking back there, and going inside through the back meant that I didn't have to face that empty building again.

I saw Dusty's black Ford Bronco in the parking lot and

pulled up next to it. He was still inside the cab and gave me a wave before we got out of our trucks.

"Why is your shirt so tight? You look like Peter Frampton," I said when Dusty and I fell into step next to each other.

He ran a hand through his blond hair. It was long right now, falling just past his chin. "You know, no one under fifty is going to get that joke."

"You're under fifty," I said.

"Yeah, but I'm me."

"And thank god for that," I responded. Dusty slung his arm over my shoulder and left it there until we got to the door of the diner. He opened it, and we stepped inside.

"Hey, kids!" Betty called. Betty was probably in her late sixties. She didn't own the diner, but she'd worked there since before Dusty and I were born. She had short box-dyed black hair and had been wearing the same bright red lip stain for as long as I could remember. Meadowlark's own Betty Boop. "Sit anywhere!"

"Booth?" Dusty asked.

"Booth," I agreed. We walked toward the wall of booths on the west side of the diner, but there was only one left, and it was the booth that had the stupid broken seat. If you sat in it, you'd probably get motion sick before you got your dinner, it was so rickety, so Dusty and I slid into the same side of the booth.

"How'd your first week go as Riley's nanny?" he asked as he grabbed the menu from the center of the table.

"Fine," I said. "And I'm not her nanny—I'm a part-time babysitter, basically."

"Is there a difference?" he asked, and I shrugged. "Nanny" felt a lot more official—I felt like I was just hanging out at my favorite place with a kid I liked. "Are you missing the boutique? We haven't really gotten to talk about it since it closed. How are you doing?"

I was saved by answering that impossible question when Betty came over to take our orders. "What can I get for you, honey?" she asked me.

I got my usual. "Patty melt with jalapeños, please. And fries—can you put cheese on them? And a Diet Coke."

"Hot beef, please," Dusty said, "and a regular Coke." Dusty looked at me. "Do you want a rainbow?"

"Oh my god," I moaned. "Yes." A rainbow was a Meadowlark delicacy—a disgustingly sweet artificially sweetened slushy topped with soft serve vanilla ice cream.

Betty smiled. "Blue raspberry for you"—she looked at Dusty—"and peach for you?" she said to me.

"Yes ma'am." I nodded. Betty smiled again and walked away to put our orders in, leaving a flash of pink in her place.

"Teddy!" Riley squealed and jumped onto the seat next to me.

I laughed. "Hello, Sunshine. What are you doing here?"

"Eating dinner and getting shakes," she said. "Dad and Coach and Sara are over there." Riley pointed to a table toward the center of the diner, where Gus was sitting with Nicole and the girl who had been waiting with them when I picked Riley up.

*Go, Nicole,* I thought. She'd pulled off a dinner—a dinner that Gus had probably reluctantly agreed to, judging by the shitty look on his face, which only got shittier when he saw where Riley had gone.

Gus's emerald eyes met mine. I waved at him. His eyes shifted to Dusty, who also waved. Gus's frown deepened just a bit, but he recovered quickly to just a normal frown.

I didn't know why he was frowning at Dusty—those two were friends. Gus liked Dusty a hell of a lot more than he liked me.

We were all connected in our weird little small-town web, but Dusty and Gus's connection was the weirdest, I think. The woman Dusty was in love with was the mother of Gus's child. Did they ever talk about that? Probably not. Men.

And now Gus was Dusty's boss and Cam was getting married to someone else. I guess life doesn't always work out the way you expect it to.

Oh, and my dad was dating Dusty's mom. Small towns were a trip.

"Patty melt with jalapeños, cheese fries, a hot beef, and two rainbows." Betty had made her way back to the table with our food. "And it looks like you've got yourself a straggler," she said, smiling at Riley. "How was soccer, honey?"

"Good," Riley said. "I knocked a girl over."

"Your mom would be proud." Dusty laughed, and so did Betty. It was well documented that Cam was competitive.

Betty set down our food and said, "You kids enjoy," then walked over to Gus's table to take their order.

"Better skedaddle if you want dinner, kid," I said. "Your dad is waiting for you."

Riley sighed—it was hard being six. "Ugh. Okay. 'Bye, Teddy. 'Bye, Dusty."

After she scampered off, Dusty turned to me. "Is it just me or does Gus look like he has a stick up his ass more than usual?"

I glanced over at Gus, whose frown had deepened again. "Yeah, kinda," I said. A wave of disappointment flowed through me; we had learned to coexist in a more neutral way this week, but apparently our truce didn't extend beyond the borders of Rebel Blue.

"What's going on with him and that woman? She looks familiar."

"Nicole James. She's Riley's soccer coach," I said. "And she has a big fat crush on Gus—definitely wants to fuck him, and is perfectly positioned to do so because she has a daughter Riley's age that Riley seems to like." My voice was more bitter than I meant for it to be—I wasn't sure why—but Dusty noticed.

"Not a big Nicole fan, huh?"

I scoffed and popped a fry into my mouth.

I looked back over at Gus's table, at him and Riley sitting across from Nicole and Sara. They almost looked like a real family unit.

"Do you ever feel like you're behind?" I blurted out.

His brow furrowed this time. "I'm not following, Ted. I'm not Emmy—you might have to use a couple more words for me to catch on."

*Solid point.*

"Like . . ." I hesitated. "Does it bother you that everyone else is falling in love or getting married or having babies or planning on having babies and you and I are the same people we've always been?"

"What's wrong with the people we've always been?" Dusty asked.

"Nothing. It's just . . . I thought I would be settled by now. Not like married or with babies, but I thought . . . I would have a better idea of where I was going."

"I don't know. Sometimes I wonder what my life would've been like if I'd stayed here." He was thinking about Cam, I was sure of it. "But if you hadn't gone off to college, if I hadn't gone and seen the world . . . I don't think either of us would've been real happy with that, right?"

He had a point. I loved my small town, but I think that was partly because I'd gotten out of it for a bit, experienced life somewhere else. Meadowlark had the same drawbacks as all the others. It was like a room with a low ceiling and no windows, but you wouldn't know that unless you left and saw how big other rooms could be. Most people who never left had ended up married young to their high school sweetheart and had had at least two kids before I had even graduated from college, which wasn't a bad thing, but it hadn't been something I wanted for myself. Not then, anyway.

Leaving didn't make me love Meadowlark less—it had actually had the opposite effect—but it did make me understand why people like Dusty had stayed away for a long time, why the others had left and stayed gone.

But not me, I wanted a life right here in Meadowlark. But now the home I had loved so much was feeling less familiar than ever. I didn't regret any of the decisions I had made in my life so far, but I couldn't help but worry that I'd missed my shot at something bigger because I had always been so content with what I had. Those pieces that I always thought would eventually fall into place when I was ready—a partner of my own to share my life with, the family we'd build—were no longer waiting for me on the horizon.

"Yeah, maybe you're right," I said quietly. I kept my eyes on a drop of condensation that was making its way down the side of my glass.

Dusty picked up his drink and took a swallow. "But just because you thought you'd be 'settled' by now—whatever that means—doesn't mean you're behind. Maybe everyone else is just ahead." I nodded, but I couldn't form a reply.

He bumped my shoulder with his. "Hey. This is really bothering you, isn't it?" he asked.

I put down my patty melt after a couple of bites. "If we're both not settled by the time we're forty, do you wanna get married?"

Dusty laughed loud enough that we got several looks from other diner patrons. Including Gus and Nicole.

"Way to let a girl down easy," I murmured. He was laughing, but I was mostly serious.

"I love you to death, but I'm not your type, and you're not mine," Dusty said, still chuckling. I knew he was right. It'd be like being married to my brother. Even in small-town USA, that probably wouldn't fly.

"Of course," I said. "I forgot that your type is tall, dark, and"—I counted off each thing on my fingers—"engaged to another man."

Dusty's eyes fell, but he played it off—always unruffled—by putting a hand over his heart as he said, "You wound me," but I still detected a hint of real pain in his voice.

Now I felt bad for bringing Cam up, but he kept talking before I could say anything. "You're going to be okay, Teddy. You won't need me to marry you when you're forty. Plus, forty is not old. I've heard it's the new thirty."

"Well," I said as I brought my hand up to touch the right side of his neck. There was a tattoo there—an Old English *A*. He'd never actually confirmed to me that it was for Cam's last name, but I knew. "My offer still stands. We can tell everyone that that *A* on your neck is for Andersen."

# Chapter 15

## Gus

Before today, I could've confidently said that seeing Teddy Andersen in her stupid fucking running outfit was the worst thing to happen to me since that night years ago.

Not anymore.

Because at that moment, Teddy was sitting in a booth in the Meadowlark Diner and flashing a smile that she's never given me at another man. I watched them walk in with Dusty's arm draped over her shoulder. I don't know why it bothered me—I'd watched men fight for Teddy's attention for years.

Teddy is a flirt, and for once, I don't mean that as an insult. It's just how she is. She has a flirty personality. She likes attention. She basks in it.

So I don't know why seeing her touch Dusty's neck made me feel like I could breathe fire. Maybe because when she touched his neck, in that moment, I wished it was mine.

I'd always kept Teddy at arm's length—exactly where she should be. But now she was living in my house, eating my food, and prancing around in her stupid outfits that felt like they were designed to drive me crazy.

And to top it all off, my kid fucking loves her.

It was officially doing things to my head.

Teddy laid her head on Dusty's shoulder as she popped a fry into her mouth. The movement made a white strap peek out from the tank top she was wearing.

I hated how comfortable those two seemed to be with each other, and I hated that I hated it. I had no reason to. Dusty was my friend, and Teddy was my part-time babysitter. If they wanted to *canoodle,* or whatever, while they got dinner, they had every right to do that.

But that white strap was like a light in the dark—just like it was a few years ago.

I felt my breath quicken. I should've looked away before Teddy could catch me staring, but I didn't.

When she lifted her head from Dusty's shoulder, her blue eyes locked on mine. For a moment, she looked confused, probably wondering why I was still looking at her.

*Believe me, Theodora, I'm wondering the same thing.*

She held my gaze and absentmindedly went to move the white strap back up her shoulder.

"Gus?"

I'd forgotten Nicole was talking. She talked a lot, but not in a way that made me want to listen. I always listened to Teddy—mostly so I could think of a comeback for whatever bullshit she was spewing.

"Sorry," I said. "What were you saying?"

Nicole looked where I'd been staring. Teddy wasn't looking at me anymore; she was dipping her fries in her ice cream and laughing at something.

I wondered what she was laughing at.

"Are Dusty and Teddy dating?" Nicole asked when she turned back to me. "Wouldn't that be something!"

"What do you mean?" I asked. My tone was harsher than intended.

Nicole shrugged. "I mean, both of them are kind of hard to pin down, wouldn't you say? Kind of irresponsible?"

"Teddy isn't irresponsible," I responded. Fuck, someone better write this day down in the Meadowlark history books, because I'd never said that before. I'd never believed it before. But then Teddy started being Riley's nanny or whatever, and I believed it now.

As much as I was loath to admit it, Teddy Andersen was good shit—just not to me.

The look Nicole was giving me was full of confusion. *Same,* I thought. Why was she even at this table with me? When I'd picked Riley up, she asked what Riley and I were going to get up to, so I told her we were heading to the diner. Next thing I know, her car pulls up behind my truck when I park on the street and she and her daughter walk in with me and Riley, and Nicole asks for us all to be seated together.

"Maybe you know her better than I do," Nicole responded. I didn't like her tone when she was talking about Teddy—not one bit.

"I do," I said without thinking. "I mean, she's my little sister's best friend. I've known Teddy her whole life, basically."

Betty's voice saved me. "Chocolate shake for you," she said, placing a tall glass in front of Riley, whose eyes had gotten just as big, taking in the whipped cream and the red cherry on top of it. "And strawberry for you"—she set mine in front of me.

"And an order of fries, extra crispy." She put that right between us.

"We didn't order yet," Nicole said, annoyed.

Betty smiled at her as she pulled her notepad out. "Gus and Riley always get the same thing after soccer," she said. "Now, what can I get for you two?"

Riley and I switched our shakes after we took our first sips. We always took our second sips of each other's.

"Chocolate is damn good today," I said as I slid her shake back to her.

Riley giggled. "You have ice cream in your mustache."

"Do I?" I smiled. I wiped a finger over my mouth, and sure enough, pink strawberry shake coated it. I licked it off, and for some reason when I did so, my eyes flicked to Teddy, who looked away as soon as our eyes met.

I didn't have time to think about it—thank god—because Nicole's voice pushed through the Teddy-induced haze that had been affronting my thoughts way too often as of late.

"Don't you get any healthy food?" Nicole asked Riley. "All that sugar is bad for you."

*Fuck, no.* This woman was not about to lecture my six-year-old on what foods she should and shouldn't have.

"We don't think any foods are good or bad," I jumped in. This was something Cam was passionate about, and I was happy to support her in it. "It's all just food."

Nicole looked confused. "That's not true," she said.

"It is at our house," I said firmly, hoping she would take the hint. I looked at my daughter, who was happily sipping on her chocolate milkshake. Good. Maybe we could get the hell out of here soon.

Nicole didn't say anything else about it, just yammered on

about soccer season like she was coaching the fucking Olympic team.

I risked another glance at Teddy, who popped one more jalapeño slice into her mouth before she slid out of the booth and walked toward the back of the diner. Dusty followed her with a hand at the small of her back, and I was forced to sit with the fact that my opinion of Teddy Andersen was starting to change.

# Chapter 16

# Teddy

Week two of being Riley's babysitter was nearly in the books—just a couple more hours left today, and then I could go home. Not that I didn't want to spend more time with Riley—pretty much the opposite—but I was ready not to have to see her dad for the rest of the week.

He and his arms and his mustache and his eyes were fucking with my head.

Over the weekend, I found an old *Rocky Mountain Native Plant Guide* in my dad's garage. I brought it with me to Gus's because I liked having things to do, and I figured I could try to identify some plants while Riley was wandering around, but when she saw me looking through it while we were eating a snack in the backyard on Wednesday, she immediately took notice.

"What's that?" she asked.

"It's the *Rocky Mountain Native Plant Guide* from 1998," I said. "It's for people to learn about plants in the Rocky Mountains—recognize them, be able to name them, that sort of thing."

"Where are the Rocky Mountains?" Riley asked.

"Right here," I said, gesturing around us. "We're in the Rocky Mountains."

Riley's dark brows furrowed, and she looked confused. "No," she said, "we're at Rebel Blue Ranch."

"Rebel Blue Ranch is in the Rocky Mountains," I said. I tried to think of a way to explain this. "That's what the mountains are named—like you're Riley, you're your own thing, but your last name is Ryder, which you got from your dad, so you're part of him and he's part of his dad."

I was not the least bit good at this, and the way Riley was looking at me proved it. "So the Rocky Mountains are Rebel Blue's grandpa?"

"Kind of," I said. Amos Ryder would love that description, I thought.

"Who's Rebel Blue's dad?" she asked.

I thought about that for a second before I said, "Meadowlark, probably."

The wheels were turning in Riley's brain. I tried to think of a better explanation, but then Riley said, "So we're in Rebel Blue, in Meadowlark, in the Rocky Mountains?"

"Yes!" I exclaimed. "Excellent!" *Fuck yeah, babysitting win.*

Riley reached out her small hands, and I gave the book to her. "So we can find all of these?"

"Maybe not all of them, but probably most of them."

"I want to find them," she said. She was flipping through the pages of the book, which were worn, torn, and a few of them even stuck together. "This one," she said when she saw a picture she liked. "It's pink."

I leaned over her shoulder to look at the plant she was interested in. The science name was Androsace, but I sure as shit didn't know how to pronounce that, so I said its common name out loud instead: "Rock jasmine. It's pretty." Riley ran her hand over the picture of the wildflower. "I'm going to go grab some sticky notes, and we can mark all the ones we want to find first, okay?"

The smile Riley gave me could've powered all of Rebel Blue for a week. I quickly ran inside and dug through my purse. I knew there were sticky notes in there. I felt them and let out another silent cheer.

And they were pink. Excellent.

I jogged back out to Riley, who was still sitting on the blanket I'd set out. She'd changed positions—now she was lying on her stomach, swinging her dirty little feet in the air and flipping through the plant book.

My dad would be pleased to hear that his long-forgotten purchase was coming in handy today.

Riley and I looked through the pages together, and I handed her a sticky note to put on the edge of the page for all the plants she wanted to find. It actually took a good chunk of time—Riley had me read to her what the plants were named, where they were normally found, and if they were perennials, which I explained much better this time. (They come back every year—like Santa.)

We were so absorbed in the plants—which ones we wanted to find, where we were going to look for them, when we were going to look for them—that I didn't realize Gus was home until his shadow fell over us.

We both looked up, and Gus smiled at his daughter. The least he could do was take the chaps off *before* he came to see what we were doing. *Jesus Christ.* "Dad!" she yelled. "Me and Teddy are going to be plant pirates!"

Gus shot me a look that said, "What the fuck is a plant pirate?" I shrugged.

"That sounds great, Sunshine," he said, and squatted next to her. "What's this?" he asked, picking up the plant guide bristling with hot-pink sticky notes.

"The Rocky Mountain native plant guide from 1998," Riley said matter-of-factly. There were so many moments when I saw Gus or Cam so clearly in her, and that was a Cam moment if I'd ever seen one.

"And what are we doing with the Rocky Mountain native plant guide from 1998?" Gus asked.

"We're hunting plants," Riley said. Gus nodded, doing his best to follow along and match her enthusiasm. If he wasn't such a dick, I'd think it was adorable. But he was a dick. It was annoying how many times I'd had to remind myself of that over the past couple of weeks.

*Just because he's a good dad and sometimes looks at you like you're the only person in the room does not mean that he isn't a dick.*

I looked at him again. He was a little . . . dirty today—like actually. His face was smudged with dirt, and a sheen of dust covered his clothes. It was a reminder that Gus was a working man, and who didn't love a working man? A man who knew how to fix stuff, didn't mind getting filthy . . . *Love?* Jesus, Teddy, get your shit together.

"Teddy," Gus said, startling me. He was looking at me like he knew exactly what I was thinking, but of course there was no way he could, so I shook it off.

"Sorry," I said. "What did you say?"

"I'm home early. I was wondering if you were staying for dinner tonight or if you wanted to head out."

"Do you need help with that?" I asked, even though I wasn't sure why. Yeah, the dirt made him look hot, but he also looked tired. "Maybe I can do dinner while you take the night off?"

Gus looked at me for a few seconds, and I felt my heart rate quicken. I couldn't tell if the way he was looking at me made me want to stay or to get the hell out of there.

"I'm good," he said after a few beats of silence.

"Okay," I said quietly. I didn't know why that stung—that he didn't want me to stay or didn't want my help. Time to go home, I guess.

"Stay, Teddy! Please! We have to finish looking at the plants," Riley said. I swear to god, this kid was the only person on the planet that could make me want to spend more time in the presence of August Ryder.

"Not tonight, kiddo. I'm going to spend some time with my dad, okay?" I said as I pulled her into my side for a hug.

Riley pushed out her bottom lip and started to pout. "But I want you to stay here," she said. *Well, just take a knife to my ribs, why don't you?* "I want to talk about the plants."

"We'll talk about the plants on Monday, okay? I promise."

"No, I want you to stay." Riley hit her little fist on the ground. I'd seen this little temper flare a few times. Remember how she had a Cam moment earlier? This one was all Gus.

"Riley," Gus said, his tone soft but firm. "Teddy gave you her answer. She'll be back on Monday. It's important for her to spend time with her dad, too, okay?"

Riley huffed before she murmured "Fine" and threw herself into my arms for a hug. "I'll miss you."

"I'll miss you, too, Sunshine. And we're going to hunt the shit out of those plants on Monday, okay?"

Gus grumbled something under his breath—probably

complaining about the swear word, but he truly had no leg to stand on with that argument, so I ignored him.

"Okay." Riley nodded. I kissed the top of her head, then stood up.

"I'll see you soon," I said to her, then walked toward the back door—not bothering to say goodbye to Gus.

# Chapter 17

# Gus

Riley and I were going to Emmy and Brooks's house for dinner. After my blowup at Emmy during family breakfast, I was surprised that I'd even gotten an invite.

I felt like shit about it—especially because Teddy had mostly been fine, and having her around was actually really fucking helpful. When she offered to help with dinner the other night, I'd wanted to say yes, because making dinner was the last thing I felt like doing. I wanted to shower and rub the tension out of my muscles, but the line between my historical dislike for Teddy and the way I'd been feeling about her recently was already way too blurry.

Then there was that shit about the plants and how excited Riley was about hunting down a bunch of flowers with Teddy that made my throat tight.

I wasn't about to admit it outright, but Teddy filled in some gaps that Cam and I couldn't. Neither Cam nor I had a creative streak. Both of us were logical and competitive—two things that Riley definitely picked up, but she also liked to do things with her hands—make shit—and I didn't know how to help with that. I didn't want Riley to grow up thinking she could be only one thing or that her only choices were things her parents or family were.

Teddy was good at that creative shit. Last week, she and Riley went to Teddy's and got a bunch of fabric scraps and brought them back to my house. They spent all day nailing them to flat pieces of wood that they'd found, trying to make landscapes.

When I got home, and Riley told me what they'd been doing all day, my first thought, which I obviously didn't say out loud, was that that sounded stupid.

But Riley thought it was the best thing ever. Then, when she actually showed me what she'd created, I was floored. What they'd created was interesting and . . . fun. I wanted to hang it up somewhere. That night, we called Riley's mom and told her all about it. Later, I'd gotten a text from Cam that said, "I think Teddy was a good call."

And I told her I agreed.

But Teddy didn't need to know that.

Emmy and Brooks lived in a small bungalow deep in the holler behind the Devil's Boot. Brooks's dad left him the bar and the house when he died. It was the only thing he'd ever done for Brooks.

My truck rolled to a stop in front of the bungalow, and before I'd even turned the engine off, Riley had unbuckled herself from her booster in the backseat, opened the door, and jumped out.

My little lunatic.

By the time I got out of the truck, Riley was already opening the front door. As soon as she did, she looked back at me. "Auntie and Uncle are kissing!"

Of course they were. Lucky that's all they were doing.

Emmy appeared in the doorway a second later and waved. I made my way up the stairs to her front porch and pulled her in for a hug. "I'm sorry about breakfast," I said.

"I know." Emmy hugged me back. "I was just trying to help."

"I know," I sighed and pulled back. Emmy and I looked a lot alike—more than her and Wes or him and me. It was weird, because I was the spitting image of Amos Ryder, so you'd think Emmy would be too, but the older she got, the more she looked like our mom. "And you did," I said. "Help me, I mean."

"I did?" Emmy smiled.

"You did." I may be a hardass, but I have a soft spot for my sister. The thought that I'd made her feel like she messed up by trying to do something nice for me had been tying me up in knots.

"You helped me, too," she said with another quick squeeze.

"How?"

She shrugged. "Teddy needed this." I didn't know what that meant, but I wasn't going to push. My feelings about Teddy—old and new—were complicated enough without bringing whatever Emmy knew into the mix.

Emmy and I walked into the house. When you entered, you were right in the living room, but you could see all the way to the kitchen, where Riley was on a stepstool next to Brooks helping him do . . . I couldn't tell what.

"We bought a pasta maker," Emmy said. "He's obsessed with it."

"So are you," Brooks called to us. "Pasta is one of her hyper-fixation meals right now."

Emmy and I made it to the kitchen, and I saw that Riley was helping Brooks shape some of the pasta dough into little spirals.

"Did you wash your hands?" I asked. My daughter looked at me, and you want to know what that little shit did? Rolled her eyes.

Apparently, she'd been spending way too much time with Teddy.

"Yes, Dad. I always wash my hands."

"Just checking," I said.

Emmy laughed under her breath. "Your stubbornness and Cam's matter-of-factness make for a hell of a combination, don't they?"

"You're telling me," I said.

"You two all good?" Brooks asked, looking over his shoulder at Emmy and me.

"All good," Emmy said. She walked up behind Brooks and put her arms around his waist. He turned as best he could and kissed the side of her forehead. "How's it going over here?"

"Good," Brooks said. "We'll be rocking and rolling in ten."

"Gus and I will set the table." Emmy grabbed plates and silverware. We went out the kitchen door to the small deck at the back of the house. When Jimmy Brooks owned this house, it had fallen into disrepair. When we first came here after Jimmy died, the windows were broken, the front door was hanging off its hinges, and the floors were as sticky as the ones at the Devil's Boot. It was the first time I had ever seen Luke cry. But he spent a few years fixing up the house, and he'd done a good job. He had built the back deck during his renovations, and Emmy had strung up twinkle lights around it.

It felt so calm back here. They had a good view of the

mountains but were also backed right up against the edge of the forest. There was a small pond back here too.

Emmy and I set the table and talked about our weeks. She was excited about the new dude horses we'd rescued and bought. There was one named Huey that she was particularly fond of.

"Good dude horses are worth their weight in gold," I said.

"And we somehow ended up with ten of them," she responded. "There's one, Alrighty, that we'll probably want to put more experienced riders on. He's great once you're mounted, but he's a little sensitive about his hind end, so whoever is riding him needs to have a good leg swing."

"Have you told Wes?" I asked.

"Yeah, he was with me when we discovered the hind end thing." Rescue horses usually came with baggage. Most of the time, we didn't know where they came from or what they'd been through. We learned as we went, building trust with them along the way. Emmy was the best at it, next to my dad.

"I need to check in with him," I said. "I can't even remember what the Baby Blue calendar looks like." Since Teddy started, I'd been able to work through most everything I'd been behind on—and made a lot of apologies to ranch hands and cowpokes—but I hadn't quite made it to Baby Blue yet. When I thought about Baby Blue, I thought about what Teddy said—that Wes was capable and would tell me if he needed me.

"He's got it covered," Emmy said confidently—unknowingly echoing Teddy's words. "You can't be everywhere all at once."

"But I need to be," I said quietly. Full responsibility for Rebel Blue would fall to me one day, and I had the world's biggest boots to fill when that day came. Emmy tilted her head and looked at me with concern. I didn't know how to let go of any part of it. For the first time ever, I wondered if I was clinging to it all a little too tightly.

Before she could say anything, Brooks and Riley came out the back door. Riley was carrying a tray of garlic bread, and Brooks had a big bowl of pasta with pesto and a salad.

After dinner, the sun was starting to set in the Wyoming sky. The sound of crickets echoed through the trees, and Emmy and Riley were sitting on the grass down by the pond trying to spot fish.

Brooks and I were on the deck, each with a beer.

"So how's everything with Teddy?" Brooks asked.

"Fine," I said, and took a swig of my beer.

"That's all I get?" he asked. "The two of you are living under one roof for half the week, and as far as I know, your house is still standing, and all you have to say about it is that it's fine?"

"Yep."

Brooks shook his head. "How's Riley liking it?"

"She loves Teddy," I said.

"God, that must suck for you," Brooks laughed.

I grunted.

"But it's good, right? To have some extra help?"

"Yeah." I sighed deeply. This was my best friend. If I couldn't talk to him about it, who could I talk to? "It's nice, actually." Brooks raised a brow. "She's good with Riley. She keeps her busy and is thoughtful about what they do together. I don't know." I rubbed the back of my neck. "I've never seen this side of Teddy before."

"Or maybe you just haven't wanted to," Brooks said with a shrug. "I've never had an issue with Teddy. I've always liked her. But I liked her more after I saw more of her and Emmy.

The way they treat each other. I'm willing to bet she treats Riley the same way—just Emmy in smaller form."

"That's a good way to put it, actually," I conceded. "It's a good thing she's only there half the week, or I might not even be needed anymore." I didn't actually think that was true—Teddy liked my cooking too much—but it was true that Teddy was exceeding all expectations. Even though my expectations of her had been historically low, I kept them sky-high when it came to my daughter.

"Whatever." Brooks laughed. "You're a good dad, Gus." Brooks was quiet for a second and then asked, "Do you think I'd be good at it? Being a dad?"

"Is this your way of telling me something?" I asked. I felt my heart rate kick up a little. Were they . . . ?

Brooks shook his head quickly. "No," he said. "God, no. We're a long way off from that, but we've just been talking about it lately—if kids are something we want."

"And do you?" I'd never heard Brooks talk about kids before. It was kind of jarring. I mean, sure, I knew that it was probably in the cards at some point, but I didn't think they'd start thinking about it so soon.

Or maybe it wasn't soon. Maybe it was right on time. I looked around the backyard, the beautiful land, the care that he and Emmy had put into their home. Sometimes, as much as I hated to admit it, I felt jealous of the life that they had started to build with each other. Of course I was happy for them, but I still felt a weird ache in my chest about it.

I'd always imagined I'd have a life like this, with a partner. Maybe not the white picket fence thing, but you know, the traditional family unit. I'd put that dream on hold when Riley was born. It was more important for me to be there for Cam, and we had formed our own version of a family that worked for us. But now that Cam was getting married and we had gotten the hang of this parenting thing, I had started to feel those old stirrings. Every now and then, I'd find myself imagining what it might be like for someone else to be in my and Riley's life. Someone who could help me remember to turn on the coffee maker before I went to bed because sometimes I forgot. Or someone to talk to about my day who wasn't six.

Even though the six-year-old was great.

Someone who could make that six-year-old a big sister.

I had always told myself that I had too much in my life to want anything more. But now, hearing Brooks talk, I realized that I'd never imagined he would get what I wanted before I did.

"Yeah, I definitely want kids. But, man, I'm fucking terrified of it." Brooks rubbed a hand down his face. "I'm scared of ending up like him."

I knew who he was talking about. Brooks's dad—Jimmy—was a piece of work, and so was his stepdad. Before Amos Ryder, I don't think Brooks knew what it was like to be loved by a father.

"You're not your dad, Brooks," I said. "And for the record, I think you'd be a fucking incredible dad." Just as I hoped I was, too, even if I was on my own. I loved Riley enough to make up for any holes in our family. And that was enough for me. *Right?*

# Chapter 18

## Teddy

My uterus felt like a war was being waged inside it—a war with knives and spears and other pointy objects. Honestly, it was a miracle I made it over to Gus's house in one piece, considering I was doubled over in the driver's seat the whole time.

When I pulled onto the gravel drive, the porch light was on, and I could hear music coming from the house—Conway Twitty.

I made my way up the steps with my small backpack. I'd been leaving most of my stuff here, except for the laundry I took home, but even that had gotten left this time around, since my washing machine was being a little shit. But it made it easy to go between my house and Gus's. Honestly, I thought the back-and-forth would be more annoying, but it wasn't bad. I think it's because I was genuinely enjoying my time with Riley. She was a good kid—a funny kid, a smart kid, a kid who I would miss seeing every day when the summer was over.

I didn't want to think about that right now—that this whole thing had an expiration date.

When I walked into Gus's house—I was way past knocking at this point—I felt a warm glow that momentarily made me forget how much pain I was in. It felt like home.

The farther into the house I got, the more I felt like something was different. Even though music was playing, it felt quieter. And it was past Riley's bedtime, so I didn't know why Gus was even playing music.

I walked into the living room, slightly hunched over thanks to the cramps that were continuing to ravage my insides. I found Gus sitting on the floor, surrounded by piles of laundry and wearing a pair of round-framed glasses. I hadn't seen Gus wear his glasses since I was in elementary school, and maybe blame my hormones, but damn. He looked good in them. Hot nerdy cowboy with a mustache was not something I thought would do it for me, but . . .

"Hey," I said.

Gus looked up. He looked surprised to see me, and then concerned.

"Are you okay?" he asked. "You look like shit."

"Thank you," I said sarcastically. "It's so hard to believe you're single."

"Not like that," he said. "You're . . . you know. You always look like . . . you." He was stammering. I liked it. "But you're pale—like really pale—and you're walking like someone just punched you in the stomach."

"I'm fine," I said. "Your music is a little loud for nine at night, don't you think?"

Gus sucked in his cheeks. "I forgot to text you," he said.

"Riley is at a soccer sleepover tonight. I was going to tell you that you didn't need to come until tomorrow night."

My heart dropped a little, even though I'd still be seeing Riley soon. "Oh," I said. "Okay. I'll just—um—head home, then."

"You don't have to go home," Gus said. "You're welcome here, Teddy." For some reason, the way he said it made me believe him. There's a first time for everything. "Plus, I don't think you should be driving." Gus got up from his spot on the floor and walked over to me. Before I knew what he was doing, he reached out and put the back of his hand on my forehead. "You don't have a fever, but you're definitely clammy."

I should've shrunk from his touch, but I didn't.

"I'm not sick," I said. "I just have cramps. The first day of my period always knocks me down and out." As if to emphasize my point, a sharp pain hit the base of my spine, and I doubled over a little bit more.

"Christ, Teddy. Sit down." Gus put his hand on the small of my back. That was twice he'd touched me in the past minute.

"I'm good," I said. "I'm going to go home. I can pick up Riley tomorrow if you need me to."

"Theodora," Gus said firmly.

"August." I tried to mirror his tone but failed miserably.

"Sit down." He was already moving me toward the couch. He took my backpack off my shoulder while we moved, and once we made it to the couch, I collapsed onto it.

Now that I was horizontal, I brought my knees up to my chest and closed my eyes.

"I'll be right back," he said, and walked down the hallway toward our rooms. When he returned less than a minute later, he had a heating pad and a bottle of Midol.

"Why do you have Midol?" I asked. Advil or Tylenol would've been fine, but a specific period painkiller?

Gus shrugged. "I have a sister. This was always in the medicine cabinet growing up, so it's always in my medicine cabinet now." He plugged the heating pad in next to the couch and handed it to me. I took it gladly. I only unstretched from my balled-up posture long enough to lay it across my stomach.

"I'll get you some water." Gus's house was open concept, so I could hear him grabbing a glass in the kitchen and filling it from the fridge. He even got me ice.

He came back and handed me the water, along with two white pills, which I took dutifully. I wasn't used to this—to somebody caring for me this way. I was used to getting the pills and the water and making sure my dad swallowed them.

I didn't know until right now how nice it felt to be taken care of—how badly I craved it, to just relax and let go. But I didn't know how I felt about the fact that Gus was the one who was granting me that.

He resumed his spot on the floor, among the laundry piles, his back against the couch where I was lying.

"You say they're always this bad?" he asked. He looked back at me. He looked truly concerned.

"Yeah," I responded. "On day one at least. They're more manageable as the days go on, but yeah, it's kinda debilitating at first."

"And you were just going to push through for Riley?"

"People with uteruses do it every day, August," I said wearily—even though I don't think they should have to. "Plus, I'll probably be fine tomorrow."

Gus just grunted in response, like I was being ridiculous, and went back to folding.

"You know," I said after a while, "I thought you'd be one of those guys who think periods are gross."

"Okay, ouch," he said. I got another one of those huffs that could've been a laugh, but I couldn't say for sure. "I've seen childbirth, Teddy. I know what's going on down there."

Something about that made me perk up. "You were there?" I asked. "When Riley was born?" I'd never heard that before. I didn't know why he wouldn't have been—maybe because he and Cam weren't together? I guess I'd never really thought about it.

Gus smiled. A very small smile, but a smile nonetheless. "Yeah, I was."

"Tell me about it." I couldn't explain why, but I suddenly wanted to know what the experience had been like for him.

"What do you want to know?" That wasn't the answer I was expecting. I expected him to shut me down, tell me he wanted to fold his laundry in peace, kick me out, whatever.

"Everything," I said. "Was it just the two of you?"

Gus nodded. "Yeah. Cam doesn't have the best relationship with her family"—he kept folding laundry while he talked—"or at least she didn't at the time. I think it's better now, but back then it was really bad.

"My dad, Wes, and Brooks were in the waiting room. Riley was about a month early, so Emmy couldn't get here in time, but she drove all night to be here the next morning." I remembered that.

"Cam labored for so long I thought Emmy might make it before Riley was born, but when it was time to push, she popped right out, and she had a set of lungs on her, I'll tell you what." Gus did his small smile again. "She screamed and screamed. When she was born, she was covered in, like, this weird white powder. I thought there was something wrong, but the doctor said it was normal, and to keep an eye on her skin because she'd probably have eczema."

"Does she?" I'd never heard of the powder thing before.

"Yeah, she does. Especially in the winter—the dry mountain air doesn't do her any favors."

"What else do you remember?" I asked. He sounded so soft when he talked about his daughter. I wanted more.

"I remember being totally in awe of how strong Cam was. I remember being grateful for my family because they weren't just there for me, but for both of us. I also remember exactly what it felt like to realize that I'd never love anything the way that I loved Riley as soon as I saw her." That part tugged at my heart. "I've always wanted to be a dad, probably because I have a really good one, but I didn't really know what to expect once she got here. I was wrapped around Riley's finger within a second, and my life got so much better once she was in it."

"I have another question," I said—not sure how he'd react to this one, or when I got brave enough to ask it, or why it mattered to me.

"Since when do you come with a warning?" Gus asked.

"Good point," I said. "Do you ever wish you and Cam would've ended up together? That you would've fallen in love?"

Gus stopped folding and was quiet. Damn it. I'd gone too far. I knew this talking and smiling thing was too good to last.

"No," he said softly. His voice felt like velvet against my skin—warm and smooth. "I don't." I stayed quiet, silently hoping he would say more and giving him permission to do so.

"Do I think it would've made both of our lives easier at

some points? Probably. But I like what we are now." Gus looked back at me when he said, "I wouldn't trade Cam as my friend for anything."

"And you guys were really never . . . a couple?" I asked. I only knew the story that Emmy told me—that they were never really together but wanted to co-parent their kid anyway—Cam because she needed a support system and Gus because family had always been his thing.

"No," Gus said. "We weren't. We had this phase where we were messing around a few months after Riley was born—I think both of us realized at the same time how lonely and isolating being a single parent could be at the same time." That made sense to me. I could only imagine what each of them went through with their little plot twist. "It was like we were both looking for something to cling to—but that didn't last longer than a couple of weeks."

"You guys are great parents," I said honestly.

Gus rubbed the back of his neck and looked away from me, like he didn't know what to do with my compliment. "Do you want more kids?" I asked.

"Yeah," he said quickly. "If I found the right person to have them with. I'd want to do it a more . . . traditional way this time, I guess." Those would be some lucky kids. He was a good dad—thoughtful, patient, affectionate with the one he had, and I had no doubt he would be that way with a few more, too.

"You mean you wouldn't want to knock up another woman via a one-night stand?" I joked.

Gus huffed and judging by the way his shoulders relaxed, I was starting to think those little huffs were actually laughs. "I think one time is enough."

"Riley would be a really amazing big sister," I said, even though I didn't know the requirements for big sisters—I was an only child—but I felt sure she would be. Protective and open-hearted.

"She would," Gus agreed. There was longing in his voice. "What about you? Do you want some copper-headed demons running around someday?"

I wasn't expecting his question. I thought about it for a second, chewing on my answer. It wasn't like me to think before responding, but something about the way he asked made me want to give him a thoughtful answer. "I think so," I said. "Some days I think I definitely want one or two, and then other days, I'll see something on the internet that no one ever told me about childbirth, and I'm like 'No, absolutely not, please keep that little alien out of my body'—but I think so." This was new to me—I'd never really given it much thought before this past year. I didn't know if I'd be a good mom the way Gus was a good dad. I knew how to take care of people, but taking care of a child was a whole other ball game. There were so many ways to fuck a kid up. "If I found the right person," I added.

Gus looked around at me again. He'd paused on the T-shirt he was folding, and his voice was sincere when he said, "I hope you find what you're looking for, Teddy."

"I hope you do too." And I really did.

# Chapter 19

## Gus

It turned out, much to my surprise, that Teddy Andersen was pretty good company when she wasn't being a fucking menace.

We'd never talked this way before. We'd never been able to have a conversation that didn't devolve into a petty argument, but that didn't happen, not tonight.

I liked that she'd asked me questions about Riley and about Cam. I hadn't really done a lot of dating since Riley was born—especially in the last couple of years. Things had really picked up on the ranch, my dad was starting to turn things over to me, and Riley was always my priority. It didn't really leave a lot of time to get to know someone.

But before that, when I did try to date, women were always weird about Cam. It wasn't easy. I always got the feeling they were trying to fulfill some ready-made family fantasy with my daughter and me—like both of us were just an opportunity to live out some weird dream they had about my family or Rebel Blue.

Talking to Teddy made me wonder what it could be like to

do this—talk, fold laundry, listen to music—with someone I actually liked.

Probably pretty fucking great.

Teddy had finally fallen quiet.

"How are you feeling?" I asked.

"Like a bunch of rabid raccoons are feasting on my uterus."

"That's a nice visual," I huffed, then shook my head.

"The heating pad is helping, though. Thank you." I nodded. I didn't know how to respond to Teddy thanking me for something—it was weird.

"So, is this what you normally do when you have a night off from parenting? Laundry?"

"I'm usually better at keeping up with it," I said as I folded one of my T-shirts. "But with everything lately, it's just . . . piled up." I thought about when Teddy threw in a load of Riley's laundry that first day she was here, and how inadequate it made me feel. Like I couldn't even make sure my kid had clean clothes.

I gritted my teeth.

"Laundry sucks," Teddy said. "I always forget that I put it in the washer and then it sits there for two days, and then I go to put another load in and have to rewash the first load, and then I do that cycle approximately three more times before anything makes it out of the dryer. Plus, our washer is this close to crapping out on us, so I have to choose what I wash sparingly until we can fix it or get a new one."

I wondered what was wrong with Teddy and Hank's washer and whether it might be an easy fix. "You know you can always do laundry here," I said.

"That's nice of you," Teddy responded. "Thank you."

"I like doing laundry," I said. "It's methodical, doesn't take a lot of brain power." I picked up a pair of Riley's jeans and noticed a hole in the thigh. "Fuck," I grumbled. "This is like the tenth piece of clothing of hers that has a hole in it." I skipped folding it and threw it into the pile with the other holey clothes.

"I can patch those for you," Teddy said simply. "My sewing machine is broken, so I'd have to do it by hand, but it won't be hard. As payment for letting me do laundry here." Jesus, was anything in the Andersen household not broken?

"I don't need any payment," I said. "But that would be great, actually. There's a shirt in there that she would be heartbroken to throw away."

"I'll start on them tomorrow," Teddy said. "I never get rid of clothes unless I have to."

"Thanks, Teddy," I said, and I meant it.

"Was that so hard?" Teddy asked.

"What do you mean?"

"Accepting some help when it's offered," she said. *This again?* "You try to carry everything by yourself even though you don't have to. It has to be heavy, even with your arms." Teddy glanced down at my biceps, and I flexed a little without thinking. "You have a lot of people who love you, or at least tolerate you"—she pointed at herself when she said that—"and maybe if you let them help, you wouldn't be . . ."

"Wouldn't be what?" I asked, crossing my arms.

"Such an asshole all the time." Teddy met my gaze, and even though I knew it wasn't a good look, she didn't back down. I'd started to like that about her.

I sighed. "Noted," I said. Teddy looked surprised, like she was expecting me to put up more of a fight, but she had a point—a point I didn't feel like arguing. I liked how we were right now.

The playlist I was listening to ended shortly after that, but I still had a few loads of laundry to fold, so I turned back to Teddy, who was still curled in a ball on the couch. "Do you want to watch a movie?" I asked.

"What do you have in mind?" she asked.

I shrugged. "What's your favorite?"

"*School of Rock,*" she said with no hesitation. I actually did laugh this time.

"That wasn't what I was expecting, but okay. *School of Rock* it is." I turned on the TV and bought it online. That way Teddy could watch it again here if she wanted to.

"I love Jack Black," Teddy said right when his character did his failed stage dive after an admittedly epic guitar solo. "He oozes sex appeal."

I turned and raised an eyebrow at her. "Jack Black oozes sex appeal?"

She looked at me like that was the dumbest thing I'd ever said. "Yes," she said pointedly. "He's funny and uninhibited and a hell of a musician."

"Speaking of musicians, how's your dad?" I asked. I hadn't seen Hank in a while. He'd had a bad bout of pneumonia over the winter that gave us all a good scare.

"He's okay," she said. "I worry about him, but he's spending a lot of time with Aggie." Her voice sounded kind of . . . sad, but when I looked back at her, she was smiling a little.

"That's cute," I said, and it was. Aggie's husband passed away a few years ago, and Hank had been single since I'd known him. It was nice that both of them had found someone to spend time with during their later years.

"In twenty-eight years, I don't think I've ever heard you use the word 'cute.'" Teddy reached out and touched my forehead, like I'd done to her earlier. I'd touched her a few times tonight—her forehead, the small of her back—but when she initiated contact, it was a shock to my system.

"What the hell are you doing?" I asked.

"Checking for a fever."

"You're ridiculous, Theodora." I rolled my eyes, and she laughed before she settled back on the couch again. She winced a little, and I looked at the outlet by the couch to make sure the heating pad was still plugged in.

"Drink some water," I said. The glass I'd gotten her was still mostly full. "Do you need anything else?"

"I'm good," she said. "Thanks, Daddy."

"Fuck off with that," I said, but I couldn't help smiling.

Somewhere between Jack Black getting fired from his band and then getting fired from being a substitute teacher, I ended up on the couch with Teddy—on the other end, obviously.

She was right. This was a good movie. When it ended, I turned to tell her as much, but she was fast asleep. "Teddy?" I whispered, just in case she was awake, but she didn't budge.

I looked at my phone. It was a little past midnight—shit, I needed to get to bed. When I stood up from the couch, I looked at Teddy again. I reached down to wake her up but stopped before my hand made contact. She looked so peaceful—a stark contrast to how she'd looked when she walked in here, tired and in pain. I thought about leaving her on the couch, but then I worried she'd get cold once the heating pad turned off. An image of her shivering on my couch in the middle of the night made my decision for me. I slid my arms beneath her shoulders and knees and scooped her up off the couch.

She let out a little sigh. She was always making these little noises. All of them had imprinted themselves on my brain—

not necessarily in a bad way, but in a way that had me thinking things about Teddy that I shouldn't.

When I started walking, she curled her head onto my chest.

My heart rate kicked up, and it was so loud, I wondered if it would wake her.

I thought of the only other time I'd had Teddy Andersen in my arms, and my knees nearly buckled as I carried her into her room.

I laid her on the bed as gently as I could and covered her with a blanket. I looked at her one last time before I left her room and shut the door. I couldn't help but think that the last time I accepted help—it got me Teddy. Maybe that meant good things could come from realizing you can't do it all on your own.

Because, surprisingly, Teddy Andersen was turning out to be a damn good thing.

## Chapter 20

# Gus

When I got home from work the next day, I found Riley and Teddy lying in the sun on the back porch. I'd noticed that they liked to do that—just bask in the heat at the end of the day. Honestly, I didn't think they ever spent any time indoors, and that was fine with me. I'd rather be outside than inside any day of the week, and if Riley picked that up from me, at least I gave her one good quality.

Teddy's skin had gotten a few shades darker since she'd been here. Maybe it was her copper hair, but I hadn't thought she'd tan well. The golden glow that was coming off her now proved me wrong on that, though.

I wondered whether I could taste the sun on her skin. *Jesus, Gus. Do you think you're a poet? Check yourself.*

The longer Teddy was here, the less control I had over my thoughts about her. She was on my mind all the time now.

"Hey," I called from the back door, announcing my presence. Riley ran to me and threw her little body right into my arms. God, I'd never get sick of that. I hoped she'd do it forever.

Teddy waved at me without looking back, and it annoyed me for some reason.

"What did you get up to today, Sunshine?" I asked Riley.

"We had a picnic," Riley said excitedly.

"Here?" I asked.

"No, we walked for a long time." To Riley, "a long time" could mean anywhere from five minutes to an hour. She wasn't the most patient kid. "And then we saw a butterfly, and so we followed it to our picnic spot."

"You followed a butterfly to a picnic spot?" I asked.

"Don't ruin the magic, August," Teddy piped up.

"That sounds like a good day," I said.

"And now we're getting our vitamin D," Riley said. "It's good for you. Do you need some?"

"I think I'm all good," I said. "But you keep at it. I'll come get you when dinner is ready. Enjoy your vitamin D, Teddy," I called.

"I prefer the other kind, but the sun will do," she called back. I made a choking noise, which Teddy must've heard, because she said, "Get your mind out of the gutter, Gus. There's a child present."

"What's she talking about, Dad?" Riley said.

"Nothing," I said as I set her down. "She's just being Teddy."

Later that night, Riley said, "I want to play a game."

I looked at the clock. "It's almost your bedtime, Sunshine."

"Please," Riley said sweetly. Little shit knew I was a sucker. "Teddy wants to play too."

I looked at Teddy, who put her arms up as if to say "I have nothing to do with this."

"Riley," I said firmly, "you can't use Teddy to get what you want."

My daughter crossed her arms and gave me a look that was so annoyed and so fucking adorable at the same time. "How do I get it, then?"

"Ask nicely," I said. I glanced at Teddy, who was watching this exchange with an amused smile.

Riley let out an annoyed huff, and for a second, I forgot she was six years old. "Can we please play a game?"

"Sure," I said.

"Really?"

"Really."

At that, Riley flew down the hallway. Once she was out of sight, Teddy let out a laugh, and I looked over at her. "Funny girl," she said.

"She's something, that's for sure." I heard rummaging in the hall closet, and a small "Aha," before Riley returned with the last game I was expecting: Twister.

"We have to go to the living room immediately."

"Immediately?" Teddy asked. I think she was enjoying this.

"Immediately," Riley said, and then looked at me. "Hop to," she said, face expectant, and I laughed—a big loud laugh. This kid was like a sponge, soaking up everything she heard, even when I often have no idea where she'd heard it.

"All right," I said on a chuckle. "I'm hopping to. Teddy?"

"Also hopping to," she said as she pushed her chair back from the table. Riley ran to the living room like a possessed track star and had already laid out the mat by the time Teddy and I got there.

"Do you guys know how to play? My dad probably does, because Sara said this game is old."

Ouch. Teddy snorted and said, "I might be too young for this one, then." Fucking liar. "So you'll have to explain it to me."

Riley was bouncing on the balls of her feet. "It's easy," she said to Teddy, who was listening so dutifully to my daughter that it made me rub my chest. "Two of us will play and one of us will be the spinner. You have to do what the spinner says, and if you fall, you lose." Riley finished with a firm nod.

"Got it," Teddy said with a mock salute. "I'll be the spinner first."

Riley and I got situated by the mat, and Teddy sat cross-legged with the cardboard spinner in her hands.

"You sure you're ready, August?" she said. "Do you need a few minutes to stretch? Limber up a little?"

"Spin the fucking arrow, Teddy." I rolled my eyes.

"You're not supposed to say 'fucking,' Dad," Riley said, and I had to bite back another smile. I shot Riley the sternest look I could muster, and I watched the lightbulb go on in her head. "Oh," she said. "I'm not supposed to say that either."

"Looks like we're both in trouble this time, Sunshine," I said with a shrug. I was feeling weirdly . . . light tonight.

"Sorry, Dad," Riley said looking down at her toes. They were covered in mismatched socks. I couldn't win them all—especially when it came to laundry.

"I'm sorry too," I said. "You ready to play?" Riley's smile came back and she nodded. I looked over at Teddy. "All right, Andersen, do your worst."

"Right foot red," she said. Easy enough. I put my right foot on a red circle. "Left hand blue." I bent over and put my left hand on a blue circle. Riley did the same. After staying like that for more than a few seconds, I wondered if maybe I should've stretched after all—Christ.

Teddy called out a few more colors and limbs. Everything was good until I somehow ended up practically doing the splits and lost my balance when I had to put my stupid right hand on green.

I went down, and Riley let out a whoop and a laugh. I landed right next to Teddy's legs. When I looked up at her, she was smiling.

"Winner gets to spin!" Riley said. Teddy handed her the spinner and stood up. She reached her hand out to me, and I took it without thinking and she helped me up off the floor.

It took me a few seconds to register that if Riley was calling out the moves, then Teddy and I would be playing.

Suddenly I was very aware of how little Teddy was wearing—black running shorts and a tank top.

She caught me looking at her—dragging my gaze up and down her body. "Ready, Daddy?" she said, with a look that was both fierce and playful—like a lion.

I swallowed. Hard. My mouth was too dry to call her out on the Daddy thing. Heat was already rushing through me, and it took every bit of focus I had to cool things down.

"Right foot blue," Riley called out, and Teddy and I moved at the same time. We were at opposite ends of the mat, which was a small mercy.

But that didn't last very long, because when Riley called "Left foot green," Teddy put her foot right where I was going to put mine.

When I looked up at her, she was grinning. I had no choice but to put my foot on the green circle behind hers. She kept her blue eyes on mine as I did so, and I swear to god, it was like all the oxygen left the room.

"Right foot yellow!" Riley called, and it pulled me out of

whatever fucked-up trance Teddy's blue eyes had put me in. She moved first, pivoting on her left foot so her back was toward me. I stepped on the yellow circle next to the one she'd stepped on—why I didn't distance myself, I'll never fucking know—and her back was only a few inches from my front.

My mind was going places that I shouldn't let it go.

Especially because the gray sweatpants I'd changed into after my shower wouldn't do much to cover me if any more blood started rushing south.

*Fuck.*

"Right hand yellow!" Being lit on fire would make me more comfortable than I was in this moment.

Even though it already kind of felt like I was being lit on fire. Maybe I'd have to get trampled by a horse instead.

When Teddy bent over to put her hand on the yellow circle in front of her, her ass brushed up against my dick, and I wanted to scream.

And fuck me, because that meant the only yellow circle that I could put my hand on was in front of her. I was not about to fold my body over hers—no matter how badly my body wanted to—especially right now. Not the time.

So I did what any self-respecting man would do.

I faked a fall. I bent forward a little, but not enough to have another ass-meets-dick situation, and then just collapsed to the floor.

What I didn't expect was Teddy going down with me.

I couldn't catch a fucking break with this woman, could I? My shoulder clipped Teddy hard. She stood up and tried to steady herself. I flipped to my back as I went down—an automatic reaction to my shoulder hitting hers—and then she came down on top of me.

She let out this giggle that sounded so shocked and happy that I started laughing too. Our bodies were pressed together, but I wasn't focused on that. I was focused on Teddy's freckles and her laugh that sounded like wind chimes on a summer day.

I reached up without thinking and tucked a stray piece of hair behind her ear. When my skin touched hers, both of us froze.

Our breathing was in sync, and I could feel every spot where her body was pressed against mine. And I got an urge to do something I hadn't done in a long time.

I wanted to kiss her. I wanted to grab her by the back of the neck and pull her mouth down to mine. I wanted to feel our tongues tangle. I wanted to know if she still tasted the same.

I might have done all of that if Riley hadn't chosen that moment—thank god—to jump on Teddy's back and yell "Dog pile!"

I rolled and Riley and Teddy toppled to the ground beside me. Riley put her arms around Teddy's neck as they laughed side by side, and Teddy put her head against Riley's.

I sat up and watched them, and shit, I never wanted this summer to end.

# Chapter 21

# Teddy

I think Gus and I have officially turned a corner. Or maybe we can at least coexist in a way that is less volatile?

When I woke up the morning after we watched *School of Rock,* in my bed, with a glass of water on the nightstand and the heating pad over my stomach, I was convinced I was dreaming. The last thing I remembered was Jack Black's monologue on the Man and then feeling like I was floating and then nothing.

Gus had carried me to my bed, and I didn't know how to deal with that fact.

He wasn't there when I got up the next morning, but he'd left a note that one of the soccer parents was dropping Riley off around noon.

I put the note in the book I was reading. I don't know why, and I'm not going to deal with that either.

And then there was the whole Twister situation. I loved making Gus Ryder sweat.

At the end of last week, Riley and I had started our forage

for plants. We hadn't found any rock jasmine, but we'd found a few others that the guide had pictures of—spotted coral root, lots of thistles.

So far, we'd been pressing the ones we'd found between the pages of the guide, but I'd wanted to think of a better way to track it.

Nearly a week after we started foraging, I had an idea, and I was itching for Riley to go to bed so I could get started on it.

The three of us were at the dinner table—Gus was freshly showered, wearing his glasses, and smelling like he'd just stepped out of a lumberjack soap commercial, and Riley was telling him all about Billy Idol.

"How do you know who Billy Idol is?" Gus asked with a shake of his head.

"Teddy is teaching me," she said. "She says there's a severe lack of music education at Meadowlark Elementary."

Gus looked at me with a small smile—like we were sharing our own private joke—and I smiled back.

"Well, she's probably right."

"Billy Idol is a vegetarian, so he doesn't eat meat. Is that what Auntie is?" Riley asked.

Gus shook his head. "Emmy eats some meat, so she's not a vegetarian."

"Is chicken meat?"

"Yes."

"So I'm not a vegetarian?"

"No, Sunshine."

"But I could be one?"

"If you wanted to, yes."

"Cool," Riley said. "Dad, what's your favorite Billy Idol song?"

"'Rebel Yell,' probably," Gus said, and Riley perked up.

"That's Teddy's, too!" she exclaimed.

Gus made eye contact with me again and said, "She's got good taste."

I nearly choked on my broccoli. God, this whole not arguing with Gus over everything was weird, but I have to say I liked it. Plus, Gus was a good cook, and I really loved not having to make dinner.

I'd been my dad's caregiver since I came home from college, and I didn't mind doing it, but it was nice not to have to make dinner every night for a while (though I still made sure my dad was well stocked back home).

After dinner, Gus took Riley upstairs for bath time, and I finally got to start on my plant tracker idea. Once I heard the bath start, I ran to my room and pulled out the piece of cream-colored fabric, my embroidery hoop and thread, and the list of plants Riley and I had prioritized.

I'd also finished patching up her clothes over the weekend, so I grabbed those, too. If they were in the living room where I could see them, I'd remember to take them up to her room in the morning.

I made myself comfortable on the floor of the living room and set the cream fabric—it was about two feet by two feet—on the coffee table and started drawing.

Doing things with my hands was my favorite thing. I'd always loved to draw and paint, and my dad let me do both . . . everywhere.

When I started getting into clothes, I realized that it wasn't just painting and drawing—I just liked being able to create things. I liked having a vision and executing it. I wasn't like Ada—I couldn't DIY the shit out of literally everything—but I could art the shit out of anything.

I didn't know how long it was before Gus came back downstairs, but when he did, he stopped and looked over my shoulder.

"What's that?" he asked.

"You know how Riley and I are looking for plants?"

"From the 1998 Wyoming field guide? Yeah."

"From the 1998 Rocky Mountain field guide, actually." I looked up at Gus and he rolled his eyes. But the malice or annoyance that used to accompany his eye rolls was nowhere to be found—at least right now. "She picked fifteen that she wanted to find, and I thought it would be cool to track them."

"So you're drawing them?"

"To start," I said. "And when we find one, I'm going to embroider it on this. I'm hoping we can finish before the summer is over, then I'll give it to her. Maybe make it into a pillow or something."

I looked up at Gus again. He seemed to be having trouble swallowing.

"This is . . . really thoughtful, Teddy," he said. "The whole thing." Sometimes when Gus was nice to me, it still stunned me silent. "Is this the kind of stuff you did at the boutique?"

"Sort of," I said. "I made full pieces—mostly jackets and skirts—that Cloma let me sell, and we had options for personalization and stuff online, so I got to do some embellishment work like this, too."

"Do you miss it?"

"Yeah," I said honestly, "I do. Not just making the clothes, but the boutique in general. I liked talking to people, helping them find something they felt good in, hearing about what their plans were for the pieces they picked out—that sort of thing. And I liked doing the backend stuff, too—watching the needle move on sales and finding more ways to get our name out there. I liked having goalposts that I could move as I accomplished things."

Talking about the boutique made my chest feel tight. I loved being here with Riley, but I missed my job—not having it and not knowing what I was going to do next made me uneasy. I wanted to keep moving, but I didn't know which direction to go.

"I'm sorry you lost all of that," Gus said. He sounded sincere. "I'm sure you were good at it."

"I was," I said with a shrug. "But I was also totally comfortable. I don't know"—I shook my head; I hadn't really talked about this with anyone before—"I kinda wonder if it was almost a good thing. How long would I have stayed there, doing the same thing—doing something that I always wanted to do for myself for another person?"

"So that's what you want to do?" Gus asked. He was looking at me intently, listening to everything I was saying. "Stuff with clothes?"

I nodded. "I love making things, and I love making people feel good. With clothes, I can do both—make beautiful things that make people feel beautiful. I just don't really know how I want to do it. I don't have enough money to open a brick-and-mortar store, and I don't want to just replicate what Cloma did. I don't know."

"Well, one thing's for sure," Gus said. "You'll sure as hell come up with a better name." I laughed at that. "But seriously,

Teddy. I know you'll figure it out, but I'm sorry you have to, even though I'm not sorry that I benefited from you losing your job."

"So you're not regretting letting me be your babysitter?" I asked, jokingly, but Gus sounded serious when he answered.

"Not at all."

I didn't know what to say to that, so instead I said, "Speaking of which, I patched Riley's clothes." I nodded toward where they were sitting on the arm of the couch. Gus glanced over at them and squinted.

"Do I see flowers on the back pocket of those jeans?"

I smiled. "I told you I did embellishments!" I said. Botanicals had always been my favorite things to doodle—another reason why I was so excited about this summer project with Riley—and I'll never forget when I figured out how I could wear my doodles all the time. "I used to embroider flowers all over my and Emmy's jeans in middle school. I thought Riley would like it."

"She'll love them anyway, but tell her Emmy used to wear jeans like that and she'll never take them off."

"She might love Emmy as much as I do," I laughed.

"She might," Gus agreed as he went and sat on the couch.

"It's funny," I said. "I've known Riley her whole life, but spending so much time with her lately, I've noticed so many pieces of everyone in her."

"What do you mean?" Gus asked.

"She's curious and fearless like Wes," I replied. "She has a bit of a reckless streak like Brooks. She's analytical and has the memory of an elephant like Cam. She's stubborn like you." I shot a pointed look at Gus. "She's kind like your dad, and she's brave like Emmy."

Gus made an amused sound. "You know that weird thing Emmy does with her leg when she sleeps?" he asked.

I nodded. Emmy did this thing where when she was sleeping on her back, she would bend one knee and then cross her other leg over it.

"Riley does that too. She also sleeps hard like Emmy, and fucking hates mornings . . ."

"Like Emmy," we said at the same time.

Gus got up from the couch. "C'mon," he said. He reached down and grabbed my hand, and I tried not to let the shock register on my face when I got up to follow him. "I bet she's doing it now."

Gus kept hold of my hand as we went up the stairs. Riley's door was open, and there was a soft pink and purple glow shining from it. She had a nightlight that went off on a timer.

Once we got closer to her door, Gus started tiptoeing, and I had to pretend it wasn't the cutest thing in the world. He kept me behind him while he peeked his head around the corner.

When he looked in on his daughter, I saw Gus's dimples for the first time in a long time.

I was so busy staring at him that I didn't realize he'd tugged on my hand until he did it a second time.

I stumbled forward quietly and peeked around Gus's shoulder. He was right. Riley was doing the leg thing, and I had to stifle a laugh. Gus looked at me, and there was a smile on his face, and goddamn if it wasn't the most beautiful smile I'd ever seen.

Those *dimples.*

He looked at his daughter one more time before pulling me back down the hall. "I told you," he said.

"Can't believe that type of weirdness is hereditary," I said.

Once we got back to the living room, Gus started to laugh. "There's no way that can be comfortable," he said. I didn't know if I'd ever heard him laugh before—not like this, at least. Not freely. And soon I was laughing too.

Gus and I fell silent at the same time, and suddenly I realized how close we were—almost chest to chest.

We'd been like this before. Both times, I'd written it off—the way it felt. But I didn't know if I could do that again. I didn't know if I wanted to.

I watched Gus's eyes fall to my lips, and then to where our fingers were still intertwined, and then back to my mouth.

He stepped closer to me.

I stepped closer to him.

I didn't know what was happening or why. I'd be the first to admit that I liked Gus a lot more than I had a few weeks ago, that I was starting to notice things about him that I'd never noticed before, and that I found almost all those things appealing.

But did that mean I was going to let whatever was about to happen, happen?

Well, apparently, yeah, it did.

He put his hand on my waist, and I let him. His eyes were on mine and then on my mouth again. His tongue darted over his lips, and I dragged my hands up his arms to rest on his shoulders.

Maybe after this, it would all go away. The want, the struggle that showed up in my head every time I thought about August Ryder, maybe it would stop.

Maybe I needed this.

"Teddy . . ." Gus sighed. "I . . ."

I shook my head. "No kissing," I said as I dragged my hands

down his chest. That was a split-second decision. This already felt like too much, like I was getting dangerously close to doing something that I couldn't come back from. As much as I'd promised myself I'd never admit it, I had barely come back from it seven years ago. I had drawn a line around those deep, secret places in my heart, and I had to do it again—to protect myself from the onslaught of feelings that were getting kicked up like dirt under truck tires—loud, chaotic, and lingering. "Not on the mouth."

"Why?" he asked. He sounded . . . pained?

*Because I can't get rejected again.* "Because I just . . . I can't do that again." He straightened up, and I could see that night flashing before his eyes. He did remember after all. I leaned in and kissed his neck. My thoughts were starting to fall behind my actions—they couldn't keep up with what I wanted. His breath hitched in his throat. "No kissing," I said again.

"On the mouth," Gus repeated, and I nodded. He touched his forehead to mine and breathed out a sigh. "But I can touch you?" he asked. "Like this?" One of his hands brushed over my ass and the other played with the waistband of my shorts.

It was me that gasped this time. "Yes," I forced out. The hand at my waistband dipped inside and gripped my hip.

"Like this?" he asked, and I swore his voice was lower than it was a few seconds ago.

"Yes," I said again, sounding needy and desperate. I didn't know how the situation had changed so fast, but all I could think about was Gus Ryder's hands and how I wanted them all over me.

"Like this?" he asked, brushing his fingers over my panties.

"Um," I said, not able to think. The wheels had stopped turning in my head.

"Tell me, Teddy . . . baby. Can I touch you like this?"

"Yes," I sighed. I wanted him to. I really, *really* wanted him to. He kissed the spot right underneath my ear, and I felt like I was going to combust.

I pushed on his chest and he moved back immediately. "We can't do this, August," I said. "I can't do this." *Not again.*

# Chapter 22

*Seven Years Ago*

## Gus

*I tipped the shot back and felt the burn of bourbon down my throat. After a long fucking week, this was just what I needed. Wyoming was facing the worst drought of the last century, and it was stressing me the hell out. I was worried about our animals. I was worried about our land. I was worried about everything.*

*But with every shot, with every sip of beer, my worries grew smaller and smaller.*

*That's what happened when you walked into this piece of shit bar—your concerns went away, but you had to be careful or they might get replaced with regrets in the light of day.*

*Brooks and I slammed our shot glasses down on the table at the same time. A pretty blonde was hanging on his arm and whispering in his ear, but he wasn't paying attention to her. His eyes kept shifting to the bar, where his dad, Jimmy, was sitting with a full glass of amber liquid. Those two had never had a relationship, but you wouldn't know it bothered Brooks until you saw the way his eyes found Jimmy every time we came to the bar.*

*Jimmy sat in his corner, mainlining Scotch and ignoring his kid like he'd done for Brooks's whole life.*

*The blonde didn't seem to notice that she wasn't holding Brooks's attention, because she was rubbing his arm like a feral animal. He'd go home with her eventually, though. My best friend was a good fucking guy, but he had a reputation as a womanizer.*

*Someone had lined up the jukebox with nineties country classics, and you would've thought Alan Jackson was here in the flesh, the way the bar was reacting to "Chattahoochee" right then.*

*It was loud in here, but I could still hear her. Teddy Andersen's earsplitting voice was nearby, and it was not happy. I looked around, trying to spot my sister's best friend. Emmy had stayed in Denver after she and Teddy graduated from college last year. Teddy came back to Meadowlark and continued to wreak havoc on our little town. Teddy drove me fucking insane, but the anger in her voice had me wanting to make sure she was okay—for Emmy's sake if nothing else.*

*I spotted her copper ponytail within a few seconds. She was right by the bar and—Jesus Christ—squaring up with a man twice her size. I took another swig of my beer before setting it on the tall table and walking toward her.*

*"You good?" Brooks asked over the music. The blonde's arms were around his neck now.*

*"I'll be right back," I said.*

*I made my way over to Teddy, who—much to my annoyance—was looking hot as hell tonight. She had on these tight jeans that looked like they were painted on—same with her black tank top. It was the middle of summer, and her skin was bronzed and freckled.*

*Her personality helped cancel her appeal, though. She was a troublemaker. I'd gotten my little sister out of too many scrapes to count, all thanks to Teddy Andersen—including the night that Teddy and Emmy's tears couldn't stop the sheriff from arresting them for trespassing after they got caught on someone else's property with a bottle of schnapps because they wanted to "talk to the sheepies." Emmy called me instead of our dad, so I had the treat of picking her up from the Meadowlark County Jail. Teddy, too—who thought the whole thing was hilarious.*

*She was brash, and fucking loud, which she was doing a great job of demonstrating as she got up in the man's face. I didn't recognize him, so he must've been from out of town.*

*Once I saw her puff her chest out and start pointing at him, I moved faster through the crowd gathering around Teddy and the guy.*

*"Get this crazy bitch out of my face!" the man yelled.*

*"You owe that girl an apology," Teddy spat.*

*"Fuck off," the man said.*

*Teddy pushed on his chest. Fuck. "You can't just go around playing grab-ass with random girls, you weirdo. What the hell is wrong with you?"*

*She pushed him again, and this time, he looked like he might push her back. Shit. I came up behind her just in time and wrapped one of my arms around her waist, picking her up and swinging her around.*

*Teddy started kicking immediately. "Let me go!"*

*"Control your fucking woman," the man said. This guy was a prick, I'd give Teddy that, and he deserved to get kicked out of the bar, but she didn't need to do it.*

*She was still thrashing in my arms. "Asshole," she screamed. I didn't know if she was talking to me or to him. "Let me go, August!"*

*I whistled for Joe, the bartender, who saw me and immediately started making his way over from the far side of the bar. I motioned to the guy, who was looking at me and Teddy with a hell of a lot of malice. Once Joe clocked him, I knew that guy wouldn't be in here much longer, but I still wanted to get Teddy away from him. If I let her go, she might jump on him and start clawing his eyes out.*

*You never knew with her.*

*The guy was lucky there wasn't a baseball bat anywhere in the vicinity.*

*I dragged Teddy toward the back door, ignoring the fact that she was doing her best fish-out-of-water impression. People moved out of our way, and I bumped the back door open with my hip.*

*We were welcomed by the cool Wyoming night air. It didn't matter that it was the dead of July, nighttime in the mountains always had a chill.*

*Once I heard the door shut behind us, I let Teddy go. And just like I knew she would, she tried to go back in the door, but I blocked her.*

*"Get out of my way, August!" she shouted. "I need to make sure that piece of shit gets kicked out of here!"*

*"He will," I said. I put my hands on her shoulders. "Joe's got it covered." Teddy let out a huff. Her eyes were wild and her chest was heaving. "What the hell were you thinking, Teddy? What if he'd decided to push you back and you got hurt?"*

*"It would've been worth it!" she yelled. "Let me back in there."*

*"No." She tried to shove past me, but I still had my hands on her shoulders, and I held her in place. Her tongue darted out over her lips, and I tracked the movement.*

*A white bra strap had fallen down her shoulder, and for some reason, I pulled it back up. As I did so, I reveled in how her skin felt under mine. I wondered if the air had gotten thinner out here.*

*I skated my hands down her arms to her waist and pulled her closer to me. "Are you okay?" I asked.*

*She nodded. "I'm fine."*

*"You've gotta stop squaring up with men who look like they eat raw eggs for breakfast, Theodora." This wasn't the first time I'd watched Teddy get in a man's face—I wasn't sure she had any sense of self-preservation—but it was the first time I'd been worried that she might get hurt.*

*She rolled her eyes. "Why?"*

*"Because it'll be embarrassing when they lose." That pulled a smile out of her. I didn't get a lot of smiles from Teddy. We didn't get along very well, but damn, she was pretty.*

*I smiled back at her—something I didn't do very often—and the air shifted again.*

*Teddy dragged her hands up my arms, and when they landed on my neck, something in me snapped. I pulled her body to me until there wasn't any space between us, and then I slammed my mouth down on hers.*

*I kissed her like I'd been waiting my entire life for this moment—like I might die if my mouth wasn't on hers.*

*And she kissed me back.*

*I would've kept going—I would've done more than kiss her—but right then the back door to the Devil's Boot opened and a crowd of tipsy patrons flooded out. I pulled back from Teddy and tried not to groan at the sight of her swollen lips.*

*Teddy's eyes were searching my face. Normally, when she looked at me, her eyes were like daggers—icy blue daggers. But right now, they were soft, smoldering, and dangerous. They made me want to kiss her again.*

*Maybe that's why I did it in the first place—because for some reason, I wanted to. I didn't want things very often. I didn't have the time, but seeing Teddy tonight—touching her, being alone with her, seeing how she looked in the moonlight—caught me off guard.*

*"Gus?" she said quietly. I blinked a few times, her voice and the*

*clamor of the people in the alleyway with us yanking me out of my thoughts. Shit. I'd kissed my little sister's best friend—who I didn't even like.*

*And I wanted more. Apparently, my drinks had been a little too strong. But so was this feeling rising inside me right now. It was too powerful. Too much. I knew it could consume me. I don't know how I knew, but I did. And I had too much else at stake, including the future of Rebel Blue, to let it in.*

*"I—I—" I stumbled over my words for a few seconds. "This never happened," I said finally. "Forget this ever happened."*

*And I turned and went back inside.*

# Chapter 23

## Gus

"Hi," she said when she saw me.

"Hi," I said back. We were in the kitchen. I thought that when I saw her in the light of day, I wouldn't want to kiss her anymore, but I did. I wanted it so badly I felt like I couldn't think straight.

Maybe it was the way she talked about my kid like she was the sun. Maybe it was the way she looked in her stupid little sweat shorts and tank top. Maybe it was the way her breath felt on the back of my neck when we'd gone up to watch Riley sleeping.

Maybe it's the way I realized that Teddy loved my family the same way I did. Maybe it was the fact that Teddy was so much more than I'd ever given her credit for, and I felt stupid for only just now realizing it.

So I set my coffee down and walked over to her. "Can I help you?" she said, confused.

Teddy's always been a straight shooter, so I decided to give it to her straight. "I wanted to kiss you last night," I said.

She looked at the floor. "I know," she said. "I was there."

"And I think you wanted to kiss me, too, Theodora." God, I felt like I was sixteen. Teddy said nothing. I put my thumb under her chin and forced her blue eyes to mine.

"Let me?" I said softly. "Just once."

Her eyes flicked to my lips, just like they had seven years ago, just like they had last night. I didn't even think she realized she'd put her hands on my waist.

"Okay," she said.

Wait, did she just say *okay*? She was giving me permission to break the stupid rule she made up last night? Because of the unspoken rule we had broken years before? "Really?" I asked.

"Just don't—" Teddy sighed. "Just don't walk away again, okay?" My eyes stayed on her. Had I hurt her when I told her to forget about it? I could see it now, the way I fled the scene and left her outside, alone in the cold. Was that the reason that our mutual dislike had turned so bitter?

She rolled her eyes—there she is. "You better hurry up and do it before I change my mind."

Teddy didn't have to tell me twice. I brought my lips to hers—softly, tentatively. I just wanted to know what it felt like. It only lasted a few seconds, but it was enough—more than enough. It was easy. I pulled back, not wanting to press my luck, just in case she decided to slap me instead.

But the kiss—god, the kiss. It was soft and short, but it was all I needed to confirm that I hadn't made up how good our first one had felt.

For the past seven years, I had convinced myself that our first kiss wasn't as good as I remembered—that it couldn't have been that good.

But it was.

And our second one was better. Because I knew Teddy now, and not just the Teddy that everyone else knew. I knew the Teddy that was just as fierce when she was soft and just as fun when she was comfortable. She was loyal and kind and funny. She was so much more than I ever knew. She surprised me—wanting to kiss her again surprised me.

And the thing that surprised me the most? I didn't regret it one fucking bit.

I turned and walked back to the kitchen counter. I'd poured her a cup of coffee a few minutes ago. I slid it across the counter toward her.

She walked slowly toward the counter—like she was approaching a wild animal. When she picked up the coffee, she said, "I use this cup every morning."

"I know," I said. I didn't know why she liked that one. I'd taken it from the Big House when I moved in here. I didn't know how old it was, and it was chipped.

She took a sip of her coffee, which had that disgustingly sweet brown sugar creamer that she liked.

"So," she said.

"So," I responded.

She worried her bottom lip with her teeth, and I wanted to kiss her again. I didn't know what was happening to me.

"You just kissed me," she said finally.

That pulled a smile out of me. "Yeah," I said. "I know. I was there."

Teddy huffed. "Were you? Are you sure it wasn't your evil twin who's starting to stir shit up? Or maybe you're sleepwalking? Or maybe you've actually been possessed by one of the Devil's Boot demons and you have no control over your body . . ."

She trailed off, and I shook my head. “You’re insane, Teddy baby,” I said, letting a nickname roll off my tongue. “I’ve got to go to work.” I stepped closer and moved her copper hair behind her shoulder. “I’ll see you later.”

“Oh yeah?” Teddy said, and I stayed where I was. “How can I be sure you’re not going to change your mind, make me keep a secret for seven years, and act like you can’t stand me?”

I shook my head. Teddy had laid herself bare. What I did after I’d impulsively kissed her years ago—the last time I’d done something I wanted to, probably—had stuck with her. And not in a good way. “Listen to me. I am in possession of all my mental faculties, I’m not sleepwalking, I’m not possessed, and I’m not walking away this time. Okay?”

“Okay.” Teddy’s voice was quiet. I kissed her forehead before I left.

I didn’t know what I was doing, but I liked doing it with Teddy.

I drove my truck down to the ranch hand stables. Every couple of months, the vet came to do a check on our herd, and since we were coming out of winter, we needed to check shoes too.

I saw Emmy first. She and Wes were herding all the horses from our family stables across Rebel Blue and into the large pasture near the ranch hand stables.

Wes was riding Ziggy, his gray dappled mare, and Emmy was on Huey. Huey was a new horse at Rebel Blue—he was part draft horse, which meant he was fucking massive. Emmy had taken a liking to him because he was a hell of a workhorse. Maple, Emmy’s barrel horse, tended to get hot feet when Emmy used her for ranch work. She was used to going fast and didn't have a lot of patience plodding through tasks. Maple and I didn't get along. She was a biter.

The family herd was coming from the east side of the ranch, and when I looked to the west, I spotted my dad riding Cobalt.

Cobalt was made for my dad. He was a black American Painter horse—easily the most beautiful on the ranch. When my dad rode Cobalt, in his black cowboy hat, chaps, and shearling-lined denim jacket, he looked every bit the powerhouse of a rancher that we all knew him to be. And I have to say, the sight of him on Cobalt always gave me a lump in my throat.

Sometimes I was so focused on what I thought Rebel Blue Ranch could be that I forgot that everything it was was because of Amos Ryder.

I got out of my truck as the horses approached the pasture gate.

"Well, well, well," Wes said. "Look who decided to show up for work on this fine Tuesday."

"Emmy told me that you didn't need me for herding," I said.

"And we didn't," Emmy said, shooting a pointed look at Wes. I knew this was her way of making sure I wasn't working too much. "And Dusty has the ranch hands under control. We've got a foolproof schedule here."

My dad rode up next to them. "And where have you been?" I asked him.

"My ranch, my rules, son," he responded with a wink. I gave Cobalt a pat on the neck, and he leaned into me.

"Is the vet here?" I asked.

"He should be here in thirty," Emmy said. "I think we start with our retirees, get them on the hitching posts before he gets here." We had five horses that didn't work and that we didn't ride. There were a lot of ranches out there that would give them up at that point, but not Amos Ryder. A lifetime of service was more than enough to earn a horse a comfortable retirement at Rebel Blue.

It was a big part of my dad's legacy, and over the past few years, I'd been starting to think about how I could contribute to that legacy. Maybe we could welcome more horses that needed a place to spend their later years—like a horse rescue or sanctuary. I didn't know how to execute on the idea yet—hadn't had the time.

We had so much potential here. I didn't want Rebel Blue's era of growth to end with my dad. I wanted to make it last.

Emmy, Wes, and my dad all dismounted then. Emmy was tall, but the drop from Huey's back to the ground was still enough to make my knees hurt when I watched her hit it with ease.

"He's fucking huge," I said to Emmy.

"I love him," she said. "Gets a little lazy on the lope, though."

"That's because his trot is just as fast as everyone else's lope with less effort."

"Both his trot and his lope are smooth, though. You could sit both of them. It's like riding a couch."

"He's going to make a hell of a dude horse," I said.

Wes came over and scratched Huey's ears. "Hear that, Hubert? The city girls are going to love you."

Huey nickered, apparently a fan of that possibility.

"I knew Huey would be a ladies' man," my dad chimed in. He'd bought Huey at auction—said he liked the look of him and that he had a kind eye. Not totally sure what that meant, but maybe it was just one of those things you learned with time.

"So we need Peach, Pepper, Winston, Doc, and Applejack," Emmy said, grabbing two of the halters from me. "And let's bring Moonshine out with these guys, too."

Moonshine was old—closing in on thirty—but she was in great shape. If she kept up like this, she'd probably have five more riding years in her. She was a good horse, too. Wes's girlfriend, Ada, still wasn't quite used to horses, but when she did go riding, Moonshine was her go-to.

Wes, Emmy, and I went to work haltering the six horses we were bringing out. Applejack—that old trickster—did his best to evade me, but I got him after a while.

"Looking a little rusty, Gus," Wes called.

"Fuck off," I called back.

I heard tires coming down the gravel road toward the stables. I looked up and saw a silver Dodge pickup approaching. The vet—Dr. Bowski, better known as Jake, or just "the vet"—had quite the truck for a man who came from the city, worked in town, and had never pulled a trailer a day in his life.

I didn't have anything against the vet—I just thought his truck and its stupid lift kit was a bit fucking much. And when he got out of the truck, I noticed he was wearing boots. What the fuck did a vet need boots and a cowboy hat for?

Once Jake started on his exams, it was constant movement—taking horses in, bringing them out. We had thirty horses in our family herd, so we were looking at a good chunk of time.

After an hour or so, we got through the retirees, and I went to grab Maverick—Hank's old horse.

A four-wheeler drove up and Maverick started to whinny

and nicker and swish his tail. He helped me get his halter on with enthusiasm, and when I turned to walk him out of the pasture, I saw why.

Teddy and Riley were walking toward the hitching area hand in hand. I tried not to think too hard about the way the sight of them made my stomach jump to my throat.

Teddy's ponytail was swinging back and forth as she walked. She had on a tiny pair of denim shorts that you could barely see under her oversize Dolly Parton shirt, which I was learning was a favorite outfit of hers, and a pair of cowboy boots. In the hand that wasn't holding Riley's, she was carrying a bag of . . . Twizzlers.

Once Riley saw Emmy, she said something to Teddy, and Teddy nodded and Riley took off like a shot toward her aunt, who greeted her with open arms.

Teddy started walking toward me, and I realized I'd frozen before Maverick and I made it out of the pasture. When she reached us, she put a hand out. "I've got him," she said, and I handed over the reins wordlessly—still dumbstruck.

I thought I'd have had a little more time to process our kiss this morning before seeing her again.

*Fuck.*

I'd kissed her this morning. After we'd said no kissing. And I wanted to kiss her again. And again. And again.

Maverick was making a hell of a lot of noise—excited to see Teddy—and she said, "Tell me all about it, Mav" as she hugged his broad neck.

"Hey," I finally coughed out.

"Hi," she responded. Her tone was cool. Why was her tone cool? My heart was beating at a rate that couldn't possibly be healthy and she was just . . . fine? She asked me not to walk away, not to hurt her again, and now she was just . . . fine?

She walked away with Maverick, and I stood there, dumbfounded, staring at her back.

To add insult to injury, she walked Maverick directly to Jake. When she got close enough to him, she touched his fucking arm.

I clenched my jaw and walked out of the pasture toward Emmy and Riley. Riley jumped into my arms when I got close enough.

"Dad!" This was exactly the distraction I needed while Teddy and the vet were . . . making eyes at each other.

"Hi, Sunshine. What are you doing here?"

"I texted Teddy and told her we were doing exams today. She hasn't ridden Mav in a couple of weeks, so she wanted to see him," Emmy said as I held my daughter close to my chest.

"Why does she have Twizzlers?" I asked as I set Riley down, trying to ignore the fact that Teddy had just thrown her head back in laughter at something the vet said, which meant that the motherfucker had a prime view of her neck.

I wished that things had gone further last night. I wished that I'd left a mark that the vet could see.

"Mav likes Twizzlers."

Riley tugged on my shirt sleeve. "Dad, can I go pet Sweetwater?" The filly had her head over the pasture fence with her eyes on Riley. They had a bond.

"Yeah, Sunshine. Looks like she wants to see you." Riley's curly hair bounced as she scampered toward her horse.

I looked at Teddy again, who was still smiling with the vet. What the hell were they talking about?

"What's with that?" I asked Emmy, gesturing toward Teddy and Jake.

"Hmmm?" she asked, then looked where I was looking. Why the fuck was Teddy touching that asshole's arm again? "Oh. Nothing currently, I don't think."

"Currently?" I hoped my voice was level.

"They had a friends-with-benefits thing going on for a while." I felt my nostrils flare. *Rein it in, August.*

I shook my head. "She can do better."

Emmy looked shocked when I said that. "Was that a"—she paused for a second—"compliment?"

I grunted.

"Oh my god—it's working, isn't it?" Emmy asked excitedly.

"What are you on about?" I asked. Did she know something? She couldn't know—could she? And what if she did—what then? Would she react the way I did when I found out about her and Brooks? Get angry and throw a fit? Or would she be happy? Was there even anything for her *to* know?

"You and Teddy. It's working." I hoped the way my spine stiffened wasn't noticeable. "You're actually getting along, aren't you?"

"No, Clementine," I said. "We're not."

"Liar." She smirked. I looked at Teddy and the vet again.

Yeah, I was a fucking liar.

## Chapter 24

# Teddy

Gus didn't say goodbye to me after Riley and I went to see the horses this morning, and when he got home last night, he had reverted to his first language—grunts—when talking to me. He spoke in complete sentences to Riley, but not to me.

He didn't even directly speak to me this morning when he told me that Riley was going to hang out with Emmy while she trained horses today so I wouldn't be needed. He just told Riley that's what she was doing and then glared at me.

What the hell?

I tried not to let it sting, but it did. I'd told him not to walk away again, and he said okay. So why the hell was he acting like it never happened? Again!

Stupid stubborn asshole and temper-tantrum-having man.

After he and Riley left this morning, I was free to do as I pleased, which wasn't as much of a relief as I thought it would be. But it did mean I could go help Ada at the Devil's Boot. Ada and I had met in college. We hit it off and kept in touch even though she transferred the next year.

Ada and I were on the second floor of the Devil's Boot. A lot had been done since the last time I was here—there was a smaller bar up here, and seating and a few neon signs had been installed. It felt less stuffy, but it still had that old-school dive bar charm that made us all keep coming back.

Well, that, and the fact that it was the only bar in town.

Ada and I were working together to display the newspapers that were found during the cleanout. We'd been brainstorming for a couple of weeks and had decided on a vision. For the cover stories, Ada had thrifted a bunch of vintage frames that we would hang throughout the space. For all the others, we were going to basically modpodge them to the wall behind the bar and create wallpaper out of them.

Then, the reclaimed wood shelves that Aggie made would have the newspapers as a backdrop.

We'd already washed the wall and primed it. Now we were determining our layout—we wanted it to be planned but not look planned. Let me tell you, making things look effortless takes a lot of effort.

"I don't know," Ada was saying. "I think we have to angle some."

"But do we angle them on the bottom layer, or do we create a bottom layer that's more uniform and then layer them differently on top of it?"

"Teddy Andersen asking the hard-hitting questions," Ada said, but she wasn't looking at me—she was looking at the wall—the same place she'd been looking for the past twenty minutes.

"What does the wall say?" I asked.

"It doesn't know either," Ada muttered, and I smiled.

I loved Ada, and even though we hadn't spoken a lot over the past few years, I'd been watching her grow. She'd built an interior design business, so when Wes was looking for an interior designer for Baby Blue last year, I'd pitched Ada.

He brought her on, and she created the most beautiful end product I'd ever seen. Plus, she and Wes had fallen deeply in love, so that was a bonus.

"I think we just go random from the jump," I said.

"You would," Ada said, finally looking away from the wall. "But you sound surer than I am, so let's do it."

I walked toward the wall, newspaper in hand, and slapped it right in the middle of the wall, and said, "All right, now show me how we're sticking this shit up here."

"Just like wallpaper—we'll put paste on the back, and then we'll do a sealant coat over the top, but not until we have everything up."

"I love it when you talk dirty, Ada Hart."

We started working and got into a groove, though I know it was taking everything Ada had not to impose some sort of order on the papers we were placing randomly. She got quiet when she was focused, so I had time to do one of my least favorite things lately: think.

And where did my thoughts go? Straight to August fucking Ryder, which kind of made me want to throw up.

There was a lot to unpack.

First, that the thought of him didn't immediately send me into a blind rage. Second, that I might actually . . . like him? Or have liked him? At least until he had gone back to his general assholery this morning. He was so much more than my best friend's asshole older brother or someone I didn't get along with. I liked talking to him and spending time with him, and I think he liked doing the same things with me. He was an excellent father, and he cared deeply for his family and the people around him.

I couldn't write off what I felt for him as the aftershocks of a kiss from years ago. This was something, and I think I wanted to find out what.

"Ada," I said, "can I talk to you about something?"

"Shoot," Ada said as she stuck a piece of paper on the wall.

"It's about a guy," I said.

"Oooh," Ada remarked. "The vet?"

"What? No. Why does everyone know about the vet?"

"Small town."

I rolled my eyes. "Well, you're adjusting well, aren't you?"

"I've decided that small towns are the best places for introverts because there is literally always something for me to listen to," Ada said. "The other day, I overheard two women at the post office talking about someone getting their bike stolen, so then they stole it back from the thief, and then the thief stole it back, and now they're just in this never-ending cycle—pun intended, I think—of bike theft."

"Yeah," I said. "Jeremy and Wayne have been at that for like five years."

"I love it here," Ada laughed. "Anyway, back to the guy that isn't the vet."

"It's complicated," I said, "but I think I like him. He's actually great, and I haven't always thought that, but I do now. And he's also like ridiculously good-looking."

"Okay, so what's the problem, then?" Ada looked confused.

"Well, I thought we were kind of . . . I don't know . . . starting to become friends? But then yesterday he started acting weird and standoffish. It was behavior that I would've expected from him a while ago, but not now."

"Okay, got it," Ada said. "Sounds like he has a lot of really great qualities."

"Are you making fun of me?"

"Yes," Ada said without pause. I huffed. "Teddy, you're . . . Teddy. You're beautiful and loud—I mean that as a compliment, by the way—and fun. If you like a guy, he likes you back. Unless he's a complete and total dumbass, in which case you shouldn't want him anyway."

"Fair," I said, even though she didn't know the half of it.

"What does Emmy think about him?"

I swallowed. "She doesn't know." So far, I had pushed off that thought: What would Emmy think? If she knew about something *potentially* happening between her brother and me? I didn't really know how she'd react. I didn't think she'd be mad—that wasn't her style—but I did think she'd be cautious, anxious, about what would happen if things went wrong.

Luckily, I didn't have to worry about that, because so far all that had happened between us was two kisses, seven years apart, and if this morning was any indication, it didn't look as though anything else would happen, so I pushed my thoughts of Emmy away.

I was more of an "I'll cross that bridge when I come to it" type of gal. I'd tell her when there was something worth telling, which might be never.

Ada narrowed her eyes at me. "She doesn't know?" I shook my head. "So this guy is complicated enough that you haven't told your best friend, and are instead asking for advice from the woman who was married for three months and subsequently fell in love with her boss a year later?"

"Because your boss was 'the one,'" I said. "But yeah, basically."

Ada arched one of her thick black brows at me. "Interesting."

"Never mind," I said. "Not important." Ada gave me a look that said she didn't believe me. She opened her mouth, but then we heard footsteps on the stairs.

Brooks appeared a few seconds later, wearing his signature look: worn-out jeans, backward baseball cap, and a cropped T-shirt, which he'd probably still be wearing at eighty.

Emmy used to think the muscle tees were douchey, which they would have been if Brooks wasn't such a good guy.

"Hey," he said. "I come bearing gifts." He held up a few grease-stained brown paper bags, and I smelled fries.

Ada and I each grabbed a bag from him and took it over to the bar. Brooks followed. We sorted through the bags until all three of us had a sandwich of some sort—two for Brooks—and a carton of fries.

The fridge under the bar already had mixers in it, so Brooks pulled out a couple of Diet Cokes—one for Ada and one for me—and then filled a glass with water for himself.

I cracked open the Coke. The first sip burned down my throat. Some people like to crack open a cold beer at the end of a hard workday. Me? I like a crisp Diet Coke.

"It looks great up here," Brooks said, looking around. "Thank you for helping."

"When does this part open?" I asked.

Brooks swallowed a bite of his grilled chicken sandwich. "Next weekend."

"That's soon," I said. "Are you nervous about it?"

"Kind of." Brooks shrugged. "The Devil's Boot has always only been one thing, so it's kind of intimidating to add something new to the mix, but this part of it really feels like mine."

Huh. That sounded familiar. Without even trying, Brooks had just put the storm of feelings roiling within me the past few weeks into words. My life had always felt like it was one thing, but there was so much . . . new around me. Including, it would seem, some feelings about a certain grumpy cowboy. And I had to admit . . . I was scared.

"It's going to be great, Brooks," I said. "The whole place is great."

He looked around thoughtfully. "Yeah, I'm really proud of it."

"How are you going to celebrate opening night?" I asked.

"I'm not sure yet. Got any ideas, Andersen?"

I was scared of a lot of things right now. But I've never been scared of a good time.

"Yeah, actually," I said with a smile, "I do."

# Chapter 25

## Teddy

When I got home that night, I was treated to another round of Grunty Gussy. More talking around me and avoiding any sort of eye contact. We didn't even do our secret glance thing when Riley made an unknowingly inappropriate joke about roosters.

After he put Riley to bed, he walked past the living room—again without looking at me—and slammed his bedroom door. I tried not to let my heart sink. I enjoyed the time we usually spent together after Riley went to bed. I liked talking to him, hearing about his day, laughing with him.

Something was seriously wrong with me—like I must be sick—if I was missing Gus Ryder's company. But take me to the hospital, because I was.

I waited for a while, but he didn't come back out. I texted Emmy.

TEDDY: Dude. What the hell is up with your brother?

EMMY LOML: Like in general? Or like today?

TEDDY: Today. He's being more of a shit than usual.

EMMY LOML: Probably just one of his moods. It'll blow over.

EMMY LOML: You won't believe what he said to me yesterday, though.

EMMY LOML: He saw you flirting with the vet and said you could do better.

TEDDY: I wasn't flirting with the vet.

I actually was flirting with the vet, but not because I liked him or wanted to sleep with him again—because I wanted to make sure Maverick was getting the best care possible.

EMMY LOML: Yes you were. And you were very convincing. Jake is cute, but I don't think his biceps deserve that much attention.

TEDDY: It was all for Mav!

EMMY LOML: Well, duh. I knew that, but Gus didn't. I was hoping the fact that he was even paying attention meant you two were getting along.

By "getting along," I was ninety-nine percent sure my best friend didn't mean the kitchen kiss yesterday, but I didn't know for sure.

TEDDY: We are. Well, I thought we were.

EMMY LOML: Okay then go talk to him.

EMMY LOML: You're Teddy fucking Andersen and you don't take shit from anyone.

EMMY LOML: Especially August Ryder.

TEDDY: You're right.

Without thinking too much about it, I threw my phone down on the couch and started toward Gus's room. Once I was outside his door, I took a deep breath, then called out, "You better not be jerking off in there, August, because I'm coming in."

I opened the door to Gus scrambling off his bed and saying, "What the fuck, Theodora." His flannel pajama pants hung low on his hips, and he wasn't wearing a shirt.

My mouth went dry.

*Get it together, Teddy. You've seen a lot of men without shirts.*

But not Gus Ryder—at least not for a long time. He wasn't as free with his nipples as Brooks was. The planes of his stomach were defined, and the muscles in his chest and arms were toned by years of hard work. He had two swallow tattoos—one under each collarbone—and what looked like a sun on his ribs. I'd never seen those before.

"Why the fuck are you in my room, Teddy?" Right. I was in his room. I looked around, quickly taking in my surroundings. It was dim in here—there was a lamp on his nightstand and one by the entrance to his bathroom. His bed was big—king-sized, with a lot of blankets. More blankets than I ever thought Gus Ryder would have on his bed, honestly. There was a stack of children's books on his nightstand, and a thick woolen rug covered the hardwood floors.

It was . . . nice in here. Simple. Masculine.

"Teddy." Gus's voice hit me again. Firm. Low. Annoyed.

"Why are you being an asshole to me?" I asked, not beating around the bush.

"I'm not," he said, once again not making eye contact with me. "Also, stop shouting. There's a kid asleep upstairs."

I closed the door, because even though he was an asshole, he was right about that.

Once the door clicked shut, I regretted shutting it, because apparently air was only available outside this bedroom.

"You are," I breathed. "Yesterday morning, you kissed me. Then last night and this evening you don't talk to me at all, and you slam your door like a teenage girl right after Riley goes to bed even though we normally . . ."

"We normally what, Teddy?" He was looking at me now, and it felt like too much.

"We—we—talk. And just kind of . . . hang out," I stammered.

"I didn't know my company was something that you'd miss," Gus said. I think he meant it to be sarcastic, but it came out serious.

"I don't," I said immediately. "Miss your company."

"So you're just barging into my room for the fun of it?" He took a few steps toward me, and I tried to suppress the way my breath hitched.

"No, I want to know why you're being an asshole," I said.

"I'm always an asshole—according to you, anyway."

"Well, you're being even more of an asshole than usual. And I don't know why. You can't kiss a girl the way you kissed me yesterday and then not speak to me," I said. "It's basically what you did seven years ago and it . . . it doesn't feel good. It hurts," I finally said—my voice breaking slightly on the last word.

I watched his shoulders drop—only slightly—before he said, "Well, it doesn't feel good to watch the woman you just kissed flirt with someone right in front of you." His voice was hard.

"Are you kidding me?" I said. "This is about the fact that I touched Jake's arm?"

"Yeah," Gus said. "I guess it is."

"Be an adult, August," I said. "You kissed me yesterday, and you didn't even use tongue. I didn't think that made us exclusive. I'm not even convinced you like me."

"It doesn't," Gus said. "But I don't want to watch you flirt with other guys while I'm at work."

"I flirt!" I shouted. "It's what I do! It doesn't mean anything!"

"The flirting means something to me, Theodora!"

"Get a grip, August!"

"I can't get a fucking grip. You literally make me insane!"

"Likewise, asshole!" We were close now, having drifted toward each other as we screamed. Gus's green eyes sparked and his nostrils flared. I thought he was beautiful, and that's all I remembered thinking before he brought his mouth down on mine.

I pushed on his chest—hard—and he stumbled back. Time moved slower in that moment—like it was giving both of us the chance to make our decision without being rushed.

Gus's chest heaved. His eyes were wild, and his hair was mussed. He licked his bottom lip before biting down on it.

He didn't make another move. He was waiting for me to do it.

And I did.

I stepped toward him and threw my arms around his neck—clutching at his dark hair and sealing my lips against his. The way I was holding on to him was like I was trying to pull him close and push him away at the same time.

But when my mouth was on his, all I could think about was the places our bodies touched and how it wasn't enough.

More.

I wanted more, and the frustrated moan that I let out must've clued Gus in, because he used one of his arms to lift me, and I wrapped my legs around his hips. I registered that we were moving, but I didn't recognize where until my back hit the door and his hips rolled into mine and pinned me against the hard surface.

"Slow down, August," I said against his mouth.

He bit my lip. "Shut up, Theodora."

"Make me." He kissed me harder then, so hard it would've hurt if it didn't feel so fucking good. We were all teeth and tongues and hands and skin.

One of Gus's hands was gripping my ass and the other was cupping my neck. I could feel his thumb on my throat, and I wanted him to press it down.

He pushed me harder into the door, and I moaned again. I felt his cock straining between us, and suddenly, being fully clothed and pressed against the door was the last place I wanted to be. I wanted to be naked and under him or in front of him or on top of him. For once, I didn't have a strong preference.

I reached down to pull my shirt over my head, and Gus lowered me to my feet to help. Once it was over my head, he tossed it aside without taking his eyes off me. There was nothing but eye contact now. I wasn't wearing anything under the oversize shirt and sleep shorts that I'd put on for bed.

He uttered a low growl, and I felt it all the way down my spine. The way he was looking at me was like he had poured me into a glass and was gulping me down.

I'd never felt anything like it.

I thought he was going to kiss me again, but instead he

brought his hand up to my face and lightly grabbed my chin between his thumb and forefinger. "Do you want to do this, Teddy baby?"

"Yes," I breathed.

"Are you sure?" He brushed my hair behind my ear. "Because I don't know what's going to happen when I get inside of you. I don't know if once will be enough."

I dragged a finger up his bare arm. "Maybe you'll only want it once, but I don't think . . . That's not what this is for me."

"That's not what this is for me, either, Teddy," Gus said earnestly.

"Take me to bed, then." Something shifted in him then—his gaze went from soft and earnest to hungry and heated. Suddenly his hands were on my waist, and they flipped me so my stomach was against the door.

"Not yet, baby," Gus said as he moved my hair to one side of my neck and bit down on the spot where my neck met my shoulder. His hands were everywhere all at once—roaming up and down my back, over my shoulders, under my arms, gripping my breasts.

I could feel him hard against my ass, so I pushed back into him, and he groaned. "I want to make you come with my fingers and my mouth," he said against my ear. God. "I can't wait to feel you come."

Gus traced a knuckle down my spine. Once he got to the waistband of my sleep shorts, he pushed them down past my ass, and they fell to the floor. I kicked them out of the way. "Spread your legs, baby." I did what he said and was rewarded with two of his fingers brushing over my center. It wasn't enough, though. Not nearly.

"Fuck," Gus gritted out. "You're making a mess, Teddy baby.

Is this all for me?" Instead of answering, I pushed my ass against him again. He knotted the fingers of his other hand in my hair and tugged my head back so my neck was exposed and I was looking up at him.

"Is this all for me?" he asked again. He pushed his fingers inside me this time, and I had to fight to keep my eyes from rolling back in my head.

"That seems obvious," I managed to say. His fingers pushed in and out, and I was starting to forget how to stand.

"What if I want to hear you say it?"

"Then you'll have to do better than that."

"God, you're annoying," he said as he bit down on my neck. Hard. My knees buckled, and Gus supported me with an arm around my waist.

"You can't give out on me yet, Teddy baby. We haven't even started." With that, he flipped me around again and crushed his lips against mine. I tried to push his pants down as he led me back toward the bed, but he said "Not yet" against my mouth.

For some reason, I complied.

I couldn't orient myself when Gus was moving me around. He was so sure, so in charge, that I just let him lead me. Throughout my life, Gus had often been hard for me to like, but he'd never been hard for me to trust.

When the backs of my legs hit his bed, I let myself fall—even though my mouth immediately missed his. I looked up at him, aware that I was totally naked and he was only half. I could see the outline of his cock pressing against his pants, and I desperately wanted him to strip down.

I reached my arms above my head and stretched, arching my back, showing him all of me.

"You're perfect," he said huskily, and then he was on me. One of his hands roamed my body, his mouth found one of my nipples, and his fingers were back inside of me. "Fuck, Teddy," he said against my skin, and I clutched at his hair.

"Make me come, Gus. Please," I breathed. He bit down on the nipple he'd been circling with his tongue, and I gasped.

"How should I make you come first?" His fingers were moving faster now, and he had his thumb pressed against my clit. "Talk to me, Teddy. Tell me what you want."

Damn. Gus Ryder's mouth should go down as one of the seven wonders of the world—no kidding. So that's what I said. "Your mouth," I moaned, even though his fingers would also be great. I wasn't a picky gal.

"Where, baby? Where do you want it?"

I huffed in frustration. Jesus Christ, was he going to make me spell it out for him? I looked up at him, and the blinding grin Gus Ryder flashed me told me that yes, yes he was.

"I want your mouth on my pussy. I want you to go down on me until I come, and then I want you to kiss me, so I can have a taste."

Gus smiled at me again, then flipped onto his back. "And I want you to ride my face. So I think we can both get what we want here."

"August Ryder," I breathed as I sat up. "Are you offering me a mustache ride?"

Gus smoothed two of his fingers over his mustache and said, "Saddle up, baby." I kissed him again before I scooted myself higher on the bed and swung one of my legs over his face.

"Should we have a signal?" I asked. "Like if you need to breathe?"

Gus laughed, and I preened at the sound. "If getting suffocated by your perfect cunt is the way I go, then let me," he said. "Now sit on my face. I want my last supper." He gripped my hips and pulled me down.

I gasped. I felt his tongue inside me, and my hips rolled against his face. He groaned, and I felt it all the way through me. One of Gus's hands made its way between my legs, and he stuck two fingers inside me as he sucked on my clit.

My head tipped back on a moan, and Gus's fingers dug into my hip. I hoped they'd leave a mark. I continued to roll my hips against his tongue and grind against his face. Every time I tried to hover, Gus pulled me back down. I rode the fingers that were inside me and loved the way his tongue swirled around my clit.

The movement of my hips started to get more erratic, my breaths came quicker, and I wasn't sure where the sounds I was making were coming from. I could feel my orgasm barreling down my spine, and I started to chase it.

Gus must've felt it because he slid a third finger inside me and used the flat of his tongue to apply pressure to my clit. "Fuck," I panted. "Fuck."

When Gus sucked my clit between his lips—hard—I came. My whole body shuddered. I felt like I was coming apart. I collapsed into a heap beside him.

I could feel my heartbeat in my ears, and when I was flat on my back, Gus's mouth found mine, just like I'd asked. God, he was so fucking good at this.

Annoyingly good, honestly.

I gave a slight push on his chest, and he pulled back immediately. "Are you okay?" he asked.

"Fine," I breathed, and huffed a laugh the best I could. "I

just need to catch my breath." The smile that graced his face at that was wicked and lovely and didn't really help with the whole breathing thing.

"Am I too much for you, Teddy baby?"

"Fuck off," I said as I pushed him again, but he just held on to me and laughed. I felt the fabric of his pants brush against my legs, reminding me that he hadn't taken them off. I reached over and tried to push them down his hips.

"Did you want something?" Gus asked, in that same annoying voice that made me want to punch him and kiss him at the same time.

"Take your stupid pants off, August." He quickly kissed my forehead, then rolled off the bed and stood.

I took him in again. His hair was mussed and his stupid fucking mustache was gleaming in the warm glow of his room. I couldn't believe that he'd been walking around all this time with those perfect tattoos under his clothes and I'd never seen them.

I rose to my knees and moved toward the edge of the bed so I was facing Gus as he slipped his pants down his legs. I looked up at his face, and he was smirking at me again.

"Like what you see?" he joked. I just licked my lip in response. Gus tracked the movement and his nostrils flared.

Why was that so hot?

I grasped his hard length and gave it a stroke. Gus let out a strangled noise that made me want to do it again.

And again.

So I did, until Gus's mouth came back down on mine, taking and taking and taking. God, why was he so good at kissing? He could probably kiss me to orgasm.

"Are we doing this, Teddy? Do I need a condom?"

I thought about that for a second—the second question, mostly, because we were absolutely doing this, even though I wasn't ready to think about what that meant or what it would mean afterward.

"We're doing this," I said against his mouth. "And you don't need a condom unless you want one. I'm on the pill and get checked regularly. I want to feel you."

The same strangled noise came out of his throat at that, and whatever hold he had on himself was gone. He wrapped his arms tight around my body. "Tell me how you want it, baby. Should I fuck you against the wall? Put you on your back? Bend you over this bed and fuck you until your legs give out?"

I didn't know if he was looking for an answer, but I gave him one anyway. "Bend me over the bed," I said.

Gus lifted me off the bed and spun me so my back was to him in one fluid motion, and I let out a gasp as my body hit his.

"Fuck, Teddy." His mouth was at my ear, and his hands roamed my body again—up over my arms and breasts, down over my hips, until one of his hands slipped between my thighs again. I jerked as one of his fingers brushed over my clit, and Gus laughed against my ear as his fingers dipped inside me. "You ready for me, baby?"

"Yes," I breathed. "Just fuck me already."

"Say please," Gus said. I could hear the smirk in his voice, and I wanted to slap him. He added a second finger inside me, and I wanted more.

I needed more.

A frustrated groan came out of me, and Gus bit down on my shoulder and repeated, "Say please, Teddy baby." The way his breath skated across my skin made me shiver.

"Please," I gritted out.

"God," he muttered, "I like that." The hand that wasn't between my legs came around to my back and pushed me down, my chest against the mattress and my ass in the air.

I felt the tip of his cock against my entrance, and when he started to guide himself in, I thought my legs actually might give out. He pushed himself all the way into me on a groan, and the only thought in my head was that I felt full.

"Fuck," Gus ground out. "Your hot little cunt is perfect, baby." He thrust once, and I cried out. "I already love being inside of you. Shit, you feel like heaven."

He thrust again and again and again. The rhythm he struck was relentless, and I had no choice but to just go along for the ride.

"Oh my god," I groaned.

"Tell me how my cock feels, Teddy." His voice was gravelly. "Tell me what it feels like to have me inside of you."

"So-o-o good," I breathed out—at least, that's what I tried to say, but I wasn't exactly an effective communicator at that moment.

"Fuck, I can't wait to fill you up." Another shot of heat went through me at his words. Did I . . . like that? From the way I could feel the spot at the end of my spine coiling, I think I did. I think I liked that a lot. Might as well tell him that.

"Fill me up, Gus," I said. "I want your cum inside of me."

"Jesus," he huffed, and the brutal pace that he'd set started to get more erratic and sloppier—like I was undoing him.

That made two of us.

"Can you come like this, baby? I want you to come again while you're wrapped around my cock. I want to feel you."

I was pretty sure I could, but I never had before—I was a clitoral girlie—so I brought one of my hands between my legs and applied pressure.

There were so many sensations—him, bare, inside me, his hands gripping my hips in a way I knew would bruise, the cool air of his room hitting the sweat that had started to gather on my skin—all of it coiled my insides tighter and tighter. He drove into me harder and faster, and the coil finally snapped.

I came with his name on my lips and his cock buried deep inside me.

"Teddy, holy fuck, you're gripping me so tight," he said. "Fuck, fuck, fuck." I felt his body shudder behind me as he came.

For a while, our breathing was the only sound in the room. I couldn't believe what had just happened.

Gus slipped out of me and collapsed on the bed beside me. He wrapped his arms around me and pulled me to him, adjusting us so we were both fully on the bed and my head was on his chest. I traced one of his swallow tattoos with my fingers.

"I didn't know you had these," I said quietly.

"I got them when I was twenty-one, I think," he said. His lips were against my hair.

"I like them," I said.

"I like you," he responded.

I let out a laugh. "No, you don't." When I said it, he held me tighter.

"I do." He kissed the top of my head. "But I'm not sure I get it yet."

"Me neither," I whispered.

We stayed like that for a while. Under the cover of the night, I let him hold me, and he let me stroke his tattoos and kiss his chest and I tried not to think about what this meant for tomorrow.

# Chapter 26

## Gus

I woke up with Teddy in my arms and my phone buzzing on my nightstand. It stopped after a minute, then started again. I reached for it, trying not to jostle Teddy.

When I moved, she moved with me—like there was a magnet holding us together.

The screen of my phone was lit up, and when I saw the name I was confused and worried. "Dad?" I asked. "Everything okay?"

"It's Hank, August." My heart dropped, and I hoped the woman sleeping on my chest couldn't feel it. "The hospital has been trying to call Teddy. They got ahold of me since I'm his next emergency contact."

"Is he okay?" I whispered, holding Teddy a little tighter.

"He's stable. He had a heart attack. Luckily, the nurse was there. He's going to be okay, but I need you to wake Teddy up and bring her down here. I already called Wes. He's going to come watch Riley."

"Yeah, of course."

I looked at the woman in my arms. She looked so peaceful.

"And August," my dad said. "Be gentle, please."

*No shit,* I wanted to say, but I didn't. Instead, I just said "Yeah" and hung up.

I looked down at Teddy's sleeping face, lit only by the moonlight coming through my window. Her hair was a mess, her mouth was slightly open, and she looked completely content. I swallowed, knowing I was about to obliterate her peace.

I had the urge to rub my chest—my heart was hurting for her. And Hank. Though Teddy and I hadn't always gotten along, Hank was a hell of a man. I respected him and admired him as much as I did my own father.

And I knew Teddy loved him more than she loved anyone else in the world.

I took a deep breath. "Teddy baby," I whispered as I put my hand on her face, "you've gotta wake up." I jostled her a little more.

She let out a frustrated noise that sounded like some version of "No."

I gently rubbed her cheek with my thumb. "Please, baby." There was a lump in my throat. I didn't know when it got there, but it felt impossible to swallow.

Teddy's eyes fluttered before they opened—well, not quite opened, but they weren't closed all the way anymore. "Is it morning?" she asked on a yawn. "There's no way it's morning."

"Not quite," I said, still stroking her face. "We've gotta get up, though. It's your . . ." I trailed off. Suddenly Teddy was wide awake.

"What?" she asked.

"It's your dad, baby." I saw her jolt, ready to throw herself out of the bed, but I held on to her. "He's okay," I said. "He's okay. He's stable. He's fine, but I'm going to take you to the hospital."

She looked up at me and all I could see was blue.

"He's okay?" she said. I'd never heard her sound like that before—timid, scared. As far as I knew, Teddy was fearless.

"He's okay."

"Why didn't they call me?" she asked, but then swore. "My phone is on the couch."

"They got ahold of my dad. He called a few minutes ago," I said. "Wes is coming to stay here with Riley, and then we'll go." She tried to move again, and this time I let her, even though all I wanted to do was hold her and comfort her and tell her that everything was going to be okay.

I stood up with her. She'd put her Dolly Parton shirt back on before we fell asleep. "I'm going to change," she said—her voice hollow. I didn't like the sound of it one bit.

"Okay," I said. "I'll meet you in the kitchen." She nodded, then opened my bedroom door and was gone.

This all felt wrong. I should know what to do—I should be doing more for Teddy right now. *Be gentle, August.* My dad's words echoed in my head, and I couldn't help but think I'd let him down.

Ten minutes later, after I'd changed, put my contacts in, and run upstairs to make sure Riley was still sleeping, I met Teddy in the living room. She had changed into a pair of leggings, a hoodie, and a shearling-lined denim jacket.

I'd never seen the expression on Teddy's face at that moment. I wanted to reach for her, to wrap her in my arms, but for some reason I didn't. Of all the new versions of Teddy that I'd been getting to know, this one, the one that was so . . . *blank*, was the most jarring.

"You ready?" I asked. She just nodded when there was a soft knock on my front door. I opened it to find my brother, Wes, still in his pajamas, his hair sticking out in every direction. He nodded at me, but his eyes sought Teddy.

Once he saw her in the entryway, he pushed past me and pulled her into a hug. Teddy wrapped her arms around his waist, and jealousy prodded at me—jealousy toward Wes and Teddy's friendship, that he instinctively knew how to comfort her, that she let him.

I wanted to do that for her. And more.

"He's going to be fine, Ted," Wes said, and Teddy just nodded as she pulled back. Still, there were no tears, no signs of distress, just her blank expression.

"Yeah, he's going to be fine," she said quietly.

I cleared my throat. "Let's go," I said. Wes shot me a look, but Teddy didn't seem to notice. She just walked out the front door. I had to fight the urge to put my hand on the small of her back as she walked by.

"Hey," Wes whisper-yelled, and I rolled my eyes as I turned back to him. "Be nice," he said.

*Jesus Christ.* Did everyone think I was truly incapable of being nice to Teddy? "Thanks for watching Riley."

"No problem." Wes nodded. "Keep me updated, okay?"

"Will do," I said, and headed out after Teddy. She walked toward her Ranger, but I gently took her elbow and shifted her toward my truck. She didn't fight me. I opened the passenger door for her and made sure she was settled inside before I shut it.

Once I was in, I started her up, and we were on our way. It was reassuring that Hank was at Meadowlark General Hospital. If things were really bad, they would've taken him to Jackson or another larger hospital. I wanted to tell Teddy that, but I didn't.

I wanted to grab her hand and hold it, but I didn't.

It was like this was the last part of the wall between us. We'd gotten closer: We'd broken the no-kissing rule, we'd had sex tonight, for Christ's sake—the type of sex that makes you understand all the books, paintings, and songs about it, by the way—but comforting her in a moment that was so intense and so incredibly vulnerable felt . . . different. Like once we crossed that line, we wouldn't be able to take it back.

So we sat in my truck and drove in silence.

When we rolled in to the hospital parking lot, Teddy unbuckled her seatbelt and was out of the truck before I'd even put it in Park and cut the engine. I'd barely set foot on the pavement when she walked through the automatic doors.

When I walked in, the woman at the reception desk was looking up Hank's room number. "It looks like he's in 108, honey," she said. "Just down the hall and to the right."

Teddy took off again, and I followed her. The fluorescent lights beat down on us as we walked. They made her hair look lighter than it was. The hospital was quiet—the only noises were our footsteps, the beeping of machines around us, and the occasional whisper.

I hated hospitals. I hated the way they smelled—like disinfectant and despair—and I hated the way they made me feel—helpless.

When we got close to Hank's room, I caught up to Teddy and grabbed her by the elbow. She tried to shake me off, but I held on.

"What are you doing?" she asked coldly.

"Take a breath, Teddy," I said. We kept walking, but I kept the pace slower. Teddy rolled her eyes and didn't respond. "Please, baby." I let the term of endearment slip without thinking. "Just one deep breath before you go in there. For his sake."

Teddy's blue eyes met mine, and even though she didn't say anything, she made a show of taking a big breath in, and then out.

We kept eye contact for a few seconds longer before I let go of her elbow. Once she was out of my grip, she rounded the corner to room 108.

The door was ajar. Teddy paused for a fraction of a second before she pushed it open and went inside. I stayed in the doorway, unsure if she wanted me to follow her inside.

My dad was sitting in one of the chairs at Hank's bedside. He had his glasses on and was reading the newspaper. When Amos saw Teddy, he immediately stood with arms wide open.

Teddy hugged him, but her eyes were on her father, who was asleep in the bed. When I saw Hank, it felt like I'd gotten the wind knocked out of me.

Hank had used a cane or a wheelchair for the past few years, and time had started to show on him, but I'd never seen him look like this. Hank was badass, but right now, in a white hospital gown, with tubes sticking out of him, he looked fragile. It was hard to see that.

My dad looked over Teddy's head at me and nodded. The expression on his face was sad and tired. His best friend of nearly three decades was lying in that bed.

"What happened?" Teddy asked. She sounded the way

Hank looked, and hearing her voice like that made my chest crack wide open.

Teddy pulled out of the hug, and my dad put his hands on her upper arms—like he was trying to steady her. "He had a heart attack, but he was able to yell for his nurse. She called 911, and they got him here in record time. They're going to keep him for observation for a few days—just because of his history and his age—but he's going to be fine, Teddy."

"I should've been there," she whispered, and my dad pulled her to him again.

"It wouldn't have made a difference, Teddy," he said. "You will not blame yourself for this, do you hear me?" My dad was using his firm but soft voice. It was one that he'd mastered over the years and one that I'd tried to replicate with my own daughter.

He guided Teddy to the chair he'd been sitting in and told her to sit down. She grabbed her dad's hand as she did. Her face was still blank. She hadn't even cried yet. "We'll get you some coffee, okay?" my dad said, looking at me, and I nodded.

I turned and walked out the door and heard my dad's boots follow. He shut the door behind us. "Thanks for getting her here so quick, August," he said with a pat on my shoulder and a squeeze.

"Yeah," I said. "He's really going to be okay?"

"He's going to be okay," my dad responded. "You can head home if you want. I'll call Emmy when it's not the middle of the night, and we can cover it."

"No," I said immediately. "I want to stay with her."

## Chapter 27

# Teddy

I heard the door to my dad's hospital room click shut, and as it did, my shoulders slumped. I felt so unbearably exhausted.

For someone who was feeling that her life was boring a few weeks ago, it sure as hell wasn't boring right now. In the past four hours alone, I'd had enough happen to keep me satisfied on the events front for a good long while.

We weren't going to unpack the other event right now, though.

I reached out and folded my other hand over my dad's. His skin felt like paper against mine, and I couldn't swallow.

*Don't cry, Teddy.*

My dad's chest rose and fell as he slept. He looked so small in his hospital bed. His hair wasn't tied back the way it normally was, and his beard was loose. It was almost like I was looking at someone else's version of my dad and not my actual dad.

I'd seen my dad in a hospital bed a few times, and every time, I'd wished I'd never have to see it again. It made me feel like there was broken glass in my chest where my heart should be. Dads were supposed to be invincible, and even though I knew my dad wasn't, I still wished he could be.

He'd been through a lot over the past couple of years—problems with his lungs, liver, and kidneys. All of that had taken a toll on his body, and he didn't move around as well as he used to. He still played the guitar, but it was a lot more difficult for him to sit behind a drum kit—his true love. It broke our hearts, but both of us tried not to let it show.

I couldn't pinpoint the moment when the dynamic between us shifted, when I started taking care of him in the ways he always took care of me—making sure he was eating and sleeping, or that he was warm enough and taking his vitamins. I didn't think twice about doing it because I owed him everything.

And today, I wasn't there. For the first time ever, I wasn't there for him.

My lower lip quivered, and I let out a shaky breath. I thought about my dad, alone in his bed while his heart betrayed him. I thought about how scared he must've been, and I felt so guilty.

I should've been there. I should always be there.

It had always been my dad and me against the world. He'd always said that he and I were a two-man band—the favorite band he'd ever been part of, and he'd been in a lot of them. He had been in a band when he first came to Meadowlark over thirty years ago. He'd passed through on a tour bus and it stuck with him—the Welcome sign, the small main street, and the rancher and his cowboys wrangling escaped cattle on the side of the road.

That rancher, in his black cowboy hat, atop his black horse, was an image my dad said he'd never forget—especially as a city boy from Seattle.

My dad was a drummer for nearly twenty years. He started doing gigs with his first band when he was seventeen. They hit it semi-big and were able to open on a large North American tour, but they broke up before my dad turned twenty-two.

There were more bands, more tours, and more opportunities for bad decisions—at least that's what my dad said. He didn't shy away from the rock star lifestyle, and he didn't shy away from telling me about it, because my dad has been clean since the day my mom showed up with me in her arms.

I don't know much about her—just that her name was Evelyn Jones, her name is on my birth certificate, and she was one of the girls who followed the band around. My dad didn't know her very well either (sex, drugs, and rock and roll, I guess), but he noticed when she disappeared from the tour.

Nearly a year later, she turned up at a show in Chicago with me. She told my dad that she was too young to have a kid—that she didn't want me, and he needed to take me or she'd drop me off at the fire station.

According to Hank, who loves a good exaggeration, he saw my blue eyes—blue eyes that looked just like his—and said yes on the spot.

Once I was in his arms, he asked my mom what my name was. She told him I didn't have one. He said that was the only time in his life he'd felt truly heartbroken.

He named me after a jazz singer that he loved and left the tour the next day. He stayed in Chicago with me for a few days—enough time to get his knuckle tattoos that I was so fond of. There's an old photo from that day that I love: my dad getting his hands zapped as one of the other tattoo artists—big, brawny, inked all over his face—holds me.

He eventually decided that he wanted to raise me in a small town, and he remembered the town he'd passed through a few years earlier. I remember asking him why when I was a kid. He said, "It just seemed like the best place for us to start our life."

So he came back to Meadowlark, this time with his three-month-old daughter in tow. He asked around about the rancher, and of course everyone knew he was talking about Amos Ryder and Rebel Blue Ranch. My dad drove to Rebel Blue that day and asked for a job.

Truly, I don't know why Amos gave him one, but I have a good guess. Stella had passed away a few months earlier, and Amos had three kids and a ranch to take care of on his own. I think when he saw my dad, he saw someone else who was doing it alone, and one thing about Amos is that he can't resist a stray—horse, cat, dog, human, it doesn't matter. He always has enough room to take them in.

Neither of us ever saw or heard from my mom again. Hank said he wrote to her once—told her where we were, and that if she ever decided she wanted to be part of my life, she was welcome to join us—but she never replied. I wondered about her sometimes—especially when I was a teenager. But I didn't miss her, and I didn't have any desire to find her because I never felt that anything was missing from my life.

I wasn't mad that she didn't want me, because she gave me to someone who loved me more than anyone else in the world and showed me that every single day—plus she gave me my copper hair. And I was grateful that she had semi-decent taste in men, because my dad was the best man I'd ever known. Because of him, my life was full. He was the only parent I needed—as long as we had each other, we were okay.

I blew out another shaky breath and looked down at my dad's left hand. My vision got blurry when I read the tattoo on his knuckles, THEO, and when I thought about the other side that said DORA, I blinked the tears back.

*Don't cry, Teddy.*

The hand I was holding squeezed mine, and my eyes shot up to my dad's face. His eyes were still closed, but his lip twitched.

"Dad?" I said softly.

"Teddy Bear," he said. His voice was barely audible—reedy and thin—but his blue eyes blinked open, and relief flooded through me, though not quite enough of it to drown out the guilt. Not yet.

"How are you feeling?" I asked.

"Surviving," he said.

"Scale of one to ten?"

"Three," he said, and my heart swelled. I knew he was lying, but if he felt good enough to lie, that was good enough for me.

"Good," I responded. "Because, Hank Andersen, if you die on me, I will fucking kill you." A wheeze came out of my dad. I think it was a laugh. He slipped his hand out of mine and lifted his arm.

I stood and crawled onto the hospital bed with him—careful of all the tubes—and curled into his side. His tattooed left hand rubbed my shoulder. "The devil will have to drag me kicking and screaming, Theodora," he whispered, and I let myself relax into him.

No matter how old I got, I would never be too old for this.

After a few minutes, my dad went back to sleep. His breathing got slow and even. I stayed awake.

I watched his chest rise and fall, and I listened to his heartbeat—the kick drum that I couldn't live without.

## Chapter 28

# Gus

When my dad and I returned with coffee, I peeked inside Hank's hospital room. Teddy was lying beside him on the hospital bed. I couldn't tell whether she was asleep, but I didn't want to wake her if she was.

Something about seeing them that way hit me. Teddy wasn't my little sister's annoying best friend and Hank wasn't someone who used to work for my dad. They were a father and his daughter, curled up on a bed in a hospital, and as a father myself, it gave me a lot of feelings.

My dad and I went to the small seating area just outside Hank's room, and I texted Wes.

GUS: Give Riley a kiss for me.

Surprisingly, Wes responded a minute later, even though it was three-thirty in the morning.

WES: You got it you big softie.

GUS: Jackass.

WES: How's Hank? How's Teddy?

GUS: Both okay. Hank's sleeping. Teddy's with him.

WES: And Dad?

GUS: Okay, I think.

WES: Is he doing the nose scrunch thing?

Amos Ryder was steady as a river, as grounded as a deep-rooted tree, and as calm as a pond on a sunny day. But he did have the nose scrunch thing—his tell that his emotions were overwhelming him. I saw it when Riley was born, when Emmy raced her last race in Meadowlark, when Wes showed us Baby Blue for the first time, when Brooks graduated from high school, when Cam got into law school, and whenever it was time for one of our horses to move on from this life.

My dad felt things deeply. I think all three of us had a little bit of that in us.

GUS: No, but he was here for a bit before we got here.

WES: Keep an eye on him.

I thumbs-upped Wes's last message and slid my phone back in my pocket. I leaned back in the couch I was sitting on. It was hard and uncomfortable—like the tile floors and harsh lighting. My dad sipped his shitty hospital coffee and read his paper. Every few minutes, I heard him flip the page.

Me? All I could do was think about Teddy.

I was still unsettled by how she had been on the way over here. It was so different from the Teddy I knew and the one I'd gotten to know over the past month and a half.

For as long as I'd known her, Teddy had been larger than life. She was animated and fearless and so goddamn fucking loud. The Teddy I'd gotten to know recently was all of those things, but she was also thoughtful and creative and cared deeply about the people around her—including my kid, which was obvious every time I watched them together.

But the Teddy from this morning? I didn't know how to face her. Withdrawn, like she wasn't allowed to let her pain show—like she wasn't allowed to feel anything.

I dozed off to those thoughts, and woke up to my sister shaking me awake. "Gus," she said. "Wakey wakey."

I blinked the sleep out of my eyes.

Emmy was sitting next to me on the uncomfortable couch with a few bags between us. I smelled food—good food, not hospital food. My stomach rumbled, which told me it was probably way past the time I normally ate breakfast.

"Food?" I asked.

"Good morning to you, too," Emmy said with a small smile. "But yes, there's a breakfast burrito in there for you." She pointed at a brown paper bag. I reached in and grabbed one.

"Where's Dad?" I asked, noticing that he was no longer in the chair across from me.

"He stepped out to call Wes and Dusty—to make sure everything is good at Rebel Blue without you two."

"Wes has Riley," I said.

"Luke went and picked her up. They're going fishing." That brought a smile to my face. Riley would love that. "He was going to go anyway, and when Dad told me you brought Teddy here and had been here all night, I figured you'd probably need some rest."

"Thanks, Em." I nodded. "What else you got here?" I gestured to the large canvas tote bag she'd brought with her.

"A few snacks and supplies," she said. "And I stopped at Teddy's before I came to grab a few things for her and Hank."

I don't know why that pushed on my chest—I was going to have to get that checked out—but it did. I set my breakfast burrito down and leaned across the couch and pulled Emmy into my arms.

She let out a little laugh. "Are you feeling okay, August?"

I pulled back after a few seconds. "You're a good friend, Emmy," I said. "You guys are lucky to have each other."

Emmy narrowed her eyes. "You realize that you just complimented Teddy—again."

So much had happened since my first compliment.

I shrugged in response. The way Emmy was looking at me was very reminiscent of our father, and I tried not to sweat.

I stayed quiet, not wanting to accidentally blurt out that I'd given Teddy *a lot* of compliments last night. It's a good thing I wasn't a blusher like Wes, or thinking about *that* would've been a dead giveaway.

*Get it together, August. You're in a hospital.*

"Well," Emmy said after a minute, "c'mon, then." She patted my leg and picked up the paper bag with the food in it, leaving the canvas bag and the cupholder with coffees on the small coffee table in front of the couch.

"So you want me to grab everything else, then?" I said sarcastically as I picked it all up. Emmy walked toward the door and pushed it open slowly.

"Ted?" she said quietly, then pushed the door open all the way and walked in. I followed.

Teddy was back in the chair at Hank's bedside. Hank's bed had been positioned so he was sitting up. There was a tray of hospital food in front of him—I must've been asleep when they brought it by.

It looked like he and Teddy were playing games on one of the napkins—tic-tac-toe and that game where you connect the dots to make squares. Emmy walked over to Hank's bed and gave him a kiss on the cheek, then put her arm around Teddy's shoulders and gave her a hug.

"Hank," Emmy said. "How the hell are ya?"

"Survivin'," he said, with a smile that made him look more like himself.

"And looking damn good while doing it," Teddy chimed in. She smiled too, and some of the weight that'd been on my chest all night lifted. "Please tell me you brought something edible."

"Of course I did," Emmy said. She set the bag of burritos on Hank's bedside table. She pulled two out and handed one to Hank and one to Teddy. "And I brought coffee. Hank, I love you, but you can't have any."

"Understood," Hank said with a sigh.

"Gus," Emmy said to me, "Teddy's is the—"

"—the brown sugar one," I finished for her without thinking.

"You know," Emmy said to Teddy, "I'm starting to feel pretty confident that my maid of honor and best man might actually be able to walk down the aisle without trying to trip each other."

I risked a glance at Teddy. Her eyes brightened, and she smiled a little. It was the first sign I'd seen all day of the Teddy I knew, and I wanted to breathe a sigh of relief. "Is that so?"

"Don't get your hopes up," I said, and when Emmy looked at me, her eyes narrowed.

"August Boone Ryder," Emmy said, still squinting—like she was trying to see me better. "Is that . . . a smile?"

"No," I lied. I could feel the smile creeping up my face.

Emmy stepped toward me and poked me in the cheek—right in the dimple that rarely showed itself. "It is!" she exclaimed. "Teddy, what are you doing to him?"

*Please god, don't answer that.*

"I don't want to know," Hank chimed in.

Teddy laughed. "What else did you bring?" she asked, artfully changing the subject.

Thankfully, Emmy showed me mercy and pulled the bag off my shoulder.

"Some necessities," Emmy said. "Hank, I brought you shirts. I didn't know what you'd be in the mood for, so I brought Thin Lizzy and the Doors. And," Emmy added as she dug in the bag again, "a blanket from home." She unfolded it and draped it over Hank with Teddy's help. "And last but definitely not least . . ."

"A speaker!" Teddy exclaimed with a whoop.

"Thank you, Emmy," Hank said. Teddy had already grabbed the speaker from Emmy and was connecting it to Hank's phone. After a minute, Fleetwood Mac started playing softly—"Sarah" was the song. "I'm feeling better already."

Teddy started braiding Hank's beard and Emmy sipped her coffee. Teddy told us about the plants that she and Riley had found so far, and Hank was happy to hear that his Rocky Mountain field guide was getting some use.

My dad came in then, and when I looked up at him, I saw it—the nose scrunch.

"Sounds like a party in here," he said. As Emmy, Teddy, and Hank turned toward him, it hit me. Look at this special thing

Amos Ryder had created—all by giving a wide-eyed drummer a job.

Emmy stood and went to hug our dad. "Hey, Daddio," she said. "I brought you a coffee and breakfast."

"Thanks, Spud," he said with a kiss to the side of her head. "Hank, I just talked to the doctor."

"Let me guess," Teddy said with a pout. "Party's over?"

My dad's gravelly laugh traveled through the room. "Party's over. Hank"—he looked over at his friend—"you need to rest."

"Party pooper!" Hank muttered.

"I can stay," Emmy said. "You and Teddy can go shower and change—maybe rest for a bit."

"I don't need to change," Teddy said, and Emmy shot her a pointed look. I think they had an entire telepathic conversation in that moment, because Teddy just grumbled, "Fine."

"I'll take you home," I said quickly, which earned a look from both my sister and my father. And Teddy's father. And Teddy.

*Jesus.*

I ignored all of them and kept my eyes on Teddy. "Okay." She nodded. "But I'm coming back."

"Duh," Emmy said.

## Chapter 29

# Teddy

It wasn't until Gus's truck pulled to a stop in front of his house that I realized everyone probably expected Gus to take me to my place, and I should have too.

But I hadn't.

When he cut the engine, neither of us got out right away. Instead, we sat in silence. It wasn't uncomfortable like it was earlier today. It was nice. I wasn't sure why, but I felt comfortable sitting with Gus like this.

At the hospital, I had to be a daughter, a caretaker. I had to be on point there, around everyone else. Here, in the cab of his truck, I could just *be.*

I didn't have to be Teddy the daughter or the caretaker or the best friend or the flirt. Here, with him, I could just be Teddy.

I sighed.

God, I was so tired. I closed my eyes.

I heard Gus get out of the truck, but I stayed. I couldn't move. After a few seconds, my door opened, and the warm air of the summer morning hit my face. I didn't open my eyes until I felt Gus's arms—one slid under my knees and the other behind my shoulder blades—and he lifted me out. I blinked up at him, and he looked down at me. "I've got you, Teddy baby."

I believed him, so I closed my eyes again. His steps crunched on the gravel, and I swayed slightly with each of them. I felt it when he went up the stairs and when he pushed the front door open.

The smell of his house was comforting. Like Gus.

He turned left, down the hallway toward my room, but he walked long enough that I knew we'd gone past it.

Another door.

His room.

And then, boots on tile. A light. Bathroom.

Gus sat me down on the closed toilet seat and knelt in front of me. His hands were on my knees, and when I saw his green eyes, tears welled in my blue ones.

His face was soft, and he rubbed his palms up and down the sides of my thighs.

"Don't cry, Teddy," I accidentally said out loud. My lip quivered, and my throat hurt.

Gus tilted his head and brought one of his hands up to my face. "You can cry, Teddy," he said. "I've got you."

"I'm so tired," I whispered. My voice was trembling. I felt a tear slip over my cheek, and Gus wiped it away.

"I know," he said.

"My dad," I hiccuped.

"I know," Gus said again.

"I'm—scared—" I stammered. "I'm—scared of having to live without him."

"I know, baby." Gus's thumb stroked my cheek again and

again. More tears fell, and my vision was waterlogged. I looked up at the bathroom ceiling, trying to keep them at bay.

Gus stood, and my eyes stayed on the ceiling. I heard the shower start. When Gus came back to me, he took my hands and pulled me to my feet. He slid my jacket down my arms, and I heard it drop to the floor. The metal buttons hit the tile with a small clink.

"Arms up," Gus said softly, and I obeyed. He pulled my T-shirt over my head and dropped it on the floor too. He knelt again, unbuttoning my jeans and tugging them down my legs along with my underwear. I put my arms on his shoulders to steady myself.

There wasn't anything sexual about the way he was touching me and undressing me now. He was doing it with so much tenderness and care that it was a miracle I hadn't melted into a puddle on his bathroom floor next to my discarded clothes.

He guided me inside the glass shower door. When the warm spray hit my body, I felt such a rush of release that I almost collapsed. Gus was still holding my hand and keeping me steady.

"Will you be okay for a minute?" he asked. I nodded, closing my eyes and turning my face toward the water. He left the shower door open, not caring that water was soaking his bathroom.

I didn't know how long he was gone, but when I heard his footsteps come back, I turned to look at him. He was carrying stuff from my shower—my shampoo, conditioner, face wash, body wash, lotion—everything. He reached into the shower and set them on a shelf. Then he started undressing.

He was beautiful.

Once he was naked, he stepped into the shower with me

and shut the door behind him. When he put his hands on my waist, I sighed. He pushed on one side of my waist and pulled on the other to turn me around.

He kissed my neck before he brought his hands up to my shoulders and massaged them for a few moments. Then I heard him pick up a bottle and squeeze something out. When I felt his hands on my head, I realized what he was doing.

His fingers worked the shampoo through my hair. His fingers on my scalp made me groan. My head unconsciously tilted back, but it didn't make it too far because Gus was still massaging my scalp. When he made it to my temples, I closed my eyes.

"Tip your head back, baby," he said in my ear, and I did. He put one of his hands on my forehead to shield my eyes from the shampoo that he was rinsing from my hair.

When he was done, he moved on to conditioner, and then I smelled the familiar scent of my cucumber and mint body wash. I reveled in the way that his hands felt as they roamed over my body—taking care of me. He was very thorough.

I looked down and watched the white lather rinse off under the water and go down the drain.

"Turn around," Gus said, and I did. He was putting some of my face wash in his hands. He rubbed it together on the tips of his fingers before he put it on my cheeks, and something about the gesture made me smile. He was so focused, so soft.

He gently rubbed the gel around my face and then said, "You might just have to go for it and put your face under the spray for this one." I thought he was smiling a little. I did what he said, and a laugh bubbled out of me when I wiped my eyes.

Gus pulled me into him, and I laid my head on one of his swallow tattoos.

We stayed in the shower for a while—until the water changed from hot to lukewarm. At that point, Gus turned it off, and we stepped out together. He draped a towel over my shoulders, wrapped another one around his waist, and led me out of the bathroom.

He opened his dresser and pulled out a big T-shirt, which he pulled over my head, and then he slipped a pair of boxers on.

Then he kissed me. Quickly, softly. He grabbed my hand and pulled me to his bed, where we both collapsed.

When I curled into his side, I felt his lips in my hair. "You can cry, Teddy," he said.

And so I cried. And cried.

And August Ryder held me the whole time.

## Chapter 30

# Teddy

My dad got to come home last Saturday. The doctors prescribed some new medications and told him he had to watch what he was eating—no red meat, no fried food, no cheese. It was safe to say that Hank was not thrilled.

I had set up a command zone in the living room. The small table next to my dad's La-Z-Boy held his medication sorted by day, time, and frequency. It also held a giant water bottle and a basket of doctor-approved snacks.

He was sitting in his chair now—he had dozed off, and I had scrolled through TV channels until I finally settled on some *Criminal Minds* reruns. I swiped the book I was reading off the coffee table and flipped it open—more hot demons.

It was cooler outside today, so I opened one of the living room windows. The mountain breeze combined with the sound of Hank's wind chimes on the front porch made me feel so content.

Yeah, my life was quiet, but it was also mine.

Whenever I thought about what I wanted my life to look

like, Meadowlark was always the backdrop. But I still needed to figure out what I was going to do next here.

I had a little over a month left at Gus's. Honestly, Emmy was right. It had been a really great summer.

But it was going to end. Like everything else in my life lately.

Thinking about it made me sad—for a lot of reasons (one big grumpy one that I wasn't ready to think about yet), but also because I was going to have to start from square one again. I'd been inadvertently using my time with Gus and Riley as an escape—as a way to avoid thinking about the things I was supposed to be thinking about.

My dad's snoring brought me out of my head, and I realized I'd been reading the same paragraph for god knows how long. Hank's snore was also robust enough to wake himself up.

I looked over at him—his shocked expression made me laugh. "Well, shit," he muttered.

"I thought a freight train had crashed into our living room."

"Smartass," my dad grumbled. He was looking more like himself today. There was color in his cheeks, and seeing him in his chair was so much better than seeing him in a hospital bed.

"How are you feeling?" I asked.

"Incredible," he said. "A healed man. Ready for some chicken-fried steak."

I arched a brow at him. "Nice try."

"It was worth a shot." He shrugged. "What about you? You look deep in thought over there."

"I was," I said honestly.

"Care to share with the class?" Hank asked.

Before I could answer, there was a knock at the door. *Saved by the bell.* I wasn't really in the mood to unpack everything with my dad—at least not yet. I wanted to keep all of this in my head a little longer. I had a lot of stuff to sort through up there.

I put my book back on the coffee table and walked to the front door. Through the small window I could see Aggie and Dusty.

Even if I didn't know them, I'd know Aggie and Dusty were mother and son. Dusty got his blond waves, and enviable cheekbones, from his mom. Aggie's wavy hair was all silver now, and still beautiful. It fell all the way to the middle of her back. She was wearing the same thing she always wore—Carhartt coveralls, with an excess of turquoise and silver earrings, bracelets, and necklaces that somehow all looked perfect together. She didn't wear rings, though. Aggie was a carpenter; she kept pretty things off her hands.

Aggie was holding a casserole dish, and Dusty had two armfuls of brown grocery bags.

"Well, look what the cat dragged in," I said as I moved out of the doorway, making room for them to come inside. I took the casserole dish out of Aggie's hands as she walked through the door.

"That's just chicken and vegetables," she said. I was grateful it wasn't lasagna—poor Hank would've been heartbroken, and his heart had been through enough in the past week. "Three seventy-five for thirty minutes covered, twenty uncovered."

"I'll put it in now," I said. "We can have it for dinner."

Aggie smiled. She reached out and touched my cheek. "You're a good one, Teddy Andersen," she said, then walked over to sit on the end of the couch that was nearest to my dad's chair.

He was beaming at her.

I walked toward the kitchen and Dusty followed with the groceries. "What did you guys buy?" I asked as I set the casserole dish on the stove.

"The entire store, basically," Dusty responded. He had his hair pulled halfway up today. "My mom's been stressed as hell. I think she and Amos spent a total of five minutes not at the hospital this week."

"I'm happy she's here," I said. "And you, too." I bumped Dusty with my shoulder, and he bumped me back.

We put away the groceries together, and I preheated the oven for dinner. "So," he asked, "how is it going?"

"Fine. Hank gave us a real scare, but it's good now."

"Really?" He nudged me, and I remembered how he'd done the very same thing at the diner, with the same concern, when I was spiraling about the future with him.

All I could do was shrug.

"You'll be okay, Teddy," he said.

"I feel like that's the problem, though," I sighed. "Everyone always just expects me to figure it out. Like 'Don't worry about Teddy, she'll be fine.' " I opened the pack of Oreos that Dusty and Aggie had brought and took a bite of one. I don't do the whole split-in-half, lick-the-cream thing (too sexual). I just like to eat them as is.

Dusty stayed quiet while I ate my cookie. "And yeah," I continued once I swallowed (on a roll with the sex things today), "I'm going to be fine. I'm always fine, but it just"—I paused for a second, trying to word my next bit carefully—"it just sucks to feel like I don't have any other choice but to be fine because even if I wasn't, people would expect me to be eventually, and so I don't know if they would take it seriously that I wasn't. Does that make sense?"

Dusty shook his head. "Not really."

"Stupid man!" I huffed.

"But are you?" Dusty asked. "Fine, or whatever? Like actually fine and not this fake fine that you think people won't care about?"

"I don't know," I said truthfully. I felt fine sometimes—like when I was at Gus's—and other times I didn't feel fine. I don't know.

"Roll with the punches, Teddy Andersen. And punch back if you need to," Dusty said as he took an Oreo from the package. He was a split and lick guy (ha).

"Is that a cowboy proverb?" I asked. "It's good."

"No," Dusty said. "It's something Emmy said about you once. That you roll with the punches and punch back if necessary."

It was hard to swallow after that. I felt like I'd been punched a lot lately, and I didn't know if I had the strength to punch back this time.

Aggie and Dusty stayed for a few hours. We ate dinner in the living room, and watched *The Wedding Date,* which was one of my and Hank's favorites, and I ate a lot of Oreos.

"So, Teddy, how are things going at Rebel Blue for you?" Aggie asked with a smile. My dad nearly blew a gasket when I told him I wasn't going to Gus's last week because I couldn't be responsible for another heart attack (I felt guilty enough about the first one), so I did spend Monday and Tuesday at Gus's, but not Wednesday. I had placated Hank enough with two days (during which I worried about him the whole time), so I came home.

"Good," I said. "Riley's an easy kid to hang out with." Aggie looked at me expectantly, like she was waiting for me to say more. It clicked in my head a second later: I'd forgotten a crack about Gus. "It's her dad that's a challenge," I added quickly. Aggie chuckled.

Shit, I was really rusty on my Gus insults.

"Always been a hard head, that one," Aggie said fondly. "How is Cam doing?" At the mention of Riley's mom, Dusty stiffened.

"She's good," I said. "She's getting ready to take the bar again and is feeling a little more confident."

"That's good to hear." Aggie leaned back on the couch. "Isn't that nice, Dusty?"

"Yeah, Mom," Dusty muttered. Suddenly, adult Dusty was gone. The look he was giving his mother was teenage dirtbag Dusty all the way through. It made me laugh.

It was a nice evening. I was happy Aggie and Dusty were here, but I couldn't help but miss a couple of things—a couple of people, rather: a curly-headed little girl and a grumpy cowboy.

## Chapter 31

# Gus

This week had been weird. Everything with Hank aside, things had changed between Teddy and me, and I was stuck between not wanting the summer to end because so would our arrangement, and wanting it to end so I could ask Teddy for more. I wanted more than just a part-time babysitting arrangement. I think . . . I think I wanted it all.

I liked having her around, and not because she was helping with my kid but because—and I'll be damned—I liked her. We just . . . fit. We balanced each other out in a weird way. And the truth was, I'd rather fight with Teddy than be happy with anyone else.

I don't know how or when it happened, but Teddy Andersen made me want something for myself: her. I wanted her. And it terrified me.

My phone buzzed with an incoming FaceTime call. It was Cam. "Riley," I called, suddenly nervous that my daughter had been so quiet for a while now. "Your mom is calling." I swiped on the screen to answer.

"Hey," I said.

"Hi," Cam responded. Her hair was pulled up into a bun, and she had her glasses on—probably called in the middle of studying. "How's it going?"

"Good," I said. "I don't know where your daughter is, though."

"Probably out drag racing or getting a barbed wire tattoo on her biceps," Cam said. I heard Riley's light footsteps coming down the stairs.

Her curly hair was flying behind her as she ran through the kitchen. When she made it to the living room, Riley popped onto my lap, holding a piece of paper that she'd folded in half, and there was a lot of glitter on it.

Fuck. That was going to be a fun mess to clean up.

"Hi, Sunshine," Cam said with a bright smile. "What have you been doing today?"

Riley held up her piece of paper. "I made this card for Hank," she said, pride oozing from her. She'd made Hank a card? On her own? Well, shit. I didn't know what I did to deserve a kid like her, but damn, I must've done something right somewhere.

"What's up with Hank?" Cam said. Shit—I'd forgotten to tell her. I'd been a little preoccupied with, what, realizing my enemy is maybe actually the thing I've wanted in my life this whole time?

"His heart hurt him," Riley said. "Dad and Teddy said it attacked him." Cam's eyes flashed to mine. They were full of concern.

"He's going to be okay," I said quickly. "He's home now, but he gave us all quite the scare." I thought about Teddy, how she'd cried in my arms until we both fell asleep, how she'd stayed there all night, and how I kissed her forehead before I left for work the next morning.

God, I missed her. There was a Teddy-shaped hole in the house when she wasn't here.

"I'm so glad he's okay," Cam said. "How's Teddy?"

"The first day or two afterward were tough, but it sounds like she's managing his recovery well," I said before focusing my attention on Riley. "Let's see this card, Sunshine."

Riley held up her card to my phone screen so Cam could see it too.

"Shiny!" Cam said with a laugh. "I love it so much. What does the inside look like?"

Riley opened the card. "That's Hank," she said, pointing to a drawing of a man in a bed, "and that's his heart. I drew a smiley face on it because it's not mean anymore. And that's me," she said, pointing to a shorter stick figure by the bed. "And that's Dad, and that's Teddy."

"You did so good, Sunshine," Cam said, looking closer at the card. "Are your dad and Teddy holding hands?" Cam laughed, like she couldn't believe it.

"Yeah, they do that sometimes," Riley said, and I froze. Did we? And did Riley see it? When? Fuck.

Cam's eyes flashed to mine and she arched a brow. "Do they?" she asked. I broke eye contact—a dead fucking giveaway.

"Yeah," Riley said with a shrug. Little gossip—turns out Riley picked up a habit or two from Luke Brooks.

Cam didn't take her eyes off me as she said, "Well, I'm sure Hank will love it. Maybe your dad can help you write something on there."

Riley turned her face up to mine. "Can you?"

"Of course, Sunshine. We can take it to him today," I said. "Go get your shoes on." Riley was off my lap in an instant.

"Is there something you want to tell me?" Cam said once Riley was out of earshot.

I rubbed the back of my neck. "Not particularly," I said. "It's nothing." Even though it wasn't. It felt more like everything.

"I know you, Gus," Cam said. "And if you've let your guard down enough that Riley was able to sneak a peek at you and a woman holding hands, when I can't even remember the last time I saw you give a woman the time of day, I'm going to bet something's going on."

Still not looking Cam in the eye, I lied again. "It's nothing."

"Liar," Cam said. "Remind me never to call you as a witness."

"Okay," I said, annoyed. "It's . . . it's something, I think. Or it could be. I don't really know," I breathed. "I think I want it to be."

"Does anyone else know?" Cam asked, and I shook my head. "Well, shit."

"Yeah," I said. "I've got myself into a bit of a pickle, haven't I?"

"Good thing you love pickles," Cam said. I did love pickles—one of my top five favorite foods. "But in all seriousness, if you want it to be something, you need to say something sooner rather than later. And, Gus"—I finally looked back up at her—"if this is what you want, I'm really happy for you."

After we hung up, I texted Teddy. I don't even want to talk about how long it took me to draft the message, and it would've taken me even longer if my kid hadn't been asking me every three seconds when we were going to leave.

Gus: Hey. Are you home? Riley wants to bring something over for Hank.

Gus: But it's fine if you don't want company.

Gus: Totally fine.

Gus: But Riley would love to see you.

Nice, Gus—use your kid. But Teddy responded a few minutes later.

Theodora: We're home. Hank would love that.

Gus: What about you?

Theodora: Just come over, August.

I smiled at my phone like an idiot as I read her message over and over again. *Just come over, August.*

Don't mind if I do.

"All right, Riley," I said, standing up from the couch and looking at my daughter, who was practically vibrating with excitement. "Let's rock and roll." Before we went outside, I remembered that Teddy had said something a while ago about her and Hank's washing machine being on the fritz, so I grabbed my toolbox out of the hall closet, and we were on our way.

As we drove to Teddy's, I rolled the windows of my truck down and turned up the music. When I heard Riley start singing along to Linda Ronstadt, I smiled. I loved every season in Wyoming, but my favorite was the early to midsummer. It was like the mountains woke up to bask in the sunlight, and the result was lush green forests and running streams and blooming wildflowers.

And there was something about a summer day, my daughter's voice coming from the backseat, and the Wyoming skyline in front of me. All that was missing was a loud redhead beside me.

We made it to Teddy's faster than I thought—maybe I was speeding a little. Teddy was out mowing the lawn—just finishing, it looked like—when we got there, and I immediately wished I'd gotten here sooner, so I could've done it for her.

She was wearing a pair of denim shorts—a pair I'd come to know and love for the way they made her ass look—and a light blue tank top. It was short, so I could see a strip of her tan skin between where her top ended and her shorts started.

I wanted to put my hands on that strip of skin, pull her in, and kiss the hell out of her. Instead, when Riley and I got out of the truck, I gave her my best casual "Hey."

She pulled white earbuds out of her ears and returned my "Hey" as Riley wrapped her arms around Teddy's legs. Teddy looked down at my daughter, which gave me a chance to really take her in. I dragged my gaze down her body and tried not to make it too obvious that I wished I was the drop of sweat that was making its way down her chest and disappearing inside her top.

"We made Hank a card!" Riley said happily. "My dad helped me write on it." Riley looked at me. "What did we write, Dad?"

"Get well soon," I stated.

"Hank is going to love it," Teddy said, smiling down at my daughter. The way she stroked Riley's curly hair made my knees go wobbly. Riley slipped her hand into Teddy's, and they walked hand in hand up to Teddy's front door, and I thought I might collapse.

I wanted to see that sight over and over again for the rest of my life.

Teddy looked back at me. "Are you coming?" she asked with a smile. I nodded and followed her and Riley inside.

The house hadn't changed much since the last time I'd been here. You walked right into the living room, which had mismatched pieces of furniture and an old oak coffee table that made the room feel warm and homey. You could see through the doorway that led to the kitchen, where Hank was leaning against the counter with a smoothie in one hand and his cane in the other.

"Gus! Riley!" he said with a blinding smile. "It's good to see you." He set down the smoothie and started toward the living room, and I put a hand on Riley's shoulder to keep her from charging him. God bless her, but my kid would knock him over from sheer excitement alone.

Once Hank got close enough, I reached out and shook his hand. "Sir," I said, "how are you feeling?"

"Good, good," he said. "Sit down, please." I led Riley over to the couch as Teddy helped her dad get settled in his chair.

When he was situated, Teddy said, "Riley made something for you, Dad," and my daughter bounced with anticipation next to me, and Hank gave her a warm smile.

"Did she now?" he asked, and Riley nodded eagerly. I gave her leg a tap to let her know it was okay to go to him now. She popped up with no hesitation, made her way to his chair, and handed over her creation. Teddy came over to the couch and sat down next to me—not close enough, but that was probably a good thing.

"Well, I'll be damned," Hank said as he took the card gently from Riley. "This is quite the card," he said. "I love it."

"You have to open it," Riley told him. "There's drawings inside."

Hank opened the card dutifully and smiled when he saw what Riley had drawn. "My heart is very happy right now," he said, pointing at the heart with a smiley face. "Is this you?" he asked, pointing at one of Riley's stick figures.

"Yep," she said. "And that's my dad and that's Teddy," she said, pointing at the two other stick figures. I watched Hank's eyes zero in on the card, but he didn't say anything.

"Riley," he said, "you're an artist." My kid, who I'd never known to be bashful or shy, was suddenly red as a tomato.

"Thank you," she said. "So your heart's better?"

"Much better," Hank said with a smile.

I turned to Teddy. "Is your washer still being an asshole?" I asked her.

She looked confused for a second before she said, "Oh, yeah, it's super busted," with a wave of her hand.

"I, um . . ." I didn't know why I was feeling nervous all of a sudden. "I brought my tools. I can take a look at it. If you want."

Something flashed from Teddy's eyes before she said, "That would be really great, thank you."

"You got it," I said. I lifted my hand to push her ponytail back over her shoulder, desperate to see her collarbone for some fucking reason, but I stopped myself when I realized that it wasn't just the two of us. Teddy looked at my hand paused in midair between us, then back at me. I pulled it back quickly and looked forward.

"Dad!" Riley exclaimed, jolting Teddy and me out of our trance. "Hank is going to show me how to play the drums!"

My kid and a drum set? Honestly, that sounded like a bad idea for anyone with ears, but her wide smile had me convinced it was the best idea ever. Hank went to get out of his chair, and Teddy immediately went to help him.

I wondered if she ever got tired.

Once Hank was upright, Riley grabbed the hand that wasn't holding on to his cane and started walking with him—slower than I'd ever seen her walk. "C'mon, Teddy!" she called back. They were headed toward the kitchen, probably to go out the side door that led to the garage, which is where Hank had a music store's worth of instruments, if memory served.

"I'll be right there, Sunshine," she said. "Your dad's going to fix something for me, so let me show him where the laundry room is, and I'll be right there."

I knew where the laundry room was—right behind the kitchen—but I didn't say that.

Teddy and I followed Riley and Hank until they went out the side door, and we kept walking toward the back of the kitchen. There was a pocket door right next to the fridge that led to a small laundry room.

Teddy flicked on the light switch and the soft white light above us flickered a few times before staying on. "So here's the culprit," she said, turning back toward me, and I couldn't help myself. I grabbed her by the back of the neck and brought my mouth to hers.

I think I shocked her because it took her a second to catch up, but once she did, she wrapped her arms around my neck and kissed me back. She kissed me like it was the easiest thing in the world. There was no hurry or urgency in this kiss. It just felt . . . right, I guess.

After a while, I pulled back and rested my forehead on hers. Her eyes were still closed, like she was taking this moment in.

"Riley missed you," I said. *I missed you,* I thought.

Teddy's eyes fluttered open. So fucking blue. "I missed her, too," she said. "Hank's going to keep that card on the fridge for the rest of forever. I'm surprised your household has so much glitter," she chuckled.

"I haven't looked in her room because I know it probably looks like a fucking unicorn projectile-vomited all over everything," I said, shaking my head.

Teddy pushed up on her toes to kiss me again, and it took me off guard. I liked this, though—the way we were feeling things out. Everything we'd done had been well—hot as fuck, really—but I wanted this, too.

The quiet moments. The normal ones.

And this moment, when our foreheads were pressed together in Teddy's laundry room, felt like the type of moment that made you want more, and fuck, I wanted it all.

"How are you?" I said. She'd been with me half the week, helping take care of my kid, and then she'd come home to take care of her dad. She had to be exhausted.

Teddy shrugged. "I'm okay," she said. "Your dad has been by a few times with food, and Aggie and Dusty came over last night. My dad was really happy."

I brought my hand up to her cheek and looked right in those baby blues. "How are *you,* Teddy?" I asked again.

"I'm good," she said, and I gave her a pointed look. "I'm tired," she finally said after a few beats of silence. Her words were emphasized with a slight sag of her shoulders. "It's hard to sleep. I check on my dad a million times a night—just to make sure he's breathing."

I pulled Teddy close and cupped the back of her head with my hand. "Riley got sick once," I said into her hair. "It was just the flu, but she had this insane fever that made her almost lethargic. I did the same thing—checked on her all night every night. Even after she was better, I did it for a long time." Teddy pulled back and looked up at me, and I stroked her cheek and fiddled with the end of her ponytail. "It's hard, sometimes—to be the one people depend on."

She nodded, and her eyes looked glassier than they had a second ago. I traced the pad of my thumb underneath one of them before I kissed her forehead.

"Your dad is lucky to have you, Teddy," I said. "And so am I." Because I was, and I wanted to have her forever. It scared the shit out of me—knowing that I might've found exactly what I'd always wanted—because that meant I could lose it.

## Chapter 32

# Gus

After Teddy left the laundry room—Riley came looking for her—I went out to my truck and grabbed my tools and started looking at the washer. Teddy and Hank's washer was a piece of shit. Honestly, I should just buy them a new one.

Nearly an hour and a half later, after a lot of curses and a good number of kicks to the side of the thing, I figured out that the spin suspension was way out of whack and the drum belt was shot. Luckily, it was something I could fix myself.

I stood up straight and lifted my arms above my head to stretch my back and thanked my lucky stars that I was a rancher and not a Maytag repairman. My body hurt when I got home from my work, but in a good way. This washing machine business had just pissed me off.

I wiped my hands off with a rag and moved the washing machine back to where it was. I hoped it would work.

Now that I wasn't focused on the washer, I could hear sounds coming from Teddy's garage. I left the laundry room and went out the side door. The garage door was open. Riley was sitting behind a drum kit, drumsticks in hand, banging the ever-loving shit out of them. Hank was sitting in a camping chair, plucking at the strings of an expensive-looking electric guitar, and Teddy was leaning against the garage door. I couldn't see her face, but her shoulders were shaking.

I walked up behind her and put my hand on the garage door right above her head. "What's going on out here?" I said, and Teddy jumped—guess she wasn't expecting me.

"Dad!" Riley yelled. "Watch!" And then proceeded to hit each drum in front of her twice before finishing with a nice tap to the cymbal.

"You're a pro, Sunshine," I said. I was surprised Riley wasn't levitating over her seat with joy.

"Did you know Hank was in a band?" Riley said.

"I seem to remember he was in more than one," I said, nodding and smiling at Hank, who I hoped wouldn't think anything of the fact that I was standing a little too close to his daughter.

"I want to be in a band," Riley said. "Can girls be drummers?"

Before I could say anything, Teddy said, "Hell fucking yeah, girls can be drummers!" And a grin broke out on my face.

Riley giggled. "Dad says we're not supposed to say that word."

"We'll let it slide," I said, trying not to laugh. Riley nodded.

"There are a lot of amazing drummers who are girls, Sunshine," Teddy said. "Meg White, Karen Carpenter, Sheila E"—she was getting excited. "We'll listen to them, and you'll see how badass they are."

"Can you drum?" Riley asked.

"I can," Teddy said. "But I haven't for a while."

Riley's eyes went wide. "Drum, drum, drum!" she said. She looked at me—she was vibrating again. God, she was going to be tired tonight. "Dad, tell Teddy to drum!"

Teddy flipped to face me, and her ponytail hit me in the face. "Hey," I said, "watch where you swing that thing." I didn't really care, though. "You can't leave us hanging," I said. Teddy rolled her blue eyes, but it looked like she was trying not to smile. She walked over to the drum kit. Riley immediately vacated her seat and handed the drumsticks to Teddy.

"What do you say, Hank?" she said as she sat down. "Should we give them a duet?" Hank's eager nod was accompanied by a hearty laugh. He looked twenty years younger with the guitar across his lap.

Teddy took a deep breath and cracked her neck like she was gearing up for the biggest performance of her life. She nodded a few times, counting her way in, then hit it. The beat sounded familiar—I couldn't place it until Hank started picking at his guitar—"Fortunate Son" by Creedence Clearwater Revival.

I watched Teddy and her father in awe. They were connected by the music. It was like Teddy was playing the drums with her entire body—not just her arms or her foot on the kick drum.

Hank's face had gone full rock star. I knew he'd been a drummer, but damn, he was playing the shit out of that guitar! When Teddy's and Hank's eyes met, they grinned at each other and got even more into what they were doing—letting the music totally take over.

Riley was jumping and clapping and dancing in the middle of the garage, and I pushed off from the garage door to meet her on her makeshift dance floor.

She squealed when I grabbed her hand and gave her a twirl. Her delighted giggle was the only thing that sounded better than the music Teddy and Hank were playing. As my daughter and I danced together, I knew this moment would be one of those memories that I thought back on at every big moment in her life—when she got her driver's license, graduated from high school, college—when she got married, if that's what she wanted. I'd put it in the same place as all the other memories I had of Riley, as well as of my mom, my dad, and my siblings, holding it close to me.

I'd think about the time my daughter and I danced together in Teddy Andersen's garage.

I picked Riley up and held her close to my chest. I looked over her shoulder at Teddy, who was smiling at us as if she was thinking the same thing, and I was struck with an overwhelming feeling of happiness, and something else I couldn't name, that Teddy was here too.

## Chapter 33

# Teddy

When I was a kid, I had a bad habit of drawing on—well, everything, including the couch and especially the walls. I drew on them constantly—paper was too small a canvas for what I wanted to create, especially when I was upset, which is when I drew the most.

My dad could've yelled at me or gotten mad—honestly, he probably should have—but he didn't. He redirected me. He told me that if I stopped drawing on the walls, the outside of the garage was all mine. He said I could draw on it, paint on it, throw glitter on it—anything I wanted—as long as I stopped drawing on the walls (and furniture) in the house.

As a kid, the garage seemed so much bigger than the walls in the house, so obviously—much to Hank's relief—I picked the garage.

After that, the back of the garage became my own little world—at least when it was warm enough for me to be outside for long periods of time without risk of hypothermia or loss of limb. I planted flowers and hung twinkle lights, and I painted.

I painted when I was happy and I painted when I was sad, but mostly, I painted when I needed to think. And right now, I desperately needed to think.

So today, I was painting. I hadn't done it in a while, not like this. I pulled my hair up, put on an old pair of shorts and a paint-stained T-shirt, pulled out my paints, and got to work.

When I painted, the same thing happened as when I was listening to music or working on clothes; it was like the front half of my brain turned off, which made room for the things that were all jumbled in the back of my brain to start working themselves out.

And my brain was filled to the brim with thoughts of August Ryder. A man I'd always respected but had never liked until recently, and I think the feeling was mutual.

I tried to pinpoint it—the moment things had changed—but I couldn't. There wasn't one moment that stuck out for me—just a bunch of little ones, like lit matches I'd kept throwing onto the box of dynamite that was Gus, and eventually one had hit the fuse and blown up everything I'd ever thought I knew about him.

Or maybe we were the lit matches.

Before, when I thought about Gus, I thought about who he was in relation to other people—Emmy's brother, Brooks's best friend, Riley's dad. Now, when I thought about him, I thought about who he was in relation to me—someone who understood my fears and wants and burdens and didn't scoff at them or even try to take them away—I think because he knew that they could be heavy, but it was the heavy things that I loved the most.

It was weird, to feel so strongly about Gus in one way and

then in an entirely different way. I wondered how I could have crossed the spectrum of feelings that I felt for him so quickly, but those feelings also felt like two sides of the same coin.

There was this little voice in the very back of my head that wondered if my desire to be loved and settled in my life was pushing me to feel something that I otherwise wouldn't, but I didn't think that was the case.

Everything with Gus felt so . . . real.

Because I felt real when I was with him. I didn't feel I had to be all of the things people expected me to be when I was with Gus. I loved being those things sometimes—but I didn't have to be. This idea that I could shed my skin, that I could—god, this is so stupid—let my hair down, made me crave him.

I liked who I was—I liked, or at least respected, every part of me—and it felt good to show someone the parts that I kept to myself, whether it was out of necessity, or love, or insecurity, or whatever else it might be.

But there was another important layer to this entire situation: Riley.

I'd always loved the kid, but just like my feelings for Gus, my feelings for his daughter just kept growing. I didn't know the first thing about being a parent, and Riley already had two really good ones, but I did know that there wasn't anything I wouldn't do for her.

A landscape was taking shape on the side of the garage—I didn't do those very often—next to the portrait I'd done of my dad last summer. I didn't have the heart to cover that up.

"That's pretty," Emmy said. I looked up, and she was walking toward me, looking like a regular cowboy sweetheart in her boots, shorts, and Coors Light cropped T-shirt.

"Thank you," I said. "I'm not sure what it is yet."

"I brought you guys dinner from my dad. It's inside, but Hank said you were out here."

"You sound tired," I said. Emmy looked kind of . . . low.

She sighed. "Mommy issues got brought up in therapy today—absolutely exhausting."

"Ah." I nodded. "Those will get you, won't they?"

"So annoying, really," Emmy said, smiling slightly.

"At least your mom died," I said with a shrug, repeating a line I'd said to her many times before. It always made us laugh, even though it probably shouldn't.

"True," she laughed airily, and I knew what was coming. "She didn't just give me to a drummer and head on her way."

Emmy and I broke into a fit of giggles. Our mommy issues were different, but if we didn't laugh about them, we'd cry. And we did do that—sometimes—but mostly we laughed and held each other upright when we thought we'd fall. It was nice that we still had this, even though our friendship had changed over the past couple of years. This would be one of the ways she would always need me, and I would always need her.

But then Emmy looked at me, and the last hint of a giggle stopped abruptly.

"What is that on your neck?" she asked, getting closer to me. "Is that . . . a *hickey*?"

I immediately brought my hand that wasn't holding a wet paintbrush up to cover the red mark on the side of my neck—right where it met my shoulder—that I thought was too faded for anyone to notice.

"No," I said quickly.

Emmy swatted my hand away from the hickey I was covering up. I tried to bring my hand back to it, but she had hold of my wrist.

So I did what any normal person would do: I raised my other hand—the one that was holding the paintbrush—to my throat and painted over the hickey.

"Teddy!" Emmy exclaimed. "What the hell is wrong with you?"

"What the hell is wrong with *you*?" I countered. "This is quite literally battery, Clementine!" I was trying to push her away, and she was trying to get closer.

"I know you're not sleeping with the vet anymore." Her green eyes bored into mine. "So who the fuck is sucking your neck?"

Without thinking, I told my best friend the truth. I didn't know how to lie to her. "Your brother!" I blurted.

Emmy went still. Her eyes were still on me, but I don't think they were seeing me. I knew the signs of an Emmy spiral, and I could see one starting. After a second, she shook herself out of it and smacked my arm lightly. "You're lucky I'm not like Gus, or I would've punched you in the face! Did you think about that?" Her voice was elevated.

"It's not my fault you won't let me have a secret!" I said back. "But I think this is a good time to bring up how upset you were when Gus punched Brooks in the face, so maybe you should stop yelling at me."

"I'm not yelling!" I watched her realize that she was in fact yelling. She took a deep breath. "I'm not yelling," she said, this time at a normal volume. "I'm just . . . This is a lot to take in, okay?"

"Understood," I said. "I was going to tell you."

"When?" Emmy snapped.

"Soon," I said, which was probably true. I hadn't known whether there would really be something to tell, but then my dad had a heart attack and I cried in Gus's truck and things changed.

Emmy blinked slowly. "Just so we're abundantly clear—you are"—she gagged a little bit—"sleeping with my brother?"

"I thought Luke Brooks would've fucked that gag reflex right out of you by now," I quipped.

"Not the time, Ted," Emmy said, holding up her palm.

"Sorry," I muttered.

"So," she said after a second.

"So, what?"

"Are you sleeping with my brother?" she asked.

I folded my arms. "I don't like this," I said.

"Me either," Emmy responded. "It's not fun being on the other side of the interrogation, is it?"

"No," I said, feeling chastised. "And yes. To the other thing."

Emmy gagged again, and I had to bite back a smile. I felt bad that she'd found out this way, but honestly, watching her reaction was entertaining.

"So is it like a forced proximity thing? Or is it like a hate-sex thing?"

That rubbed me the wrong way—like those were the only two reasons that Gus and I could ever enjoy each other's company. The energy shifted. I wasn't entertained anymore. I was mad.

"It's neither of those things," I said, shaking my head in annoyance, my tone no longer playful and lighthearted.

"So what is it?" Emmy asked as she in turn folded her arms.

"I don't know," I said. "But it's not just a sex thing or a convenience thing. It's more than that. It's just . . . more, okay?"

"I don't get it," she said. "You guys don't even like each other."

"You're one to talk, Emmy," I said, my voice having more bite than I'd intended. "I don't know how to explain it to you, but we just kind of work, okay?"

"I didn't even know being in a relationship was something you wanted, Teddy. You've never brought it up. I think it's valid that I'm having trouble wrapping my head around this."

"It's not that you're having trouble," I said. "It's that you automatically assumed that because it's me that's doing this, it means that Gus and I are temporary—a cheap knock-off of a relationship instead of something real and meaningful." It was both of those things, and I hated that Emmy seemed already to have written it off.

"I just—" she started and then paused again. "I just mean that Gus has told me a million times that he's fine on his own. And you—" Another pause. A sigh. "I love you so deeply, Teddy. You've never taken a relationship seriously. I don't even know if you've ever actually been in one, and I don't know if my brother is the best place to start."

"Are you hearing yourself right now?" I asked. I couldn't think of anything else to say. This wasn't how I'd thought this would go. Granted, I'd thought that I might have a little bit more time to think about it, that I wouldn't have been forced into spilling the beans before I'd talked to Gus about it, but still, I didn't like where this was going.

"How did you expect me to react, Teddy?"

"Honestly," I said, "I thought you'd be happy for me—like I've been for you for the past few years. I didn't expect you to throw a party in my honor, but damn, Em, I really thought you'd give me the same energy that I gave you when you fell in love with your brother's best friend." I was getting more confident now—more angry, too. "But I guess this is just another example of how our relationship has changed."

"What are you talking about?"

I took a deep breath; I guessed now was as good a time as any. "I've been having a hard time lately," I said, and Emmy tilted her head, looking at me like she already knew that. "And it wasn't just the job or the sewing machine or whatever. I've been feeling stagnant and sad and struggling with the fact that our friendship is different now."

"No, it isn't," Emmy said. She was feeling defensive too. I saw it in her tense shoulders and narrowed eyes.

"Yes, it is," I said. "And I don't think it's an inherently bad thing. I think it's what happens when people grow up and end up in different places—physically or otherwise. You and I are in different stages of life, Emmy. And it might not be obvious to you, but you don't need me the same way you used to. You're getting married. Brooks should be the person you feel the most comfortable with, the most safe and secure with. But I don't have that. I have you, and you have someone else.

"It just really sucks to be on unequal footing with your best friend. It sucks to feel like you don't need me anymore, and it sucks to feel like I can't talk to you about it because I don't want you to feel bad for focusing on building a life with the person you love.

"And do you want to know what sucks the most? The fact that maybe I have a chance at that—a chance at a person who gets me and wants me—and you respond by trying to talk me out of it."

"I'm not trying to talk you out of it," Emmy interjected.

"Aren't you?" I asked. "Then what are you saying?"

"What I'm saying is that at the end of the day, I don't know if this thing with you and Gus is going to work out or go past the summer. Cam is going to come home, and you'll go back home. You won't have Gus to distract you from figuring your shit out, and when that happens, I'm still going to be Gus's little sister, and I'm still going to be your best friend. I need both of those relationships to survive this. And Gus, he's just got a lot of responsibilities . . ."

I don't think Emmy meant to hurt me—I mean, she didn't throw a punch like Gus, but her blow landed nonetheless.

And it landed hard.

There weren't a lot of things that people could say that would hurt me, at least enough to provoke any sort of response from me. I had a thick skin, but my best friend basically telling me that *I* was the problem here made me feel like my chest had just been cracked wide open with the hilt of a knife—the pain of it made me lurch forward slightly.

It was quiet for a minute, as my best friend and I surveyed each other. Emmy held her ground, but I'd expect nothing less from her. She was fierce as hell.

Well, so was I.

"Have you ever thought," I said gently, "that maybe Gus tells you he doesn't want a relationship because he's afraid to let himself want it? Because he feels like all his focus should be on taking care of all of you, and he's terrified to let himself slip?" I wasn't trying to hurt my best friend with that, just to tell her something.

"And as for me . . ." My voice was still soft, but the gentleness had gone. This part wasn't about Gus and me, or Gus at all. This was about my best friend and me—about the fact that she seemed to see me exactly the same way that everybody else did. "Maybe I've never taken anybody else seriously because no one has ever taken me seriously, but Gus does. Both of us take care of other people, our families, our friends—you—and that makes us the only people who know how to take care of each other. It makes us good for each other. It makes what we're doing worthwhile.

"And it hurts that you don't see that. It hurts that you're more worried about how this relationship is going to affect you than how good it has been for me." I looked up at the blue sky and took another deep breath. "Because it's been the best thing, and I thought you'd be able to see it. I thought you could see me."

I saw it then, the regret in Emmy's face.

"Ted—" Emmy said, but I held my paint-covered hand up.

"No," I said firmly. "You said what you needed to say, and so did I. I'm fine. We'll be fine. I just need a beat. Okay?"

"Okay," Emmy whispered.

And so my best friend reluctantly walked away, and I went back to painting the back of my garage.

# Chapter 34

## Gus

The night had arrived. Brooks had finally gotten his goddamned mechanical bull installed at the Devil's Boot, and tonight was the first night that people could ride it. It was also the first night in a long time that I was leaving my house not with or for my kid.

Riley was hanging out with my dad tonight. They were having a sleepover in a tent in the small patch of forest behind the big house. Riley was fucking stoked about it.

I spent a little extra time picking out a shirt—a white Henley that Emmy bought me—and shaving. Normally, I'd just throw something on and go—all of my clothes were mostly the same. There wasn't really anything that wouldn't match—but I was sure Teddy was going to be there, and I just wanted to look nice or whatever. I didn't fucking know.

I'd seen Teddy work the Devil's Boot, and if I wanted to hold her attention, I needed to put in a little effort.

Honestly, I was a little nervous about seeing Emmy. I hadn't seen her since I'd heard from Teddy the other day. When her name lit up my phone screen, I grinned like an idiot. When I picked up and Teddy asked, "Do you have time to talk something through with me?" I grinned even bigger because it felt so ordinary, but also a big step toward a relationship that felt real—the type of relationship that would last.

That's when she told me about Emmy and the fight they'd had.

"I don't know," she said. "Everything about it sucked, and I didn't think it would suck. And the way the conversation started was fine, but the way it ended just . . ."

"Sucked?" I finished.

"Yeah," she sighed and then was quiet for a second. "Is it okay?" she asked. "That I told her about us?"

It was probably one of the best things that had ever happened: Teddy wanted to tell her best friend about us, which meant that we meant something. But I tried to be chill. "Yes, Teddy. I'm happy you did."

"Me too," she sighed. "I'm just bummed at how it went down."

"I'm sorry," I said. "You guys will be okay, though." I had no doubt in my mind about that. Emmy and Teddy were inevitable. But of course I was worried about my sister, too—about how she felt about all of this and how she felt about me right now. I felt responsible for Emmy. No matter what, I'd always been protective of her, but after our mom died, the three of us—my dad, Wes, and me—tried to fill the hole that she left as best we could. We were all devoted to the youngest Ryder. So it wasn't exactly easy that not only was the woman I could see as my future hurting, but so was my little sister—even if it wasn't permanent.

"I know. I just wish we didn't have to be not okay first."

The way Teddy's voice sounded made me swallow hard. I wished she was here with me. I wanted to comfort her and keep her close, especially because I was part of the reason she was feeling this way, and I hated that.

"What can I do, Teddy baby?" I'd do anything.

"Nothing. Telling you helped. Thanks for listening."

"Anytime," I said. I wanted to listen to Teddy talk forever.

It took about fifteen minutes to get to the Devil's Boot, and when I pulled in to the dirt parking lot, it was already almost full. I didn't see Teddy's red Ford Ranger, but I saw Wes's truck and Dusty's Bronco.

I hadn't seen the inside of the bar since everything had been moved around, so when I walked in, it took a second to orient myself. The bar and the stage were still in the same spot, obviously, but most of the seating had been moved to make way for the bull—which Brooks had named Sue—"a bull named Sue, get it?" he'd said, referring to the Johnny Cash classic—in the center of the room.

I also clocked a new neon sign that said YOU CAN GO UPSTAIRS NOW. Emmy's idea, probably. She was good at stuff like that—little touches that Brooks wouldn't think of. I spotted Wes and Ada at the bar and made my way over to them.

Seated nearby were Brooks's crew of regulars, which he called his horsemen. They came to the Devil's Boot nearly every day, sat at the bar, and gave him shit.

When the four men saw me, they raised their glasses and let out a cheer. "Look who decided to grace us with his awful presence!" one of them said.

"Brooks, get this guy a beer!" another one said. Brooks looked up from where he was pouring Fireball into shot glasses. He gave me a nod.

"Hey, man," Wes said with a slap to my back. "Nice shirt."

Why did Wes have to be so observant and care so much about me that he knew when I was wearing something new or out of the ordinary?

Fucking irritating, honestly.

"Hey, Gus!" Ada smiled at me and waved. "You going to ride that thing tonight?" She gestured toward the bull.

"Maybe if we get enough drinks in him." Her voice blared behind me, and I turned to see Teddy Andersen in the flesh.

And she looked beautiful.

She was wearing some tightass jeans, and her silver cowboy boots were poking out of the bottom of them. I dragged my gaze down her body. Was she wearing . . . *chaps*?

She was, but they were a shiny silver leather, like the kind rodeo queens wore—fashion chaps, I guess. She also had on a tight silver halter top and had lined her blue eyes with silver liner.

Her hair was up in her signature ponytail, which looked like it was dusted with silver glitter.

Fuck. *Fuck.*

Teddy Andersen was a knockout.

She basked under my perusal, and when our eyes met, she winked at me. And that wink went straight to my dick.

"You look . . ." I said. I didn't even know how to put into words how she looked.

"I know," she said with a feline smile. I didn't even care that Wes and Ada and everyone else were watching this all go down. Teddy had already told Emmy, and that meant that this was real to her, too.

"World's hottest disco ball," I said with a small smile.

Teddy rolled her eyes, but it was half-assed.

Wes cleared his throat behind me, and I heard him mutter, "What the fuck." When I turned around, Brooks was sliding my beer across the bar. He looked at me questioningly for a second before he shifted his gaze to Teddy.

"Tequila soda?" he called, and Teddy must've nodded, because he started making it. One of the horsemen raised his hand and said, "Teddy's on my tab."

The possessive part of me wanted to tell that man exactly where he could shove his tab, but the flirty smile Teddy was giving him, along with a polite "Thank you," stopped me.

Teddy Andersen was coming home with me tonight. I was going to make sure of it. So who cared if someone else picked up her drinks?

Teddy shone in this dingy bar. She said hi to everyone as they moved out of her way, making them feel special that they got to bask in her light for however long they were talking to her.

If I wanted this thing with Teddy to go anywhere, I'd have to remember that she was built to shine and glow and shimmer, and I couldn't take that piece of her only for myself. She didn't shine just for me. I got a different part of her—the part that was comfortable enough to turn down the brightness when we were alone, the part that wanted me to see past what everyone else was blinded by.

There were parts of Teddy that would always belong to the world around her, but that didn't matter because there were also parts of her that were all mine.

*Mine.* That word rang through me like a victory bell. Shit, I wanted that.

Teddy took her drink from Brooks and gave my arm a squeeze before she turned and walked away.

"Hey," I called after her.

Teddy looked back at me, and my heart stopped dead in my chest. "Those chaps are really working for you," I said.

"Yeah?" She smiled.

I nodded. "They're working for me, too."

I watched Teddy fight a smile, and I felt like I was floating. She shook her head, rolled her eyes at me, and kept walking to do her rounds.

I let her go, knowing that's what she wanted. I turned back to Ada, Wes, and Dusty, who were all looking at me like I'd just grown a second head. Brooks was looking at me with concern.

I shrugged. "What?"

"So I guess the babysitting thing really worked, then?" Wes said with a tentative laugh.

As I shrugged again, Emmy appeared next to me.

She pushed up on the bar and leaned across it to kiss Brooks. A few people cheered when they saw it.

"You're hot as hell, sugar," Brooks said to her when her feet were back on the ground. Gross.

"Back at you," she said. Again, gross. And then she turned to the rest of us. "Hey," she said. Then she turned to me. "Where's Teddy?"

"Around," I said. Everyone had gone back to their own conversations and Brooks had moved down the bar, so it felt safe to talk to Emmy. "Are you two okay?"

"We'll be fine," she said.

"Emmy, I'm sorry. I didn't mean—" But Emmy held her hand up.

"August, I love you, but my and Teddy's friendship is bigger than you. I hurt my best friend. I'm dealing with it," Emmy said. "This is between her and me, okay?"

I nodded. "Okay."

After that, the night picked up. The Devil's Boot got even more full and even more loud. It seemed like the whole town was here.

I stayed where I was, but lots of people came up to say hi to me or Wes, and especially Emmy. I'd heard Emmy referred to as Meadowlark's sweetheart before, and I thought it was fitting. Especially now, when people seemed to think of her and Brooks's engagement as Meadowlark's royal wedding. Every now and then I'd scan the room for Teddy, but it seemed she was constantly swept up in the crowd.

After a while, Brooks disappeared from behind the bar and reappeared onstage. The lead singer of his house band handed him the microphone.

"Hey, y'all," he said. "Welcome to the Devil's Boot!" The place erupted in a cheer.

"Tonight is the first night that our upstairs is open." Another cheer. I looked over at Emmy, who had her hands clasped under her chin. I felt the pride rolling off her as she looked up at Brooks. "And it's finally time for Sue's inaugural ride." The loudest cheers yet.

"I'm not much of a talker, but Sue's first rider deserves a little bit of an intro, and I think you'll agree. She is incomparable, she is fearless, and well, she's loud as fuck. It's Teddy Andersen, everyone!"

The cheer that erupted from the bar probably caused seismic activity throughout Meadowlark. One of the people on-stage shifted a spotlight, and I followed its beam. It landed right on Teddy, who was at the back of the bar, alight with the attention that was on her.

She flashed her signature Teddy smile, and my heart thundered in my ears.

The band started playing as she made her way toward the bull pen. I didn't think I'd ever heard the Devil's Boot band play anything but country, but right now they were playing "Strutter," by Kiss.

Which was the perfect song, because Teddy was strutting toward the pen, the light hitting the silver of her outfit and sending glittering orbs throughout the bar.

It had never been more obvious that she was the daughter of a rock star, even if she couldn't sing for shit.

Everyone was zeroed in on her—including me. She waved and twirled and blew kisses, giving everyone a show, and goddamn, I could've watched her all night.

Between the vibration of the bass and kick drum and the cheers from the crowd, there was so much Teddy. A few months ago, I would've said it was too much, but now it didn't feel like enough.

She made it to the bull pen at the start of the second chorus. Brooks helped her step in, and then she mounted.

The way she slung her leg over the bull and then did this little hop to get situated made me want her riding other things. My things. Mouth, cock, hand, whatever. I didn't care.

"Ready, Ted?" Brooks asked into the mic, and Teddy gave him a "Hell yeah." It wasn't audible above the crowd noise, but I read her lips. I looked over at my little sister, who was cheering louder than anyone else for her best friend.

Teddy lifted her right hand and held on to the bull with her left. The guitar solo in "Strutter" had just started when Brooks said, "One hand, for eight seconds, in three . . . two . . . one!"

Sue started to move, around and up and down. There was a countdown on the bull pen.

Teddy looked a little shaky on the first buck, but she recovered. She got hit with two hard bucks immediately after that but stayed on. I never thought I'd be so invested in a mechanical bull ride, but I didn't think I was even breathing.

Teddy got thrown to the side and everybody in the room hollered some version of "Hang on," and she did. With two seconds left, Teddy let out a "Yeehaw," and everyone else did too. Sue gave her one final buck, and I thought Teddy might go down, but she didn't.

When Sue came to a halt, Teddy was still firmly mounted.

The crowd clapped and whistled and cheered. And Teddy, who wasn't one to let a moment go to waste, stood on Sue's back with her arms stretched out to each side, which caused the cheers to get louder and louder. She put her hand to her ear in an "I can't hear you" gesture, and the crowd took that to heart, giving it their all.

I was grinning. My face actually hurt, which I don't think had ever happened to me before.

When Teddy jumped down from the bull, I started making my way over to the pen. I wasn't the only one; there was a line of men waiting to shoot their shot with the woman who had just ridden the hell out of that bull.

Sucked for them that she was mine, didn't it?

The band had moved on to another song, and the crowd had started to go back to their own thing. Teddy was talking to one of her many admirers when I made it to her.

When she saw me, she lit up even more. It's a miracle her smile didn't blind me.

I put my hand on the shoulder of the man who was talking to her and said, "Out of my way," and then I grabbed her by the chaps and hauled her mouth to mine. I kissed her like we were the only two people in the bar. She kissed me back with equal fervor, and I couldn't have cared less that everyone was watching.

I wanted them to. I wanted them to know that Theodora Andersen was mine.

When I pulled back from our kiss, her blue eyes were dazed and dopey. "Come home with me," I said.

"Yes, please," she said. "Now." Shit, that worked for me. I grabbed her hand and started pulling her toward the door.

I saw that my siblings' and my friends' mouths were wide open, except for Ada's. She slapped Wes on the arm, and I couldn't tell for sure, but I think I heard her say, "You owe me fifty dollars."

I didn't look at anyone else on the way out. I was a man on a mission. And that mission—to put it in the most respectful way possible—was to get into Teddy Andersen's pants.

It didn't matter that it was summer in Meadowlark, it was always cool when the sun went down. So when Teddy and I pushed through the door of the Devil's Boot, I got a blast of cool breeze.

I couldn't tell if it was the mountain air that was making me feel alive or the woman whose hand I was holding.

When we got to my truck, I pushed Teddy up against it. I covered her body with mine and pressed against her. I kissed her again. She clung to me. Her mouth moved under mine, and suddenly it didn't feel so cool out here anymore.

My hips rolled of their own accord, and Teddy gasped. I swallowed her gasp with another kiss, and when I felt her tongue in my mouth, my knees buckled. I'd never been a kissing guy. I liked it, don't get me wrong, but I didn't get all the hype around it.

Until I kissed Teddy. After I kissed her all those years ago, I understood how it could be so fucking good. Back then, I thought I'd only get to kiss her that once, but I'd kissed her again, many times, and here I was kissing her again.

I could do this all night with her, but she had other plans. "Take me home, August Ryder," she said against my mouth. Her hands had traveled from my shoulders to my chest and were now sliding down my torso.

I knew then that I'd never be able to tell this woman no ever again.

## Chapter 35

# Teddy

The drive back to Gus's house was quiet and charged. His right hand was rubbing small circles on my upper thigh and his left was on the steering wheel. God, he was hot.

Tonight felt different. Tonight, we'd chosen each other in front of the whole town.

When Gus's truck rolled to a stop in front of his house, we stayed in the cab. I let the silence fall over me like a warm blanket. I looked over at Gus, who already had his eyes on me.

"You look incredible," he said.

I huffed a laugh. "Fan of the chaps?" I said.

"Fan of the ass in them," Gus said with a grin that made my heart hiccup. "A fan of the woman the ass belongs to, too."

"Are you going soft on me, August?" I scoffed.

Gus made a show of looking down at his groin and then back up at me. "Pretty much the opposite, baby." *Baby.* The way he said it, on the end of a laugh that was attached to a smile, made my insides go molten.

We were quiet again.

After a moment, Gus opened his door and got out of the truck. I was about to follow, but he said, "Don't you dare open that door on your own, Theodora."

"Yes, Daddy," I responded coyly. I saw Gus shake his head through the windshield as he crossed in front of the truck, but he was smiling. I knew he couldn't hide those dimples from me forever.

When he opened my door, he held his hand out, and I took it. We walked up to his front door slowly, hand in hand. Once we reached the top step, Gus turned to me and said four words that I never thought I'd hear from him—"I like you, Teddy"—and then he brought his mouth down on mine. I kissed him back with urgency. I tangled my hands in his hair and pressed my body against his. He walked me back a few steps until my back hit the door.

He liked pressing me up against things.

His hands made their way to my ass, which he gripped and used to lift me up. I wrapped my legs around his waist and kept kissing him. When he moved his mouth away from mine to unlock the front door, I kissed down his neck and back up. I licked his ear and bit the lobe. I did everything that I could to feel him.

I could hear him struggling with the key in the lock. "Trouble finding the hole?" I asked.

"Fuck off, Teddy," he said as the surface against my back finally gave way, but Gus had a hold on me and I had a hold on him. He walked us inside and tried to set me down, but I held on. I felt him kick off his shoes.

"Kitchen counter," I said after I licked his neck again. He groaned but complied. He deposited me there, and I finally unwound my arms from his neck. "Take your shirt off," I commanded as I took him in. His hair was mussed and his lips were swollen. God, he was his own damn work of art.

"Someone's demanding tonight," he said, but he did what I asked.

"And your pants," I added. He didn't do that right away. He was looking at me like he wanted to fight it, so I said, "I can't suck your dick in the kitchen if your pants are on, August."

I'll tell you what: I'd never seen a cowboy's pants come off faster.

I put my hands behind me and leaned back on the counter, taking in the beautiful man before me. His shoulders were broad; his body was honed and fine-tuned from years of hard work. The veins in his forearms were popping because he kept balling his hands into fists—like he was trying to restrain himself. The tattoos on his chest accentuated the muscles there. A smattering of dark hair there made a trail toward his dick.

Which is what my eyes were on now. Listen, I didn't normally think that much about the appearance of those things, but I'd give it to Gus, he had a nice one. And he knew how to use it.

I hoped he could feel the hunger in my gaze. I hoped he could see how badly I wanted him, but just in case he couldn't, I told him. "I want you," I said. "I want you so badly all the time." I slid off the counter. "I think about you at night, when I slip my hand between my thighs. I think of your hands and your fingers and your tongue."

Gus's nostrils flared as I dragged one of my fingers up the middle of his chest. "I think about the fact that your bedroom is so close to mine, and I wish you'd open the door. Especially after that night in the living room," I said. Gus's eyes were on fire, and I knew he had felt the same way. I think it was taking everything in him not to grab me, flip me around, and fuck me right then.

I liked that he was being good. And I liked the goosebumps rising on his skin everywhere I touched him.

"Fuck, Teddy," he said. "You're killing me." I pushed up on my toes and kissed him at the same time that I fisted his cock. He jerked and groaned into my mouth. I loved the way his groans tasted on my tongue. I kissed down his neck, his chest, his abdomen, as I lowered myself to my knees.

"What do you want, Gus?" I said, looking up at him.

"I want to fuck your smart little mouth," he said as he fisted my ponytail. I opened my mouth and stuck my tongue out over my bottom lip slightly.

An invitation.

"You're going to be the death of me," he whispered. Gus used the hand that wasn't gripping my ponytail to put his cock on my tongue. I closed my mouth around him, and his head fell back. Watching his throat work made wetness pool between my thighs.

I brought my hands up to his cock and started to work his length as I sucked and bobbed my head. "Fuck," he said. "Your mouth, your fucking mouth." His hips jerked hard, and his cock hit the back of my throat, which I fucking loved. But he stilled and pulled it out of my mouth, which caused me to pout.

"I'm sorry," he said. "Oh god, Teddy, did I hurt you?"

"No," I said. "I want this. Fuck my mouth, Gus. Please I added, knowing what that did to him.

Gus stroked my cheek. "You're so beautiful, Teddy," he said. "Squeeze my leg if it's too much, okay?"

"Okay," I said, knowing he wouldn't let me get away with just a nod. When he put himself back in my mouth, I sighed around him and picked up where I'd left off. It didn't take long for his hips to jerk again, for him to start thrusting into my mouth. Tears formed in my eyes, and everything about it felt so good. I felt beautiful and powerful with his eyes on me and his dick in my mouth.

"Shit," he said. "My beautiful girl." His thrusts got faster and more sporadic, and I let him guide my head as he got closer and closer to the edge. Just when I thought he would come, he pulled out of my mouth. His hands were on me in a second, pulling me up.

"Inside you," he said. "I need to come inside you." This man had an obsession with filling me up, and I loved it. I stripped off my shirt as Gus got to work on my chaps and jeans. He pushed them down without realizing my boots weren't off yet.

"Fuck these," he said as he lifted me up onto the counter. He pulled the boots off one by one and threw each of them across the room, then did the same thing with my pants. "I'm not going to last long, Teddy, at least this round, and I need to get you close. Tell me what I need to do to get you close."

I was already a lot closer than he probably thought—getting him off got me off. "There's a vibrator in my nightstand drawer," I said.

He cursed under his breath. "I knew I heard something," he said, and I winked at him.

"Maybe that was on purpose," I said.

"Stay here," he said. "Touch yourself while I'm gone." He was walking as fast as he could toward the hallway without breaking into a sprint. I followed orders, circling my clit with my fingers, and when he came back, he was holding my purple wand vibrator.

He climbed onto the counter with me, moving me backward so my naked body lay fully along the surface. The sensation of the cool counter under me and his warm body on top of me was incredible. "I need to be inside you," he said, and notched his cock at my entrance. "Are you ready for me?"

"I'm ready," I said. "Let me feel you." He slid into me slowly and my body started to quiver. Fuck, could it be this good every time?

"Shit, Teddy, I love the way your cunt feels when it's wrapped around my cock," he groaned out. "I love it."

*I might love you,* I thought, but I pushed that thought away.

Once he was fully inside me, he balanced himself with one hand by my head and grabbed the vibrator. He turned it on and brushed it over my clit once. I jerked and he swore.

"Tease," I breathed.

He smirked at me as he laid the vibrator on my clit again and pressed it down gently. A sound came out of my mouth that I'd never heard before. "Fuck, that feels so good when I'm full of you," I said.

With the vibrator on my clit, he started moving in and out of me. Slowly, like he was making a point. I thrashed and bucked underneath him, but he didn't speed up. He fucked me deliberately. He didn't take his eyes off mine the whole time.

My body clenched as shock waves rolled down my spine. My moans got louder and louder, and finally, when I was almost to the edge, he thrust harder. And harder. It wasn't until my back arched off the counter and my orgasm rocked through my body that he sped up, fucking me into the counter until I felt him release inside me. His body went rigid and his breath came ragged.

"Teddy!" he gasped as he came. "Fuck, Teddy, I never want to let you go."

"Then don't," I whispered as his body collapsed on mine.

# Chapter 36

# Teddy

I'd picked up Riley at the Big House the next morning. Gus and I had had a long night, so I was exhausted, but in a good way. We didn't talk about the whole "I never want to let you go" thing. I knew how I felt about what he said, but I didn't know what to think about it yet, so we just lay together on the counter until Gus insisted that we shower, insisted on taking care of me.

So I let him.

I took one of Gus's four-wheelers, knowing I could leave it at the Big House, so Riley and I could walk home together—and hopefully scout some plants. There was a new patch of wildflowers down by the old arena, and I was hopeful we might be able to finish out our list.

Before I left Gus's, I looked at the embroidery project that I'd been working on over the past few months. We needed three more flowers to fill up the blank spaces, including rock jasmine, the flower that started this whole thing. According to the internet, which I figured was a little more up-to-date than Hank's 1998 field guide, it was fairly common in this part of the Rocky Mountains, common enough that we should've found one by now.

Honestly, if we didn't find one this week, I'd be heartbroken. I didn't want to fail Riley, I didn't want to feel any sense of failure, not when I still had to face what I was doing afterward.

An idea had started to snowball in the back of my mind about what was next for me, and I was excited. I liked to keep things close to my chest while I was working on them, but I also couldn't wait to tell Gus and Emmy and my dad about it.

Emmy and I hadn't talked since that day. We would soon, I'm sure. We'd had a few fights before—the great recess disaster of 2006 when Emmy picked Collin Haynes to be on her kickball team instead of me. She claimed he could kick the ball farther, which he could, but ten-year-old me was fucking pissed about it anyway. Hank picked us up from school that day, and when we got back to Rebel Blue, he got out of his truck and locked us in. He told us we couldn't come out until we weren't fighting anymore.

It worked.

Over the years, we've learned how to handle conflict in our friendship a bit more maturely. Sometimes she needed space; sometimes I did; but we always worked it out.

Riley and I walked hand in hand. It was a beautiful summer day at Rebel Blue. Every day at Rebel Blue was beautiful, but I never stopped being awestruck by it.

We'd gone off the path—cutting through a patch of aspens that would get us to the old arena slightly faster. Not that I was in a hurry—I was soaking up the time with Riley and could walk through Rebel Blue with her all day—but one thing I'd learned this summer was that six-year-olds had little legs and got tired, even when they didn't want to admit it.

I loved aspens. I loved the way the light filtered through their leaves like rain and the way their leaves sounded like thunder when they were met with wind. Walking through the aspens was my favorite type of storm.

"Papa bought me my own sleeping bag, and it's pink," Riley was saying. "And we made s'mores but we made them with Reese's instead of Hershey's."

"Mmm. That sounds decadent," I said.

Riley paused for a moment. "What does dickadent mean?"

I didn't laugh, because I didn't want to deter Riley from asking questions. At this rate, she'd be smarter than all of us by the time she was ten.

"Deck-a-dent," I said slowly. "It means super yummy—something you might not have often because it's almost too yummy."

"I like deck-a-dent things," she said.

"Me too, Sunshine." We broke through the trees then, to the large patch of plain that held an old horse training arena—the new one was covered, this one wasn't. There was a small herd of cattle grazing near the arena—right about where that patch of wildflowers had cropped up.

I love all living things, but I swear to god, if one of those little fuckers ate my rock jasmine, I was going to lose it.

"Are we going over there?" Riley asked, pointing at the cows with the hand that wasn't holding mine. I nodded. "Can we run?"

"Hell yeah, we can run," I said. I picked up my pace and pulled Riley along with me. The cows, of course, didn't care that there were two humans barreling toward them. They just stared at us, but Riley and I hooted and hollered all the way over to them. Riley must've hit a gopher hole, because she tripped and we both fell into the grass. I was worried she'd fucked up her ankle, but she was laughing, so I figured she was okay. We lay there for a second. I listened to Riley laugh and take little gasps for air.

Riley and I scoured the patch of wildflowers for a little over an hour. We found one of the three that we'd been looking for—Riley spotted it. Yarrow—it was small, short, and white. The patch that we were in was mostly large yellow blooms, so I was hoping we'd spot some evening primrose here too (no dice). But I'd take the yarrow.

We'd picked a few of them, and Riley held them like a bouquet for the rest of our walk. She'd learned about bouquets from Cam—wedding planning—but Riley informed me very matter-of-factly that she wouldn't be carrying a bouquet at her mom's wedding; she'd be throwing flower petals because she was the flower girl.

When we were nearly home, Riley wanted to run again. Over the summer, I'd noticed that every time she started to run—even if it was just from the living room to the kitchen—she let out this maniacal little banshee cackle. It had become one of my favorite noises.

I was going to miss her. I was going to miss this.

I was going to miss him.

And I was going to miss who I got to be while I was with him. It wasn't like I'd never see either of them again. I'd see them all the time, but not like this. I wouldn't get to have slow mornings with Riley or late nights with Gus while he folded laundry and I read my book. I wouldn't get to see him carefree and open in his safe place, where he could shut out all the responsibilities he carried on his shoulders.

I didn't know where we went from here. Did we try to go back to the way things were? Treat each other the way everyone had come to expect? Or would we see what would bloom from the seeds that had been planted this summer? Would we discover our own new type of flower, wild and unexpected and ours to behold? Or would it wither on the vine? I just didn't know.

But I did know I was really going to miss him. *My* Gus.

# Chapter 37

## Gus

Cam was coming to pick up Riley tonight. Teddy's bag was by the front door, and I had to fight the urge to kick it or dump it out or take it back to my room and start putting all her shit in my dresser.

I didn't want her to go.

Riley and Teddy were in the living room. They'd put out a white sheet and were carefully laying out the dried flowers that they'd collected this summer. They'd gotten lucky today and found two of the last ones they were looking for—a yellow one near the old arena and a white one on the trail back to our house. Riley was thrilled. Teddy looked happy too, but there was still one flower missing, and she couldn't seem to let it go.

"Dad! Come look!" Riley called. I quickly pulled the chicken and veggies I'd prepped out of the oven and walked into the living room. Teddy was sitting cross-legged in front of the sheet and Riley was sitting on her lap. They were both wide-eyed and smiley.

*My girls,* I thought, but quickly pushed that out of my head.

We hadn't talked about it yet—what happened when the summer was over. I hoped we'd keep moving forward. I hoped we'd keep choosing each other, because I was falling hard for her. I just didn't know what the hell to do about it yet.

"This is incredible, Sunshine," I said. "Look at everything you did this summer."

"And Teddy, too!" Riley said, looking up at me.

"And Teddy, too," I said softly. Teddy was smiling, but her smile didn't reach her eyes. When did I start noticing that sort of thing?

"Thank you," I said to her. "For all of it."

Teddy nodded and gave Riley a squeeze. "All right, Sunshine, let's get these cleaned up. I've got to get going."

My heart dropped like a rock in a lake, and I was surprised no one heard the thump. "You're not staying for dinner?" I asked, the disappointment clear in my voice.

"I told my dad I'd be home," she said. She wasn't looking at me.

"Oh," I said. "Okay."

Riley and Teddy started gathering the flowers and placing them carefully back between the pages of the field guide. I got the rest of dinner together and tried to push out the dark cloud that had settled over me as Teddy's departure became more imminent.

"Wash up," I called to Riley as I stirred together a big bowl of pasta and sauce. Once I heard Riley's feet heading up the stairs toward her bathroom, I turned around and saw Teddy leaning against the wall at the entrance of the kitchen.

"You're sure you don't want to stay?" I said as I took a few steps toward her.

Teddy nodded. "I'm sure, thank you," she said, but she

sounded anything but. Her blue eyes kept moving between me and the door—between staying and going.

Why was she conflicted? We had something here—didn't we?

"I just . . . I just want to be home with my dad tonight," she said as she pushed off the wall. "Thank you"—she wrapped her arms around my waist, and I cupped the back of her head—"for the best summer ever."

I pulled back and looked down at her. "Teddy, I—"

She shrugged out of my hold and said, "We'll talk soon, okay?"

And then she walked out the front door.

"Mama!" Riley's cry could probably be heard in the next county over as she threw herself around Cam's legs. Cam stumbled but was able to steady herself.

"Hi, Sunshine," Cam said as she bent down to be eye to eye with Riley. "Look how big you are," she said, brushing Riley's curly hair out of her face. "I missed you so much." Cam pulled our daughter into her arms and rocked her slowly.

"I missed you, Mama. I missed you. I missed you." Riley was clinging to her mom's neck. Cam stood, lifting Riley with her. She used one of her arms to pull me into their hug.

"Hey, big shot," I said. "How are you?"

"Good." Cam was beaming. She kept looking at Riley like she couldn't believe she was holding her. "It's nice to be home. Where's Teddy?"

I rubbed the back of my neck and tried not to look the way I felt. "You just missed her," I said.

"Is she coming back?" Cam asked, like maybe Teddy just

went out for groceries or something. I wished that was the case. I shrugged.

Cam tilted her head and was looking at me with a lot of questions in her eyes. Questions I probably didn't know the answers to.

She set Riley down. "Sunshine," she said as she stroked the top of Riley's head, "why don't you go grab your stuff and play for a little? I need to talk to your dad."

Riley looked disappointed, but I said, "Why don't you make your mom a picture with the paint set Teddy got you?" She lit up at that and started back toward the living room, where we'd unpacked the paints right after Teddy left.

Cam shrugged her jacket off and walked into my kitchen, which told me this was going to be a sit-down conversation. Great.

She opened my fridge, pulled out a beer and a seltzer, and sat on one of the bar stools under the kitchen counter. I sat next to her, and she slid the beer my way. I popped it open and took a healthy swig.

"So," Cam said.

"So," I responded quietly.

"What's going on with you two? You and Teddy?" she asked, even though I was pretty sure she already knew, but that also meant there was no use lying to her.

"We had a thing," I said.

"And that's all it was?" Cam asked.

"Yes." *No.*

"Liar," Cam said, and I huffed.

"Okay," I said, annoyed. "It's not just a thing."

"So why isn't she here?"

"I don't know," I said. And I didn't. I didn't know why she

left so quickly today. I didn't know why she insisted on it or why she didn't kiss me goodbye.

And it was fucking killing me.

"Ah," Cam said, as though my answer was insightful. I didn't think it was. She sighed, deeply, like she was mulling over what she was about to say.

"So, I'm getting married," she said. I looked over at her and nodded. I was aware of that. "And Graham is a great guy—in his own way. He is nice to me, and to Riley, and he doesn't ask me for more than I can give him." I had no clue where she was going with this. Also, his name was Graham? I'd been calling him Greg this whole time. "Our engagement—our life—is backed by my meddling parents, his company mergers, dollar signs," Cam said with a sigh.

She'd never said any of this to me before. I'd never gotten the impression that Cam was thrilled to be engaged, but I just thought it was because she was more reserved than most people I knew. Did she even want to marry this guy?

"And because of that, I'm very . . . picky about the relationship he has with Riley. I choose what areas of her life he gets to be part of carefully and sparingly. I think he sees her as more of a tiny roommate than a child he could potentially have a hand in bringing up," she said. "But that's by my design, because I've never had any interest in parenting our daughter with anyone but you." Cam gave me a small smile. "Until now.

"I want you to know," she went on, her voice earnest and kind—she put a hand on my arm—"that I think Teddy would make a hell of a bonus parent, and it would be an honor to add her to our team."

There was a lump in my throat that I couldn't swallow no matter how hard I tried.

"I know you better than most people, I think," Cam continued. "And I know what you look like when you're happy or sad or tired—which is impressive, because to the untrained eye, all of your scowls look the same—but I've never known what you look like when you're in love, until today." I stopped breathing. "It's okay to love her, Gus. It's okay to want her. It's okay to *want.* You have so much love to give, Gus. I see it in the way that you love our daughter and in the way you care for your family—me included—and I just want you to have someone who can love you back the same way." Cam's voice held so much emotion. "And Teddy—our lion—might be the only person I know who loves as fiercely as you do."

Cam was speaking to a part of me that most people didn't know existed—the part that desperately wanted to love and be loved.

I didn't say anything. I couldn't. I just sat there and let her words sink in.

When Teddy left today, things had felt weird between us, but I don't think that's because they *were* weird. The fact is that the whole reason we were brought together was coming to an end, and we didn't talk about it before it happened.

Now that I was thinking about it, I wondered if she thought I let her go too easily. I told her last night that I never wanted to let her go, and now I was worried that I'd done that accidentally, by letting her leave without talking. Usually I thought actions spoke louder than words. I'd done everything I could to show Teddy how deeply I cared, and she'd done the same for me, but when it came down to a future together, we needed to talk about it too. I needed to tell her that I wanted her for so much longer than the summer.

I wanted her so badly that her being gone felt like an open wound being doused with salt water.

"I don't think you should let her go, Gus," Cam said.

"I won't," I said, and I meant it. I would bring her back to me. "And, Cam—if you don't want to get married, I don't think you should get married."

Cam smiled at me, but she looked sad. "I'll be okay, Gus," she said. "Not everyone is built for love the way you are." She got off her stool then and called for Riley, not giving me a chance to push her any further.

# Chapter 38

# Gus

It had been a few days since Teddy walked out my front door. I'd sent her a few texts—checking in—but I was trying my best not to bombard her, fighting the part of myself that wanted to drive to her house, bang on the door, and ask her to come home.

She said we'd talk soon, and Teddy always did what she said she was going to do. I didn't think she'd leave us behind like that. It seemed like she had a few things to work through first.

A lot of things had changed for both of us over the past couple of months, but especially for Teddy. As much as she loved spending time with Riley, I knew she missed her job. Plus, if things went my way, she'd be spending the rest of her life with Riley.

I wanted Teddy to have it all—a job she loved, purpose, a family, whatever she wanted—and I had a few ideas about how we could at least start on all of those things when she was ready. God, I needed to see her. I needed to talk to her.

I was gazing out on Rebel Blue's land when my dad walked

into the stables to tack up Cobalt. I had been thinking about Riley and Teddy's plant project, the one stubborn flower that was still hiding from them somewhere out there.

"Morning," he said with a tip of his hat.

"Good morning," I responded, but my voice was far away. They hadn't been able to find rock jasmine. Riley had talked about it so much that there was no way I'd be able to forget the thing that was keeping them from their perfect twenty. "What are you up to today?" I asked, trying to focus on my dad.

"I thought I'd check cattle with you." A last-minute change of plan was a signature in my dad's playbook. It meant only one thing: He wanted to talk about something. He didn't have a lot of tricks, but the ones that he did have were effective—especially when they involved our being alone on an hour-long ride to find the part of the herd we were looking for.

"Sounds good," I said.

On our cattle ranch, the health and welfare of our herd was our number one priority. It was our responsibility to make sure our cattle were fed, watered, sheltered, healthy, and content. At its core, ranching could be summed up in one word: stewardship. Stewardship of the animals on the land and stewardship of the land itself. The land took care of us, and it was our greatest responsibility to take care of it.

We got tacked up and mounted together, and then we were on our way. I let my dad take the lead and set the pace for the horses, which was more leisurely than I expected. Whatever he wanted to talk about was apparently going to take a while.

Once we were up in the trees and surrounded by aspens, he asked how I was doing.

"Good," I said honestly. "Things are good."

"Thank you for working so hard over the past few months," my dad said sincerely. It went quiet between us. Ever since the kitchen table situation, I felt like my dad and I had been on shaky ground. Well, I was on shaky ground. He was fine. Steady, as usual—unlike me. "I know I was tough on you at the beginning of the summer, but everything I do has a reason, August."

"I know," I said, and he was right. His tough love had led me to Teddy, and for that I was grateful. Still, when I thought about the way he'd gotten after me that day at breakfast, I bristled a bit.

It wasn't that he was harder on me than he was on my siblings. He wasn't—or at least not on purpose. But I was the one who was supposed to take over for him someday, the one with the responsibility to make sure that Rebel Blue adapted, survived, and withstood time. His relationship with each of us was unique. Mine was just informed by more responsibility and expectation than my siblings'.

"One of your best qualities is that you go all in—you get that from your mom," he said after a minute. The mention of my mom had me tightening the grip on my reins and my ears perking up. He'd started talking about her more in the last couple of years—after Emmy moved home—but usually only when there was something important that he wanted to get across. "But you can't be all in on everything all the time when this place is yours." A few months ago, this wouldn't have made sense to me, but it did now. Teddy had helped show me that—that I couldn't be everything to everyone all at once.

"Sometimes, Rebel Blue is going to need all of you. There are going to be times when it's the only thing on your mind. Then there will be times when your family needs you more than the ranch does, and when you need time for yourself, too," my dad continued. "And when all of that happens, you'll need to be able to depend on the people around you—on your hands, and on your family.

"If you depend solely on yourself to run this ranch, you'll fail." Ouch. That was hard to hear, but I knew he was right. "Something always has to give, and it's okay to let it."

My dad sighed. "When I took over Rebel Blue, it was just me. My father passed away, my mom wasn't in good shape, and Boone was gone." Boone was my dad's oldest brother. He was supposed to inherit Rebel Blue, but he didn't want it. He bounced and left everything behind. "Rebel Blue is the biggest part of me. It's all I've ever known, all I've ever wanted to know, but I would never wish the sole responsibility for this ranch on anyone, especially not my son."

"I love Rebel Blue, Dad," I said. I needed him to know that.

"I know, and she's lucky to be left with you after I'm gone." My throat went tight. "And if you do it right, you can have a life that is made richer by Rebel Blue—not a life that's consumed by her."

"Do it right?" I asked.

"Step back when you need to. I want you to have days when you take advantage of living in the most beautiful place on earth. Maybe spend some extra time with a beautiful woman and your favorite kid."

When I looked back at him—my mouth agape—he was smiling a little. He definitely knew about Teddy and me. The whole town knew at this point; we had, after all, made out in the middle of the Devil's Boot. Even if the town didn't know, there was no way either of my siblings—or Brooks—could keep that to themselves.

"You know," he said, pointing to a small fork in the trail that we were on—I wasn't familiar with it, I didn't head up the north ridge often—"if you head up that way, there's a good amount of pink wildflowers."

I brought Scout to a halt at his words and turned us around so we were facing my dad, whose eyes were bright. "It's called rock jasmine, I think," he said. "In case someone—or two someones—are looking for them."

And then he winked at me.

I looked up the trail. I needed to get up there. I needed to get Teddy and Riley up there—today. This was what I needed—to show Teddy that I saw her, that I wanted her, and that I wanted to support her in everything. But there was no way I could check cattle and clear the trail before dark.

"Can I—" I hesitated for a few beats. I'd never asked for this before. "Can I have the day off?" The question felt foreign falling off my tongue. "This is important."

When I looked at my dad, he was beaming, like he was proud of me, like hearing me asking for time off was the best thing that'd happened to him in recent memory.

He nodded. "Of course, August," he said with a warm and knowing smile. "You deserve it."

## Chapter 39

# Teddy

I was painting the garage again. Honestly, I'd rather have been sewing, but my sewing machine wasn't fixed yet—I hadn't had time to get it looked at or sent for repair, and I couldn't sketch any more designs. I'd sketched myself out since coming back to my house from Gus's a few days ago.

Admittedly, it was my fault that I still didn't have my sewing machine in working condition or, if it couldn't be fixed, bought a new one. It hadn't been as much of a priority the past couple of weeks, my brain totally consumed by my dad and soaking up as much time with Gus and Riley as possible. But now my temporary babysitting gig was over.

And I had a plan.

Sort of.

I had the beginnings of what could potentially become a somewhat decent plan, which was good enough for me at this point. But I needed a few days before I made my next move—before I talked to Gus and told him that I wanted to give this whole thing a shot—that I wanted it all with him. And Riley.

I just hoped I'd be able to actually get words out this time.

When he'd asked me to stay for dinner, to stay and see Cam, I freaked. I felt like the foundation upon which Gus and I had gotten to know each other was crumbling, and I was in free fall. I was scared that maybe without our arrangement—part-time babysitter helping out single dad—we wouldn't be able to stand on our own.

But first I needed to feel like I could stand on *my* own.

I heard the side door open and looked around me for the first time. I'd been out here since breakfast, and it must be past lunch now. And here was Hank bearing a turkey sandwich, jalapeño cheddar Cheetos, and a Diet Coke.

"Hey, kid," he said. "Take a break. Sit with me."

I walked over to him and took the plate he'd carried out to me. Then I helped him get situated in one of the outdoor plastic chairs I'd put out here.

"That looks good, Ted," he said. "Beautiful."

"Thanks, Dad. I'm not quite sure what it is yet," I said, looking at the landscape that had started to appear.

"Really? You can't see it?"

"What do you mean?" I asked, confused.

"Never mind." Hank was smiling—it was a knowing and mischievous smile. It made me smile too, because he only smiled like that when he was feeling good. "You could do this, you know. Paint."

"I appreciate your faith in me, but I think this is one of those things I'd rather keep as a hobby, you know?"

"I do," he said with a nod, and I bit into my sandwich. "So, Teddy Bear, what's next? You've been awfully quiet the past few days. Focused. Aggie told me that Betty saw you at the bank."

"Small fucking towns," I muttered.

"Small fucking towns," Hank agreed with a chuckle.

"I was just looking into a few of my options, but it didn't work out," I said. "But I've been thinking . . . Could I make part of the garage into a workspace? If you're okay with my moving some of the instruments back inside? We could rearrange the spare room to hold them—might be easier for you to play that way," I said.

"You can do whatever you want, Teddy. What's the workspace for?" My dad was grinning. I loved his grin.

"My clothes."

"Your clothes," my dad repeated, nodding for me to keep talking.

"That I'm going to make," I said. "I love clothes, Dad. I want to make them—I want to ship my designs all over the world, with my own name on them. I used to sell on that makers' platform, but I stopped when Cloma started letting me put my clothes in the store and on the boutique's site. It felt too hard to keep up with, with everything else going on. But now . . . I want to do it again. I don't know if anything will come of it, but I think I owe it to myself to try."

My dad's eyes were glassy. Our chairs were close enough that he was able to reach out and put his hand on the side of my neck. "If anyone can make it, it's you, Theodora Andersen. I have no doubt."

"You have to believe in me," I said, rolling my eyes to keep all the things I was feeling at bay. "You're my dad."

"And a damn proud one."

"You're getting soft in your old age," I said.

"Maybe." He leaned back in his chair again. "There's something I've been wanting to talk to you about—a few things, actually."

"If you must," I said with a wave of my hand.

"First," he said, "I want you to know that I'm okay—that I am the luckiest man alive to have a daughter like you who has made so many sacrifices to make sure that I'm taken care of. But I need you to know . . . that I don't expect you to be here forever. I'm scared I've let you do so much for me that you've forgotten to take care of yourself. And if that's the case, I'd never be able to forgive myself."

"Dad, no—"

"Let me finish. What I'm trying to say is: If you wanted to move out, or go somewhere new, I would be okay. *We* would be okay."

My dad's words hit me like a kick from a horse. I couldn't tell if it was in a good way or a bad way or a both way. "Are you kicking me out?" I asked, with a tinny laugh. It was the only thing I could think to say—to do.

"Never," Hank chuckled. "But if your life takes you places outside the walls of this little red house, I'll be okay. I need you to know that. Leaving this little house doesn't mean you're leaving me behind. It just means you've got something—or someone—worth chasing."

I nodded, trying to absorb what he was saying. This aging rock star never missed a beat, even the notes of fear that I hadn't heard within myself.

"And second," my dad continued. "I think it's time you admitted to yourself and everyone else that you're in love with Gus—the two of you making moony eyes at each other when he and Riley came over was enough to make me want to puke."

"Jesus Christ, Dad," I said. "Have you ever heard of pulling punches?" I put my head in my hands. Was I really that transparent?

"Nope," he said. "And I don't think she has either." She? I looked up.

Emmy had just pulled in to our driveway and was getting out of her truck—she'd always had excellent timing. Hank got up. "I'll give you two a minute," he said, and started toward the house.

When he and Emmy crossed paths, Emmy hugged him, and they exchanged a few words before she continued toward me.

"Hey," she said when she was close.

"Hey," I responded. I set my plate on the grass and stood. Emmy and I made eye contact and then made our way to each other and collided in a hug. We held each other the way we always had.

"I'm sorry, Teddy," Emmy said in my ear.

"I know," I said.

"No," she said, pulling back. "Let me say this." Emmy took a deep breath. "I think you are miraculous, Teddy. I think that your existence—the way you care and fight and love and live—is a miracle. There is no one else like you, and I am so sorry for making you feel like I didn't know that—that I didn't see that. I'm sorry for treating you like I didn't know you the way that I do. I know that you feel things deeply, that you would do anything for the people you care about, and that you love hard." Emmy hugged me again. "And I feel like the absolute worst best friend in the world for not seeing that you were hurting. Your feelings about the way our friendship has shifted—they all make sense. I just never noticed because I was still your number one, but I also got to be Luke's. And when I thought about it that way, I realized that you should have that, too. When you told me about you and Gus, I wasn't mad that you two were . . ."

"Bumping uglies?" I chimed in.

"Jesus, Teddy," she laughed. "Sure. I wasn't mad at all. There's nothing to be mad about—the two people who have protected me and fought for me being together? That's a dream come true. It didn't feel good to think that you'd been keeping something from me, or that maybe you were trying to move on from me. Honestly, I wished you'd told me sooner. I was mad that you hadn't, and then I felt like I needed to overcompensate for that. I think I just wanted to try and protect both of you, and I did a shit job.

"I'll admit, you and my brother 'bumping uglies' "—she put that in air quotes—"was the last thing I ever thought would happen." A watery chuckle came out of me at that. "But when I sat down and thought about it, it makes so much sense, because both of you love and live the same way—with your entire heart.

"Luke is my fiancé, my partner, my everything. But you're my soulmate, Teddy Andersen, and I'm the luckiest girl in the world because of it."

I looked at Emmy with wide eyes. Hank was right, she didn't pull punches either, but goddamn, she was the best person I knew. "And you deserve to have someone else to love too. You have so much of it to give."

"You're my soulmate, too," I said. "But Jesus Christ, can you please stop talking before I need to be sedated from sobbing?"

"Love you, Ted," she finished, and then hugged me again.

"So does that epic apology mean you won't be mad if I tell you that I'm in love with your brother?" I said into her shoulder.

"No," Emmy said quickly, "but I'll be pissed if you don't tell *him*. Plus, I already knew—why else would you be painting the view from his back porch on your garage?"

I pulled back immediately, and my head snapped to my painting. Shit. She was right. The way one of the mountains sloped in the corner and how the patch of forest looked like ocean waves in the distance . . . that was Gus's view.

Right then, my phone started buzzing in my back pocket. I pulled it out. *Speak of the devil.* Emmy looked at my screen and smiled.

I swiped my finger on the screen. "Hello?"

"Teddy baby," Gus said. He sounded like he was smiling. "How fast can you get to the stables?"

# Chapter 40

# Gus

Riley and I were waiting for Teddy outside my family's stables. I'd already tacked up Scout, Maverick, and Moonshine for Riley.

"Where are we going today, Dad?" Riley asked.

"It's a surprise," I told her. "For you and Teddy." I'd spent all morning working on it—I rode out to the north ridge, and I'm glad I did. There were a good number of fallen trees that I'd had to move or, if they were too big to move in one piece, take a chainsaw to.

Once the trail was clear, and I knew where we were going, I called Cam and asked her if Riley could spend a few hours with me at the ranch today.

"Depends," Cam said on the phone. "Is this about Teddy?"

"Yes," I said without hesitation.

"Good," she said. "Riley and I will leave here in a few minutes."

As if summoned, I spotted Teddy's copper hair coming down the path. It was down, free. Once she spotted Riley and me, she waved and started walking faster.

"Can I run to Teddy, Dad?" Riley asked.

"Go for it, Sunshine," I said, and Riley took off. Her squeal echoed behind her, and I felt it in my chest. I watched my daughter collide with the woman I loved, and I watched the woman I loved catch her. I watched them laugh and smile at each other, and then I watched them clasp hands and start walking toward me—the luckiest man alive.

"Hey, Gussy," Teddy said as they approached.

"Theodora," I said with a smile. "Consider your lifetime Rebel Blue ban officially lifted."

"What's the occasion?" she asked.

"You'll see," I said. "You up for a ride?"

"Always," she said with a wink, and fuck, I wanted to kiss her, but not yet. I had a plan.

"Good," I said. "Mount up, then." Teddy smiled, and when she walked past me to get to Maverick at his hitching post, I grabbed her arm. "Thank you for coming," I said.

"Thank you for calling." I let that land. "Stop smiling at me like that," she said.

"Like what?" I asked, laughing. *Like a big, dumb, lovesick idiot* is what she meant, probably.

"Like that," she said again.

"Why?" I asked.

"Because it's freaking me out!"

Riley grabbed my other hand, and I went to seat her on Moonshine. I put a helmet on her too. I kept an eye on Teddy and the way she interacted with Maverick—lucky horse to be so loved by her.

She mounted easily, and I finished getting Riley settled on Moonshine. I had to adjust her stirrups—she must've grown this summer—and we were good to go. I tied her reins and handed them to her. Then I walked to Scout and mounted.

"All right, Sunshine," I said. "You're going to stick behind me, and Teddy's going to bring up the rear, okay?" Riley nodded excitedly.

"I love a good rear!" Teddy called. And with that, we were on our way. Now that the trail was clear, it was a pretty easy ride, but we had to do a few climbs, and cross the river at two different points.

"Keep your reins loose, Sunshine," I said when we got to the first incline. "Let Moonshine use her shoulders."

"I know, Dad," Riley said back.

"Yeah, Dad, she knows," Teddy called, and I shook my head. I was in for it with these two, wasn't I?

*Don't get ahead of yourself, August.*

As we rode, I listened to Riley and Teddy. Riley told Teddy all about the dress she'd be wearing at Cam's wedding, about how Emmy said she'd be able to ride Sweetwater soon, about Brooks taking her fishing again—basically everything that had happened to or near Riley over the past couple of days.

And Teddy took it all in. She responded, she asked questions, she let Riley talk her ear off. She was patient, and she listened. Her tone was never bored or tired—she was always engaged with what Riley was telling her. I could listen to the two of them together all day.

I pulled on Scout's reins to pull him down another trail—we were getting close. I looked back to make sure Moonshine followed—of course she did. She was a perfect horse.

Being this high up in Rebel Blue was one of my favorite things. There were fewer aspens and more pines. There were even patches of snow in some places that had withstood the summer heat. I was happy my dad told me about this.

Now that we were getting closer, I was starting to get nervous about the surprise. I'd never done anything like this before. I'd never had a reason to, but now I did.

"Five minutes," I called back to Teddy and Riley, who weren't paying me any attention whatsoever.

In those five minutes I let myself wonder about the future. If Teddy, Riley, and I would be able to do this in five, ten, twenty years—ride through Rebel Blue together. I wanted that, and I hoped I'd know soon if Teddy wanted it, too. This was the scary thing about want—the fact that it wasn't a guarantee.

It was a wish, and wishes were made of air—at best.

When we broke out of the trees, Teddy and Riley stopped talking. I didn't think they'd seen them yet—the pink flowers. There were only a few, but I knew where they were. As soon as I saw them, a weight lifted off my shoulders. Wildflowers could be fickle—there one day and gone the next.

That is why I hadn't called Teddy sooner, why I hadn't gone to her house as soon as Cam and Riley left.

I wanted to do this for her. And for Riley. I wanted them to be able to finish what they'd started this summer, and I wanted to be part of it. I wanted to show up for both of them—to show them that I'm going to be all in. Forever.

Once we got closer to the flowers, I pulled Scout to a stop. It was Teddy who saw them first. "Wait," I heard her say. "Is that . . . ? Riley, look!"

And then Riley shouted, loud enough for all of Meadowlark to hear: "*It's rock fucking jasmine!*" And I had no one to blame but myself for her impeccable use of the F word.

## Chapter 41

# Teddy

Gus and I were sitting on the top step of his porch—just like we did the night I picked Riley up from soccer. This time, Gus's head wasn't in his hands, he wasn't beating the shit out of himself for being a bad father (which, obviously, he wasn't). We sat next to each other comfortably, looking up at the night sky.

There was no night sky like Wyoming's. It was vast and sparkling and beautiful. Stars fell and shot all the time with certainty, the moon was effervescent and massive, and it featured as many colors as a sunset. Instead of reds and oranges, it was full of blues and purples and even emeralds.

"Today was perfect," I said, still looking up at the sky. After we found the "rock fucking jasmine," we'd stayed in that small meadow for a little bit. Gus had stashed a few sandwiches and apples in his saddlebags, so we ate and sat in the sun for a while. Well, Riley and I sat in the sun—Gus was a shade man—but he worked in the sun all day, so I guess that made sense for him. I'd fed my apple core to Mav and sent my dad a picture of him up in the hills of Rebel Blue. I hoped it made him happy.

"It was," Gus said. "I was fucking determined to find those flowers yesterday. I'm sorry I didn't call sooner."

"Your timing was perfect," I said, laying my head on his shoulder. "I needed to . . . figure some things out first. I talked to Emmy today."

"How did that go?" he asked, his tone thoughtful.

"Good," I said. "We're good."

"You two are really lucky to have each other, you know. I've always known that," he said. "But now that I've seen what both sides of your friendship look like, it feels even bigger to me."

"Clementine Ryder and Theodora Andersen are written in the stars," I said with a chuckle. "Doesn't get more cosmic than that."

He was quiet after that. I listened to the sound of crickets echoing around us. I'd never had anything like this before—where I felt like I could just exist in the quiet. I usually felt pressure to fill the silence, to entertain, but not here, not with Gus.

I shivered a little—I hadn't planned for a Wyoming night—just a summer day. Gus noticed immediately.

"Stay here," he said. "I'll be right back." I nodded. I was glad he didn't ask me if I wanted to go inside. I wanted to stay out here awhile longer.

I'd always been a morning person—I liked to get up and get going—but lately, I'd started to really enjoy nighttime. I got to know Gus at night. We'd sat with each other in the living room, calmly existing in each other's orbit for the first time ever, during that time. We talked. We laughed. We gave each other shit.

We'd started to see parts of each other that we liked, and

the parts of each other that we didn't like in the light of day were softened by the night. And so were we.

Gus's front door opened and he draped something heavy around my shoulders before he sat down next to me again. I recognized the weight on my shoulders. It felt familiar. How did he . . . ?

I looked down and saw camel-colored fabric—vintage suede with fringe.

"How did you get this?" I asked. My hand immediately went to the side where the hole was, but when I went to feel for it, it was gone. I whipped the jacket off my shoulders, not caring about the cold anymore, and looked at the inside of the jacket.

There was a line of small, clean stitches that I wouldn't have noticed if I wasn't looking for them.

"I got it from your dad last week. I remembered you saying it had a hole in it—and something about it being my fault."

I smiled. "It *was* your fault."

"I don't think it was, but I hope this makes up for it anyway," Gus said. He brought one of his hands up to the side of my neck and brushed my hair behind my shoulder.

"How did you fix it? This isn't shoddy sewing," I said, holding up the inside of the jacket so he could see. "See how clean it is? And how there's no tension in the fabric?"

Gus examined the stitches for a second before he said, "Cloma fixed it. Aggie helped me get ahold of her. I was lucky she was coming back to Meadowlark to tie up some loose ends last week. She was happy to do it. She adores you, Teddy."

"Most people do," I said. I threw the jacket over my shoulders and slid my arms into the sleeves. It felt so perfect—like home.

"And I was thinking," Gus said, "that maybe we could take a trip to Jackson this weekend—Riley will be with Cam—and we can get your sewing machine fixed. I assume you'll need it, since you have a workspace now."

"How did you know about that?" I asked, dumbfounded.

"Small town, Teddy baby." He kissed me then—soft and slow, like we had all the time in the world, and I hoped we did.

"Teddy," he said as he pulled back. He looked serious now—earnest. "I want to be with you. I want us to be together. This summer was incredible. I loved every second of it, but I don't want it to be over. I want it to be our beginning.

"I don't have much to offer," he went on softly. "Just a quiet life with a grumpy man from a small town, but I can promise to love you every day."

"You love me?" I said. *Don't cry, Teddy.*

"I do," he said. "And I want to show you how much I love you every single day. I want to do everything with you. I want you to be part of my daughter's life. I want you at every soccer game, barrel race, and art show. I want you there when she sneaks into my bed in the mornings"—he kissed one of my cheeks then. "I want to marry you. I want to have babies with you—little copper-headed demons running around wreaking havoc"—a kiss on the other cheek. "I want to sit on this porch with you thirty years from now and look up at the sky and wonder what I did to deserve a life this good.

"Wanting used to scare me so much, because I didn't think I had the space to want anything more than what I've got. But wanting a future with you is the easiest thing in the world. And I want it all, with you." A kiss on the forehead.

*Okay, maybe cry a little.*

Gus caught one of my tears with his thumb against my

cheek. "What do you say, Teddy baby? Do you want to do life with me?"

I nodded eagerly, but no words came out.

Gus chuckled. "Have I finally figured out how to get you to shut up?" he said. "Just gotta tell you that I'm madly in love with you, and I'll get a little peace?"

"Asshole," I breathed. "I love you." Gus's emerald eyes sparkled, and I was overwhelmed by how extraordinary this moment felt, but in the most ordinary way. It was just us, the sky, and the crickets.

Our beginning.

# Epilogue

# Gus

The ring on Teddy's finger glinted in the bathroom mirror as she put her earrings in. We'd found it when we went to Jackson in August to get her sewing machine fixed—in a little vintage jewelry shop. It was simple—just a gold band with an emerald between two small diamonds. We'd gone in on a whim—we didn't even know what the store was until we walked in, and when Teddy saw the ring, hidden in the back of a display case, she asked to try it on.

She tried to put it on her middle finger at first, but it didn't fit. After she'd tried her pointer finger, I took the ring from her, got down on one knee, and proposed to her with it on the spot.

When you know, you know.

The ring slid onto her ring finger perfectly, and it had been there ever since—except for when we told Riley. I talked to her solo first—told her that I loved Teddy, and asked her if she was okay with her being part of our family.

My six-year-old looked at me like I was the dumbest man alive as she said, "She already is" with total confidence. I told her she was right about that. Teddy joined us then. She had made the embroidery piece she was working on throughout the summer—now complete with the rock (fucking) jasmine—into a pillow, and gave it to Riley, who squealed with delight.

Then we sat on the porch as a family of three for the first time and watched the sun go down.

Afterward, I'd asked her if she wanted something bigger or newer—I'd get her whatever fucking ring she wanted. She said this one was perfect because it matched my eyes.

Teddy met my gaze in the mirror. "You look beautiful," I said. Cam was getting married today—December first. Why anyone would want to get married in December in Wyoming, I don't know, but Cam did. Teddy was wearing an emerald-green dress. It had long sleeves and hugged her perfect fucking body until it ended in the middle of her calves.

Her copper hair was down, and she'd had curlers on top of her head all morning to make it fall in large, loose waves down her back.

"You don't look too shabby either," she said with my favorite feline grin. "That suit is really working for you."

"Yeah? Is it working for you, too?"

"Definitely," she said as she put her other earring in. I stepped close to her, our bodies almost touching, and moved her hair over to one side of her neck. I liked having access to her neck—like those fucking vampires she read about all the time.

I could still see one of the marks I'd given her last night, and pride blossomed in my chest. I kissed it and then made my way up her neck. I wrapped my arms around her waist and tugged her to me. My cock was already hard, and I knew she felt it because she let out one of those little noises that I loved.

"August." I think she was trying to be stern, but her voice was breathy.

"Theodora," I said, and then bit her neck.

"We have to be at the chapel in thirty minutes," she said. "We can't be late." I dragged my hands up her torso and back down, I put them on the front of her stomach. Teddy wasn't on birth control anymore, and I was fucking determined to get her pregnant as soon as possible, which she was on board with. We talked about it a lot. When I thought about her having our baby—a little person that was half me and half her, a sibling for Riley—I was like a man possessed. I couldn't stop. I didn't want to stop. All I wanted was her.

"Please," I growled as I rubbed her stomach with one hand and started to lift her dress with the other. "I want you to be full of me while you wear this dress." My hips rolled and Teddy pushed her ass back into my cock. Fucking tease. "I want every man in the room to be able to smell me on you."

"So territorial!" she said with a laugh.

I put my hands on her waist and flipped her so she was facing me. When I brought my mouth down on hers, she gasped again. I bent her as far back over the vanity as she would go and pushed my hips against hers.

"How do you want me to take you, Teddy baby?" I asked.

"Right here," she said against my mouth. "I want you right here." Her hands were at my belt. She unbuckled it at top speed and then pushed my pants down my thighs along with my briefs. I lifted her dress up around her waist—I didn't scrunch it, I folded it up, Teddy was particular about her clothes—and pulled her white thong down her legs.

My fingers slid inside her easily. "You're always ready for me, aren't you?" I said against her neck before I bit it again.

"Hurry up," she said. "I've got places to be." I lifted her onto the bathroom counter. It was the perfect height for this, and I didn't know how we didn't notice it before.

"You're so fucking annoying," I growled as I positioned my cock at her entrance.

"You love it," she breathed.

"I love *you,*" I said as I pushed into her. Both of us moaned as I bottomed out, and I rested my head against hers for a minute. We had to be quick, but not that quick.

Her head fell back. I held on to her hips as I started thrusting into her, making sure she didn't slide across the counter.

"Touch yourself, Teddy," I ground out. "Touch yourself while I fuck you and fill you." She brought her hand to her clit, and I picked up my pace.

"Harder, Gus," she said. "Make it hurt. I want to feel you all day." Fuck, fuck, fuck. It didn't matter how many times we did this, it always shocked me how right it felt. I was convinced that Teddy Andersen was made for me.

At first, I was pissed that it had taken me so long to see it. I was mad at myself that she had been so close to me this whole time, and I never knew she was the one. I was angry that I could've had more time with her if I would've just stopped being an ass. But then I realized that we happened exactly how we were supposed to. We had the rest of our lives, and whatever came after, anyway.

"God, Gus," she moaned. "You feel so good. You feel so fucking good."

I pistoned in and out of her. I couldn't even find words anymore—I'd devolved to grunts and moans and single-syllable curses. When she clenched around me, I kissed her—hard—swallowing her moans and fucking her through her orgasm. It didn't take long for me to follow.

There was a sheen of sweat on her heaving chest. I licked it and then dragged my tongue up the column of her neck. "I love you, Teddy," I said in her ear.

"I love you too," she said. I kissed her forehead before resting my own against it, taking her in. I'd never get tired of this, of her. "What's that?" She pointed at my shirt. I looked down and Teddy brought her finger up to flick me in the nose.

I still fell for it. Every damn time.

I pulled my truck in to the chapel parking lot right on time. Teddy and I walked hand in hand toward the big wooden doors. When we got inside, I saw my family—Emmy and Brooks, Wes and Ada. Aggie and Hank were here too.

There was no sign of Dusty. I suppose that wasn't a surprise.

"Where's Dad?" I asked Emmy as we sat down. Brooks was next to her, Teddy was on the other side, and I was next to Teddy.

"Riley came and got him a few minutes ago," Emmy said. Riley had been with Cam for the past few days. We FaceTimed this morning so she could show Teddy and me her dress. She looked adorable. "Said that her mom was asking for him." Originally, Cam had asked my dad to walk her down the aisle, but that didn't fly with Cam's parents. I wondered if she was going to make it happen anyway.

I made sure to talk to Aggie and Hank before things started. Hank was doing okay on his own. Teddy went over there a few times a week. We ended up renting her a workspace in town after a few weeks. I knew she wanted that, and we made it happen. I went with her to Hank's whenever I could. Plus, he was teaching Riley to play the drums, and I was grateful, not just because it made her so happy but also because it meant I didn't have to have drums in *my* house.

I felt a hand on my shoulder. I turned to see my dad—he looked calm, but I could see his nose scrunch. Riley was with him. "Hi, Sunshine. You look beautiful."

"I know," she said with a smile.

"Can I borrow you for a second, August?" my dad said.

I nodded. Teddy took Riley, and I made sure to give both of my girls a kiss before I followed him. My dad and I walked to the back of the chapel and out to the lobby. He led me to a small alcove, and we stopped at a door with a silver plaque that said BRIDE on it.

He lifted his hand to knock, and I heard Cam say, "Come in." When my dad pushed the door open, Cam was standing in the middle of the dressing room in her long white wedding gown. She had a piece of paper in one hand, and her eyes welled with tears when she saw me.

"He's not coming," she said. I didn't know what she meant. Was she sad that Dusty wasn't here? Honestly, it was probably for the best, but then she spoke again. "Graham isn't coming. He's called it off."

Acknowledgments

"Why doesn't this ever get easier?"—Me to me while writing this book. I thought by the time my third book rolled around, I'd be better at this—better at writing books, better at being nicer to myself, just better. Gus and Teddy came with a lot of their own baggage that has been built up over the length of the first two Rebel Blue Ranch novels. I'd never felt their type of pressure before—the pressure to get a story of two beloved characters right. Honestly, I still don't know if I pulled it off, but I do know that I am deeply proud of everything this book became. It never would have gotten here without the support of the incredible people I'm lucky enough to be surrounded by.

Mom and Dad, thank you for your unconditional support of me and my dreams. You guys are the reason I believe in love stories. There are many reasons why I think I'm the luckiest girl alive, but the biggest one is that I get to be your daughter.

Lexie, I can only hope to one day believe in myself the way you believe in me. Thank you for climbing all the mountains with me—they seem smaller with you around.

Sydney, thank you for caring so deeply about me that you choose to spend so much of your time making sure that Lyla Land is running smoothly. You are my pillar. Without you, I would collapse.

Stella, my gal, thanks for keeping me humble.

Emma, it was truly an honor to work on this book with you.

The enthusiasm and care with which you do your work amazes me every day. So much of what Gus and Teddy became is because of you. Thank you for pushing me, asking all the right questions, and understanding why it was so important for me to get this one right.

Jess, there is no better champion for my books than you. Thank you for everything.

Thank you so much to The Dial Press team—Whitney, Debbie, Corina, Avideh, Michelle, Talia, Maria, and Rachel. You saddled up with me and never looked back. Thank you for everything you do to get my books out there. It's a joy and honor to work with you all.

Austin, the cover for *Lost and Lassoed* is my favorite thing you've created so far. It's actually annoying how good it is. Thank you for sharing your talent with my stories.

Angie, thank you for being here since day one. Because of you, I don't yield.

Thank you to my brothers, who have protected me and gone to bat for me my entire life. You're the best brothers on the planet, and it means the world that you're proud of me. (I'm only being this cheesy because I know you'll never read this, but if you do, I still think you guys are annoying as hell.)

I also feel the need to shoutout Diet Coke, Reese's Peanut Butter Cups, and *The Hunger Games* movie franchise. This book would not exist without any of those things (I am so serious). Thank you for keeping me going.

While we're at it, thank you to Bruce Springsteen, Chris Stapleton, the Cure, Conway Twitty, and Pearl Jam.

Thank you to ES, for telling me that some books are unicorns and others are workhorses, and that both are needed to have a meaningful and withstanding career. I think about that every single day.

Thank you to all of the reviewers, bookstagrammers, bloggers, and booktokers who love my books loudly enough that you make so many other people want to give them a try.

The most important thank you, of course, goes to my readers. Thank you for showing up for me over and over again. Truly, there is no one like y'all. I am so lucky to be loved by you. I think about you constantly. I hope I make you proud. I love you!

# LOST AND LASSOED

LYLA SAGE

Dial Delights

*Love Stories*
*for the*
*Open-Hearted*

# Lost, Lassoed, and Lane

The people I love or who have made an impression on me always find a way to make their way into my books—usually in small but meaningful ways. Amos and Gus have swallow tattoos because of a tattoo artist I met in college; Ada's favorite food is spanakopita because my mom makes the best; and Hank's horse is named Maverick because that was the name of the horse my best friend loved with her whole heart. I love that little pieces of my life get to exist at Rebel Blue Ranch, and occasionally really big pieces of my life make it there too—this is truest for *Lost and Lassoed.*

*Lost and Lassoed* came with the weight of many people's expectations. And those expectations were *heavy.* When I sat down to start writing it, all I could think about was how scared I was of letting people down—my readers, my publisher, myself. I didn't know how to balance the expectations I had for myself and the expectations that other people had for these characters that they loved.

I turned in the first draft of this book on a Friday. That Sunday, I went to my parents' house. My dad asked me how I felt about the book, and I told him I felt okay—not great, but okay. I told him I didn't quite know where this book's heart was yet. He told me I'd figure it out, and then he hugged me tight. My dad's belief in me is unwavering and steadfast—just like him.

My dad's name is Lane. He can fix almost anything. He might break it a little bit more along the way, but it'll get fixed. If you need something, he's probably got it in his garage (much to my mom's dismay), and when he talks to someone, it's often hard to tell if the person is a lifelong friend or he just met them.

He likes *Pawn Stars, Deadliest Catch,* and that one show about welding. He talks loud and fast and he can't sit still. His favorite things are pecan pie, the mountains, and, most of all, his family.

About a week before I turned sixteen, my dad pulled in to the driveway in the ugliest car I'd ever seen with a big grin on his face. It was a 1992 Nissan Sentra. Even though most of the car was white, two of its doors were black, and they stuck out from the body like they didn't quite fit. It had mismatched rims, a black plastic bumper, and an antenna that I swore could get radio stations from Pluto.

The windows were rolled down—because the car didn't have air-conditioning—and I could hear Pearl Jam blasting from the speakers; they were already blown.

I hated that car on sight. I hated it more when I found out it was a stick shift, the doors didn't lock, and it didn't have power steering. I hated that it was mine.

But my dad loved it, the way he loved me—exactly as it was *and* because of everything he thought it could be.

He was excited to fix it up—clean it out, paint the doors, get new rims (plastic ones from Wal-Mart, which I thought were lame at first, but after I hit a curb and popped one of those rims right off, it was clear they were probably a good call). He was eager to teach me to drive a stick shift, even though I almost killed both of us—several times.

Lane taught me how to check my own oil and change a tire. When I accidentally drove my car over my aunt's lawn and hit a fire hydrant, he didn't yell at me (but he did fix my bumper with duct tape and zip ties as punishment). He also bought the world's ugliest fuzzy purple steering wheel cover when I complained about how hot the steering wheel got (because purple is my favorite color).

He shows his love for me in small but significant ways, like buying three loaves of a specific brand of sourdough bread that I said I liked one time a few years ago. He is protective and kind and he's never given me the impression that there's anything I can't do. Lane has never missed an opportunity to tell anyone who will listen that his daughter is an author, even before I was a bestselling one.

He's my heart.

So of course small pieces of my dad are at Rebel Blue too. He's in the nicknames that Gus, Amos, and Hank use for their daughters because I don't know if Lane has ever called me by my full name. I don't think I ever want him to. He's in mountain breezes, and the big blue sky. Those pieces have always been there, but while I was writing *Lost and Lassoed,* they took on new meaning.

It wasn't on purpose or part of my initial plan. But while I was writing and editing this book, there came a very real and petrifying moment when I thought I wasn't going to have a dad anymore.

My dad went to the hospital a few days after I got revisions back on *Lost and Lassoed* and wasn't able to return home until after I'd turned them in. Almost every revision and edit that I made was done in a chair by his bed in a hospital room, and my dad was the only thing I could think about.

Realizing that my dad wasn't indestructible was the most terrifying thing I've ever experienced. I didn't understand how this man—this steady and strong and enduring man—could be lying in a hospital bed. He looked so unlike my dad—like a watered-down version. His voice was hollow, and he looked like a photo whose color saturation had been turned nearly all the way down. My heart broke for my mom, my brothers, and me.

I hated it.

But I couldn't change it. All I could do was sit in that chair and hope and think.

I thought about how my dad has always answered all of my phone calls, how he can fix anything that's broken. And over and over again, for some reason, I thought about that stupid car.

But it wasn't just a stupid car. My dad had made it into something big and withstanding and wonderful—a physical reminder of how much he loves me.

So, as I sat next to him in that hospital room, with my laptop open and my mind spinning as his body worked hard to heal, I ended up building my own tangible reminder of how much I love him.

And it's in the book that you're holding.

Somewhere between the first and second drafts of *Lost and Lassoed,* a tribute to my dad got layered in to Gus and Teddy's love story. The story transformed into more than just a love story between two people. It became bigger: a testament to fathers and daughters and sons. What it means to love the people in our lives deeply and truly—even when it's difficult and scary and heartbreaking.

It's about caring for our people with our entire being and how they care for us in return. It's about heavy expectations and hard choices and hope. It's about how your heart can be broken and full at the same time, and how even though time passes and things change, love doesn't.

This book is now etched deeply on my heart. I went from feeling lukewarm about *Lost and Lassoed* to loving it fiercely and passionately and madly. Where I was once scared that the weight of the anticipation would crush me, I have now embraced what I wrote and am openly and excitedly proud of it.

Because it's a love letter to my dad. But it's in a book that he's never allowed to read, so I had to write something that he could.

This.

So, Dad, you were right, I figured out this book's heart—and it's you. It's all you, Daddio.

I love you.

(If I wasn't his favorite child before—and I was—I definitely am now.)

Keep reading for an exclusive sneak peek

at the first chapter from

**WILD AND WRANGLED,**

the next book in the Rebel Blue Ranch series!

## Chapter 1

# Cam

In my opinion, there is almost nothing better than a good checklist. Crossing something off is probably the best feeling in the world, and today, my checklist was supposed to be easy—mindless, even—because, for the first time in who knows how long, there was only one thing on it: Get married.

I'd done everything I needed to do. I got the marriage license, I showed up at the chapel, and I wore the ball gown my mother picked out. It should've been a piece of cake—walk down the aisle, listen to the generic vows the officiant was told to use, and plant one on my fiancé.

So why was I sitting in the diviest dive bar in all of Wyoming drinking straight vodka while wearing my wedding dress?

As with nearly every large project, getting married required more than one person. Group projects had never been my strong suit. I should've known better than to attempt this one. I didn't like putting my fate in the hands of others, but today,

today I thought I'd be fine. How much harm can one other person do when the task is so straightforward?

A lot, actually. Because if just one key person doesn't show up, everything goes to shit.

Well, my groom didn't show up, and everything went to shit.

I thought about the note he'd left—noble of him—as I picked up my glass of vodka and took a healthy swig. I ignored the eyes of the other Devil's Boot patrons that were burning into the back of my skull as they deduced why poor Camille was sitting at the bar in her wedding dress when she was supposed to be getting married.

*Camille,*

*I'm sorry. I can't do it.*

*Graham*

I felt the alcohol burn all the way down my throat. I took another sip. And another. *He* couldn't do it? This whole thing was *his* idea. He was the one who said it was going to be okay, that we would be as happy as we could be.

And then *he* didn't show up.

He didn't even warn me, just left me a note on the dressing room table. Right when I read it, Amos Ryder knocked on the door to the dressing room. Amos was my daughter, Riley's, grandfather, but he was also the closest thing I had to a loving and steady father figure. I'd originally asked him to walk me down the aisle today, but my actual father wasn't very pleased with that, so he did what he normally did: threatened to cause a scene, take away my and my daughter's inheritance, revoke her trust fund—that sort of thing.

So I gave in. I always gave in.

But when I needed someone, my dad was nowhere to be

found. Amos, however, was always there when it counted. Ever since the day his son Gus told him I was pregnant, Amos had treated me like another daughter.

He'd spent the morning with me because I'd asked him to. Amos was a good person to have around when you were worried that nerves might get the best of you. He was calm and strong and steady—like a river, Gus had always said. I always wished he could've sat next to me when I took the bar exam—no doubt I would've passed on the first try.

"Come in," I croaked, and as soon as I saw his black and gray hair and soft green eyes, tears bubbled up in my own. Not because I was sad that Graham wasn't here and wasn't coming, but because I'd already given up so much of myself for this wedding and now it wasn't going to happen.

"Cam?" he'd said as he'd closed the door behind him and hurried toward me. "What's wrong?" His eyes zeroed in on the note in my hand, and I watched his face fall. He knew.

Instead of answering, I let out a shaky breath and hugged him. He hugged me back. Riley jumped in on the hug too, even though she didn't know what was going on.

"Let's go see if your dad is here, Sunshine," he told her. She nodded excitedly and twirled in her flower girl dress. She was so damn excited to throw petals and walk down the aisle before me. My chest constricted. How could I tell her what had happened?

"Can you . . . can you send him back here?" I asked quietly.

Amos brought Gus back less than a minute later. I told him Graham wasn't coming and that I needed him and his fiancée, Teddy, to take Riley for the rest of the day. Since I'd had a minute to compose myself, my voice was professional—unfeeling, even—but the look Gus was giving me was anything but.

"I need to get out of here," I said as I ripped the veil out of the chignon it had been secured in just a few minutes earlier. "I have to go. Can I go?"

"Go," Gus and Amos said at the same time. "We'll take care of it," Gus followed up. I trusted them to do that. I ran out the back of the church—not in a runaway-bride-on-her-way-to-freedom sort of way, but in a jilted-bride-who-needed-to-keep-moving-so-she-didn't-crumble sort of way.

And now I was here. Mainlining vodka at three in the afternoon. I was sufficiently buzzed that the tension in my neck and shoulders was starting to loosen. Maybe I'd stay here all day—listen to Hank Williams wax poetic about tears and beers from the jukebox until the sun went down. Then maybe I'd ride the mechanical bull in my wedding dress and give the town even more to talk about.

I picked my drink up again and was deeply disappointed when ice was the only thing that met my lips. I wanted vodka. And chocolate. And jalapeño cheddar Cheetos.

My eyes locked on the bottle of vodka that was on the other side of the bar right as the front door opened. I saw Gus, his brother Wes, and the man who owned the bottle of vodka, Luke Brooks, ramble through it.

I knew they were looking for me to make sure I was okay, but I didn't want to deal with it all yet. I didn't want to know what had happened at the church or how my parents reacted or what people were saying.

So I pushed myself up and over the bar, grabbed the bottle, and slid off my stool as quickly and quietly as possible. As I headed for the bathroom, I heard Wes call out, "There she is!"

"Cam!" Gus called, but I kept moving.

"Are you really stealing from my bar right now?" Brooks asked.

"You look great, though!" Wes followed up.

Only a few more steps to the bathroom. I could make it before they got to me. "Cam," Gus called again. "Let's talk!"

"I'm good," I called back without looking. "Is Riley okay?" I asked, even though I knew the answer. Gus wouldn't have come here before Riley was taken care of. He was a good dad—the best dad.

"Yes," he said right as I reached the bathroom door.

"Then we're good!" I said as I stepped into the bathroom, shut the door behind me, and made sure to lock it before I pressed my back against the old wood. I stared at the yellow tiles on the floor before I sank down on them—bottle in hand.

There was a knock. "Cam?" It was Gus. "C'mon, let's get you out of here and talk." I didn't want to talk. I wanted to drink. And eat.

"I'm good here," I called through the door. He continued to try to cajole me, but I didn't budge. I sat on the Devil's Boot bathroom floor—where probably half of Meadowlark's population had been conceived—and I didn't even care. My gaze was unfocused, my eyes heavy.

I tried to cry—really I did—but nothing came out. I *wanted* to cry. I wanted to feel something about the fact that my life just got turned upside down.

Instead, I was numb. Blissfully and comfortably numb. Maybe this was a good thing—that I didn't feel anything. My feelings had always gotten me in trouble.

I don't know how long I stayed there—my wedding dress crumpled around me—or how long Gus knocked at the door. He was persistent, but after a while, the knocking stopped.

All I could hear was the music from the jukebox—it slid its way under the door, and I welcomed it into my fortress. It felt nice being wrapped in it. I didn't get wrapped in things—music, embraces—very often.

I didn't register that the music was the only thing I could hear—no talking, no bar patrons or stools skating across the floor—until there was another knock at the bathroom door.

It was softer this time—as if the person didn't want to wake me or something. Three taps. They were on beat with the music.

"Ash?" a voice said. I straightened. I'd know that voice anywhere. If I had slipped into a coma, it would wake me up. If I was six feet under, I'd dig myself out of the grave just to be closer to it. It was dramatic and startling and tragic and stupid.

But it was real.

"It's just me out here," he said. "They cleared out the bar. They left. It's just me now." *I'll love you until we're dust in the wind, Camille Ashwood.* "I'm here, Cam."

I reached up and unlocked the door. The click was unmistakable—I knew he heard it. "I'm going to open the door, okay?" he said, and I scooted away from it as the knob turned. When the door opened, my eyes found his without even trying.

Dusty Tucker.

His wavy blond hair fell just past his chin, and his face had only gotten sharper and more angular as he got older. The silver ring through his right nostril was almost the same color as his eyes, but they were more slate than silver. He was beautiful. He always had been, but beautiful things can be dangerous, too.

Silence and the weight of the years hung between us. I was the one who broke it.

"Take me somewhere." I'd said that to him before. I didn't know I'd ever say it again. Dusty squatted in front of me so his gray eyes were level with my brown ones, and he stretched out a tattooed hand.

I took it without thinking.

LYLA SAGE lives in the Wild West with her loyal companion, a sweet old blind rescue pitbull. She writes romance that feels like her favorite things: sunshine and wildflowers and big blue skies. She is also the author of *Done and Dusted* and *Swift and Saddled.* When she's not writing, she's reading.

@authorlylasage